FOUR DARK NIGHTS

FOUR DARK NIGHTS

BENTLEY LITTLE
DOUGLAS CLEGG
CHRISTOPHER GOLDEN
TOM PICCIRILLI

LEISURE BOOKS  NEW YORK CITY

A LEISURE BOOK®

First edition October 2002

Published by

Dorchester Publishing Co., Inc.
276 Fifth Avenue
New York, NY 10001

ISBN 0-8439-5098-6

Printed in the United States of America.

1 2 3 4 5 6 7 8 9 10

TABLE OF CONTENTS

"The Circle" by Bentley Little.. 1

"Pyre" by Christopher Golden..................................... 79

"Jonah Arose" by Tom Piccirilli.................................167

"The Words" by Douglas Clegg....................................241

THE CIRCLE

by Bentley Little

HELEN

It was hard to hear the knocking over the noise of the microwave, so Helen wasn't sure how long it had been going on, but the moment her oatmeal finished cooking she heard the staccato tapping of knuckles on wood, and she strode quickly out of the kitchen and through the living room to the front door. The knocking grew louder, harder, faster as she approached. Whoever was outside wanted desperately to get in, and while her first impulse was to throw open the door and let the knocker find refuge in her home, good sense won out, and she called, "Who is it?"

"Let me in!"

It was a child's voice, a boy's, and Helen found that she was not surprised. Something about the uninhibited ferocity of the knocking indicated a non-adult origin.

"Let me in!"

The kid sounded agitated, scared, and she imagined him being chased by bullies or pursued by an abusive father. Maybe he was fleeing a psychotic killer, like that kid who'd temporarily gotten away from Jeffrey Dahmer before the police had stupidly given him back to the cannibal. Helen unhooked the latch, threw the deadbolt and pulled open the door. She had time to register that he was small, nine maybe or ten, dirty, wearing nothing but a brown loincloth, and then he was speeding past her, running as fast as he could through her living room and down the hall.

"Hey!"

She tried to follow after him, but the bathroom door was already slammed shut and locked by the time she reached the hallway. There was something unnerving about that. The kid had not hesitated, had seemed to know exactly where he was going, as though he were intimately familiar with their house.

Helen knocked on the door. "Are you all right in there?"

No answer.

She knocked again. "Hello?"

The kid didn't answer, and she wondered if she should dial 911, call the police. What if there was something seriously wrong? She'd only gotten a glimpse of him when he dashed past her, and while he'd looked unhurt, maybe he was injured and she just hadn't seen it.

"Are you okay?"

There was no response, and she jiggled the knob. Worried that he had collapsed or passed out in there, she pressed her ear to the door. From inside, she heard grunting, straining, heard the disgusting sound of plopping water.

He was going to the bathroom.

Maybe he was sick, suffering from some intestinal disorder.

She moved away from the door, wondering if she should call Tony on his cell phone and have him come home. He'd only left ten minutes ago; he couldn't be at the office yet. Besides, maybe he'd have some ideas—

Suddenly the door burst open and the loinclothed kid was running past her down the hall.

She hadn't heard the door unlock, hadn't heard any noises at all, but she didn't have time to think about that and quickly followed him through the hallway, through the kitchen and out the back door. He sped across the yard and into the garage, slamming the small garage door behind him.

What the hell was going on here? Helen stood on the stoop, torn between going back and checking the bathroom to make sure nothing was amiss, and following the boy into the garage to make sure he was all right. She finally moved forward and hurried across the lawn. To her surprise, the door was locked. She wasn't aware that it *could* be locked; the door was old and practically falling off its hinges, the pressboard peeling away in buckling layers beneath the flaking paint. She tried turning the knob but it was frozen, tried pulling on the door but it was shut tight. She could go inside and get the key for the Master Lock on the big garage door, but by that time he could be gone.

Theirs was an old garage, with a small window on the side, and she walked around the corner of the building and peered through the glass, trying to make out what was what behind the decades-thick layer of dirt. She saw the boy, in the open area between Tony's tools and lawnmower and the piled bulk of summer lawn furniture.

He was squatting on the floor, grimacing, obviously trying to go again.

Helen thought for a brief second, then glanced around the backyard until she found what she was looking for: the used cinderblocks that Tony had scavanged last week. They were piled against the fence and already covered with dead leaves and spiderwebs, but she grabbed the top one and placed it against the small door, pushing it hard against the wood. The door opened outward, and if she could put enough weight against it, the boy would not be able to get out.

Six trips back and forth, and she had all the cinderblocks piled in front of the door. She took one last look through the window—he was still squatting, still straining—then ran back into the house. She went directly to the bathroom and looked into the toilet, grimacing, prepared for the worst. She saw—

—diamonds.

Helen blinked dumbly. There were not just a few stones; there was a pile of them, a small mound at the bottom of the still clear water, their facets shimmering in the room's yellowish light. There was only one explanation for their origin, one place from which they could have come, and though she tried to think of an alternate answer, there did not seem to be one.

The boy shit diamonds.

It was the only possibility.

She reached into the water, picked up one that was as big as the fingernail on her thumb. She wasn't a lapidary expert or a gemologist; she probably couldn't tell a real diamond from a cubic zirconium. But she placed the stone against the bathroom mirror and drew it down. A long scratch followed in its wake. Diamonds cut glass. That's all the proof she needed.

4

Helen was already late for work, but she grabbed the cordless phone in the kitchen and rather than calling her office dialed her husband as she hurried out the back door. He answered on the second ring, and she quickly told him what had happened, how the dirty loinclothed boy had been pounding on the front door and she'd let him inside and he'd run straight to the bathroom and locked himself in.

"I heard him . . . *going*," she said. "I thought he was sick or something, like he had intestinal problems. Then he ran out the back door and into the garage." She paused. "The kid poops diamonds."

"Hold on, hold on, hold on." She could imagine him shaking his head with his eyes half-closed in that annoying way he had. "What did you say?"

"The kid poops diamonds." She knew how it sounded. Hell, it didn't make much sense even to her. But there it was. It happened, it *was* happening, and no amount of analyzing or rationalization could change the cold hard fact that there was a pile of diamonds sitting in the bottom of their toilet bowl.

Helen took a deep breath. "When the boy goes to the bathroom, diamonds come out. Big, perfectly cut diamonds. They're in the toilet of the small bathroom right now. And he's in the garage. That's why I called you. What do you think I should do?"

"I have that meeting with Fincher today, Hel." His voice had suddenly dropped to a low whisper, and she knew his boss was now in the room. "Do I have to come home? Do I have to come right now?"

"Tony!"

"Call Child Services or something. Look it up in the phone

book. Let them take care of him. Go across the street and wake up Gil Marotta if you're scared. He's home all day. He can help you."

"I'm not scared! I told you, he craps diamonds. The kid sat on our toilet, and went to the bathroom and diamonds literally came out of his ass."

"Hel . . ."

"I'm serious." She lowered her voice, though there was no one to overhear. "We're rich, Tony. I have him trapped in the garage right now—"

"Trapped!"

"Just 'til we figure out what to do."

"That's kidnapping!"

She was in front of the garage, and she pressed her foot against the stacked cinderblocks, gratified to find that they did not budge. "He went in there himself and he hasn't even tried to get out."

"But if he did try to get out, he couldn't. You've trapped him."

"That's why I called you."

There was a frustrated exhalation that sounded like static. "Call someone. The city, the county, the state. One of them has a department to deal with runaways and missing children. Hand him over to them. Your diamonds . . ." He exhaled again, and she knew he didn't believe her. "Do what you want with the diamonds. I'll look at them when I get home."

"Okay. Bye." She clicked off without waiting for a reply and stared for a moment at the peeling door. If he didn't believe her, what *did* he think? The only other alternative was that she was lying. Or crazy.

She didn't even want to consider that. Her world had been turned upside down as it was; the last thing she needed was to find out that Tony, to whom she'd entrusted her deepest, most secret feelings over the past fifteen years, to whom she'd made passionate love this morning before getting out of bed, could so quickly and easily be persuaded that she had lost her mind.

She walked around the side of the garage and tried to focus instead on the diamonds. They were worth a fortune. Thousands of dollars. Hundreds of thousands. Millions, maybe. But how would they explain the fact that they were in possession of the rocks? Did they have to explain it? She didn't know. Her knowledge of this stuff came entirely from movies and television, and while the jewelers to whom they sold the diamonds might not ask any questions, the IRS most certainly would. They'd have to be able to explain where they got this sudden wealth, this huge increase of income.

It was all confusing, and she peered through the dirty window into the garage.

The boy was squatting on the floor and shitting again.

Rubies.

Even in the dim refracted light they glittered redly, and Helen wondered how such a thing was physically possible. It wasn't, she knew, and she watched as rubies dropped onto the cement floor. One, two, three . . .

Maybe they had a miracle on their hands. She and Tony weren't religious, and she'd never been one to believe in any sort of supernatural claptrap, but there was nothing in the known world that could explain what was happening here, and she found herself thinking that maybe they were being rewarded, maybe this was a gift that had been sent to them from some higher power.

Inside the garage, the boy grimaced, and another ruby was squeezed out from between the cheeks of his buttocks.

Tony called after his meeting, just before noon, and Helen lied and said that she'd phoned Social Services, the Child Protection division, and a caseworker was here with her now. In truth, she was still perched outside the garage, making sure the boy did not escape. He was asleep, curled into a fetal position in the center of the open space to the right of Tony's record boxes, but he had already produced emeralds and some gemstone she didn't recognize in addition to the diamonds and rubies.

She'd brought out a folding chair and today's newspaper, as well as a water bottle and a bag of potato chips. No telling how long she was going to be out here, and she figured she might as well make herself comfortable.

She'd had plenty of time to think this morning, and she'd revised her theory as to the boy's origin. He was not a divine miracle sent to reward them for some good deed or morally upright behavior. He was a natural phenomenon who had lucked into their grasp, and if they were smart enough and savvy enough, he would make them rich.

But where had he been before this? she couldn't help wondering. And who had had him before? Weren't those people looking for him, trying to get him back? In her mind, she saw a bunch of bumbling business-suited crooks led by Joe Flynn or Cesar Romero, like in all those old Disney movies.

Tony took off work early, and she was inside the house for a quick bathroom break when he arrived home just after three.

She was using the bathroom in the master bedroom, having left the diamonds in the toilet untouched in the bathroom off the hall, and when she heard him call tentatively, "Helen?," she quickly finished and met him in the living room.

"Everything all squared away?" he asked when he saw her. "That kid gone?"

"Actually," she told him, "he's in the garage."

"What?"

"Now we have emeralds and rubies and, I think, sapphires and topaz. At least, that's what the pictures in the encyclopedia look like, but it's hard to tell."

"You didn't call anyone? You kept him prisoner in the fucking *garage*?"

Helen had never heard him so angry, and for a second she thought he might actually hit her. But instead he smacked his own forehead, palm hitting head skin with an audible slap, then ran his fingers so hard through his hair that it pulled up his eyebrows. "What the hell has gotten into you?"

"Come here." She led him down the hall to the bathroom and showed him the diamonds in the toilet. He reached in wonderingly and picked up a small handful, holding them up to the light.

"Jesus."

"I told you." She smiled and could not keep the excitement out of her voice. "We're rich."

Tony shook his head, carefully putting the diamonds down on the counter next to the hairspray. "That's still no reason to lock up that poor boy in the garage. He's not a rabid animal."

"No, but he's wild. He's—"

"I'm getting him out." Tony pulled off his tie as he walked, throwing it on the table in the breakfast nook as he headed through the kitchen and out the door. Helen followed, feeling chastened and embarrassed and . . . something else. Afraid? Maybe so, though she didn't know why. She stood on the lawn, not helping but not hindering, as he removed the stacked cinderblocks from in front of the door.

"Hello?" Tony announced. "Are you okay in there?" But there was no answer.

He carefully opened the garage door—

And the boy ran out.

"Catch him!" Helen yelled instinctively, and for a brief confused moment Tony tried to do just that, but the dirty loinclothed child slipped between his hands, ran around the lemon tree and darted into the oleander bushes that hid the chainlink fence separating their yard from the woman's house next door.

Tony moved up to the bushes, carefully parting branches, looking for the boy but apparently not finding him. He moved all the way to the back fence and the end of the oleanders, but the boy seemed to have disappeared.

"You think he went next door?" Helen asked.

"I don't see how. The branches are all tangled in the fence; I don't see how he could get over it. Maybe there's a hole underneath the fence that I missed. . . ."

"What do we do now? Do you still think we should call someone?"

Tony thought for a moment, shook his head. She could see that the decision weighed on him, that he felt uneasy about it. "Since you imprisoned him all day long in our garage, I'm not that anxious to announce our connection to him," he said. "Let someone else take care of it. Let the next person figure out what to do with him. It's out of our hands now."

Helen smiled. "And we're rich."

She walked into the garage to gather up the rubies and the emeralds and all the other gems.

They still hadn't told anyone else about their newfound riches. They hadn't even bothered to find out the going rate for precious stones. They had weighed their haul, however, placing each type of gemstone in a separate sack and placing the sacks on the bathroom scale to get a rough approximation of what they had.

Helen had decided to quit her job and never go back to work. She had not called in sick today, and no one from the office had called home to inquire about her, so she figured she just wouldn't show up again. They could send her last check through the mail.

Tony was not so optimistic. These could be fake jewels, he told her. They could be stolen.

He was planning to go to work tomorrow as always.

It was late. They'd stayed up far longer than intended, talking about what had happened, debating what to do, but not really coming to any conclusions. Too tired for her usual shower, Helen took off her clothes and put on her nightshirt. "Where do you think he went?" she wondered. She pressed her face to the bedroom window, placing her hands on both sides of her face to filter out the glare and reflection from the inside lights. It was completely dark at first, black, but then her eyes adjusted and she could make out the lemon tree, the storage shed, the oleanders.

The boy.

He was crouched in the bushes, staring at the house, staring at *her*, and his eyes seemed to be luminescent.

She nearly jumped, her heart leaping in her chest. A chill passed through her, and though she didn't know why she was scared, she was, and she wished to God that she had not decided to peek out the window.

His eyes were still staring, unblinking, and she thought that he was probably taking a shit.

What had seemed magical and wonderous in the daytime now seemed spooky and vaguely sinister. Why had he come back? Why hadn't he left for good? What did he want?

"What is it?" Tony asked from the bed.

She was afraid to move away from the glass, afraid to let him out of her sight. "He's out there. The boy. He's in the oleanders, staring at me. I can see him."

Tony scrambled out of bed, rushed over, but in the few seconds it took him to reach her, the boy looked to the right, his luminescent eyes shifting in a different direction . . . and then he was gone. She squinted at the spot where he had been, looked to the left, to the right, but he was nowhere to be seen. It was dark outside and he could have easily slid into the shadows, could be hiding right in plain sight, but somehow she didn't think that was the case.

There was the sound of frantic knocking on the front door.

"Don't let him in!" she screamed at Tony. She pushed him away from her, pushed him toward the bedroom door, and he started running, spurred by the urgency in her voice. "Make sure everything's locked! Make sure he can't get inside!"

She didn't know what had gotten into her, why she was suddenly so frightened by the child, but she had always been one to trust her instincts, and she wasn't about to question her reactions now. She had pulled back from the window, and the outside world was just a uniform black with her own reflection, horrified and ghostlike, on the glass.

The knocking on the front door had stopped, and she held her breath, listening, heart racing. She wanted to yell at Tony not to open the door under any circumstances, not even to open it a crack to see what was going on outside, but she was afraid to call out in case he had already done so.

What if the boy was in the house?

So what if he was? He'd been in here this morning and the only thing he'd done was leave them with enough diamonds to ensure that they would never have to work again.

Of course, that was before she'd trapped him in the hot garage all day long without food or water.

"Let me in."

She started at the sound of the voice. It was clear and close, and when she looked at the window, she saw the boy's dirty face next to the glass. She backed carefully toward the bed, afraid to look away.

"Let me in," the boy said, and this time his voice was a sly whisper that should not have been able to penetrate the closed window.

"No!" she screamed.

"Let me in."

They were the only words he said, the only words she'd ever heard him say, and she wondered now if that meant something, if he was like a vampire or a witch or whatever that monster was that had to be invited inside before it could do any harm. God, she hoped so.

The backyard light was flipped on, illuminating the lawn area and the patio and the front of the garage. Tony. He was in the kitchen. "Don't go outside!" she yelled. "Stay in! Don't go out!" He didn't respond, but the back door didn't open, so she assumed that he'd heard her.

In the glare of the floodlight, she could see the boy more clearly. He had moved away from the window and was squatting on the grass, going again. He cried out in pain—he was obviously passing something large—and while Helen watched, something big and dark dropped from between his legs. Vaguely round, it rolled a few inches, then stopped, caught on a straight irregular side. He reached underneath him and lifted it up.

By its hair.

Helen's hand automatically went to her mouth, and she backed away from the window, her legs threatening to buckle beneath her. The boy had just shit a human head. She still hadn't gotten a good look at it, but it was female, she could tell that much, and—

Oh, God, he was bringing it up to the window to show her!

Let me in, the child's lips were saying, but either no sound was coming out or she couldn't hear the words. He was holding the head high, like a lantern, and when he reached a spot where the floodlight's beam was not obstructed by the roof of the house, she saw that it had her own face; eyes wide, mouth open in an expression of surprise that no doubt echoed her own.

The boy threw the head at the window, and with a frightened yelp Helen ran across the bedroom to the door. Behind her, she heard it hit the glass: a muffled thump followed by a sickening squeegee sound. Was it sliding down the window? She had to turn and look, but all she saw was the boy picking up the head—

her head

—by its hair and cocking his arm to throw it again.

Let me in, his lips mouthed.

She ran into the dark hallway but stopped almost immediately. Where was Tony? He should have been back. He should have returned by now. But the house was silent. She didn't hear his voice, didn't hear his footfalls on the creaking floor.

Maybe he'd been captured. Or killed. Maybe there was an army of these boys, all look-alikes, and when the first one had run off, he'd gone to get his friends and now they were back and out for revenge.

Behind her, in the bedroom, the head—

her head

—hit the glass again.

Helen screamed, a wrenching gut-deep cry of terror and frustration, and Tony came running out of the kitchen, into the hall. She threw herself at him, held on tight. "Thank God," she sobbed. "Thank God."

"I was watching him through the kitchen window," Tony said, and he sounded rattled, his voice shaky. "He was . . . he . . ."

"He shit a head!" Helen cried. "*My* head! And now he's throwing it at our bedroom window trying to get in!" She looked up into her husband's face. "Why's he doing this? What the hell is he?"

"I don't know," Tony admitted.

Behind them, in the bedroom, the head hit the glass.

"Don't let him in!" Helen said, clutching Tony tightly. "Whatever you do, don't let him in!"

"I won't."

"Let's call the police," she suggested. "I'll tell them everything. I'll show them the diamonds and the rubies and . . . and . . . everything."

She blinked, stopped.

The diamonds. The rubies. The emeralds. The sapphires. The topaz. They were still in the house, wrapped up in bags in the den. But were they still the same? The boy had changed with the coming of night, turned into something else. Had the gemstones changed, too? Were they now eyes and teeth and fingers? Somehow, such a thing wasn't hard to imagine.

Wiping her eyes, taking a deep shuddering breath, she pulled herself away from Tony and grabbed his hand, leading him into the den. She was prepared for anything, but the diamonds were still diamonds, the rubies still rubies, all was as it should have been.

The pounding had stopped. Either he'd broken through the window with that excreted head or he'd given up that tactic and was now trying to get in some other way. She knew that he would never give up completely. He might cease a specific action, but his ultimate goal would always remain the same.

Whatever that might be.

Tony was picking up the phone to dial 911 when suddenly there was noise all around them, a papery, whispery chittering that seemed to come from every side. He dropped the phone and they quickly ran out of the room, but the noise was in the hallway, too. And the living room.

"Come on!" he said, and led the way into the kitchen. Here, through the windows, they could see the bugs. There were hundreds of them, thousands, and they swarmed over the grass, over the patio, over the house, moving up the walls, starting to cover the windows. Even through the roof and ceiling she and Tony could hear the chittering sound, and Helen was about to ask why they were making such a weird noise when she finally figured it out.

They were trying to get inside by eating their way through.

"Oh, shit." Tony pointed outside. The boy was squatting and straining, and what dropped from between the cheeks of his buttocks this time was a cascade of pitch black beetles with visibly snapping pincers. They spread out, moving impossibly fast, and they kept coming, spewing out in a torrent. These were what was engulfing the house, and even as they watched, their view of the boy was obstructed as a black mass of moving beetles inched up the window glass.

Helen started crying again. Why had she opened the front door this morning? Why had she let that boy inside? If she had ignored him, he would have gone elsewhere and right now instead of fighting for their lives they would be peacefully sleeping in their bed, just like their neighbors were.

Their neighbors! If these beetles were covering the *whole* house, the other people on the circle should be able to see what was going on. Maybe one of them would come over and try to help, maybe one of them would call the police.

Of course, it *was* late. And the chance that anyone was up

right now and looking out their front windows at their neighbors' houses was pretty damn slim.

Gil, maybe. He worked at night. He could come home and see what was happening and get help.

Tony, standing as far as possible from the blackening windows, was dialing 911 from the kitchen phone, but she could tell by the confused frown on his face that he was having no luck. The beetles had probably overrun the phone line and gnawed through it. He threw down the receiver, swearing.

"Where's the cell phone?" she cried.

"I left it in the car."

"Oh shit. Oh shit." Helen took a deep breath, swallowed her sobs. "What are we going to do?"

"I don't know." Tony got two big knives out of the top drawer, handed one to Helen. "Let's go to the front door. If it looks like we can make it, we run. If not, I guess we'll hole up in the small bathroom. It doesn't have any windows. It's probably the safest room in the house."

A loud screech cut through the low noise of the beetles. Or, rather, a loud series of concurrent screeches. The windows shattered, hundreds of the black bugs tumbling over the sink, over the counter onto the floor. Helen had time to register that the glass had broken in clean even lines; then the beetles were teeming over the breakfast nook, up the walls, onto the ceiling, a dark unstoppable wave.

She clutched Tony hard with her left hand while holding tight to the knife with her right, ready to slash at anything that came at her.

She was concentrating so hard on the hordes of beetles swarming over the floor that she neglected to keep track of the insects on the ceiling. When Tony's grip tightened on her own, however, and his knife motioned upward, she saw that the bugs had covered the area directly above them and were moving toward the open doorway into the hall. One fell on her knife hand, pincers clacking crazily. But it was the opposite end of the bug that rent her flesh, that sliced through the skin next to her thumb, and she saw, protruding from the beetle's hind end, a small sparkling diamond.

That was what had cut through the window glass, she realized.

More bugs started to fall, landing on her arms, her shoulders, her head. She tried to shake them off, tried to pull off the one in her palm, but the diamond was sunk into her flesh. Suddenly . . . it was released. The tiny gem was pushed into her and others followed, a steady stream of them.

The beetle was shitting diamonds inside her.

Screaming, jerking her shoulders, waving her knife wildly, Helen tried desperately to rid herself of the insects. Next to her, Tony was doing the same thing as beetles landed on his shoulders, scurrying both down his arms, and up his head. Pinpricks of pain erupted all over her skin as diamonds cut her, sinking into her skin, piercing through her clothes. She scraped some off of her left arm with the knife, but the diamonds remained embedded and more beetles took the place of the old ones.

She was going down.

And then the boy walked in. The insects had eaten through the door and part of the wall, and he stepped through the ragged hole, loincloth flapping, even his dirty skin looking bright against the blackness of the bugs. He carried nothing with him—no head, thank God—and the expression on his face was one of total and utter calm, a far cry from the wild agitation of the morning. His eyes still seemed luminescent, eerily so, and there was something in his poised slow approach that seemed defiantly unnatural. The wave of beetles parted before him, allowing him to pass, and even on the ceiling above a clear swath appeared.

Helen was sobbing, crying not so much from the pain but from the complete sense of defeat that had engulfed her and seemed to be the only emotion she could conjure. She closed her eyes. . . .

And the bugs were gone.

She felt their absence instantly. There was no retreat, no movement, only what seemed to be a spontaneous disappearance. She opened her eyes—they could only have been closed for a few seconds—and the kitchen was clear. Evidence of their invasion still remained. The wall and door they had eaten. The scratches and welts all over her and Tony. They were not part of a false vision or hallucination. They'd been here. But she had no idea what had happened to them.

Tony was standing next to her, dead on his feet, still clutching the useless kitchen knife. Before them stood the boy, and he stared for a moment as if studying them.

"What do you want?" Helen cried.

The child smiled, and it was the most horrifying thing she had ever seen. Slowly, he squatted down on his haunches, shifting aside his loincloth, preparing to evacuate.

"NO!" Tony cried, his voice filled with terror.

Neither of them had any idea what was coming next, but they both knew that this was the end, the grand finale, the climax of what had begun this morning when Helen had allowed the desperate child into their home.

The boy grimaced, his face turning red, the muscles in his neck bulging, and what emerged from between his legs was—

a single red rose.

It arrived perfectly, petals intact, leaves on stem, though how that was possible Helen did not know. The flower was dark burgundy, with a single white spot on the topmost petal, and she recognized it immediately. A rose with exactly that rare coloration had been growing wild in the woman's yard next door. Helen had seen it last spring when they'd trimmed the oleanders. She'd reached over the chain-link fence with her clippers and cut the rose, thinking it would make a nice centerpiece for the dinner they were having that night with Fincher and his wife, but when she put it in a vase she saw that it was overrun with scores of nearly microscopic bugs, and she threw it outside in the garbage.

The two couldn't be connected . . . yet she knew that somehow they were. The boy took the flower in his fingers and with a flourish that seemed inappropriate for both his age and the circumstances, handed it to her.

Maybe this was it, she thought, maybe it would all be over now. She glanced at Tony, who nodded slightly. Sniffling, trying hard to rein in her emotions, she reached out and accepted the proffered rose. A thorn stabbed her thumb, and where her blood touched the plant, it withered, blackened. She looked into the center of the flower and saw that it was crawling with teeny tiny bugs, and when she squinted and looked closer at them, she saw that they were miniature versions of the beetles that had been attacking her and Tony.

21

The boy started dancing. "Let me in!" he said/sang, and rather than a request or a demand, it was a jubilant announcement, a celebratory taunt. *They* let me in, he was proclaiming, although he left off that first word. "Let me in!" he said/sang/danced.

Suddenly, the child stopped dancing and doubled over in pain. A harsh spasm wracked his body and he fell to the floor. It looked like he was being hit with a hammer, and though she knew that was impossible, so many other impossible things had happened that she thought it might be true.

Yes! she thought.

She hoped that invisible hammer beat the hell out of him.

With each blow or spasm, the boy seemed to diminish slightly. He wasn't growing smaller or shrinking; he was becoming less human, his legs looking more spindly, his arms shortening and losing inner solidity, the features of his face fading into blandness. He rolled toward the hole in the wall and door through which he'd come, still buffeted by the physical impact of something unseen, and by the time he reached the ragged opening, she could not see any mouth or nose or eyes. He looked like a large piece of Silly Putty shaped into the general form of a person and tied with a piece of dirty cloth.

Then he was outside and gone, and with grateful relief, Helen threw aside the rose and collapsed into the arms of her husband. Tony was battered and bleeding, but his arms were strong and felt good, and both of them looked toward the hole in the wall, waiting to see what, if anything, would come through it next.

When several minutes passed with no sign of movement, no sound from outside, Tony, holding her tightly, limped toward the ragged opening and looked into the backyard. It was clear. No boy, no head, no bugs, nothing.

It was over.

They didn't know what had happened, didn't know how or why it had stopped, but they were grateful that it had and, still leaning on each other, they made their way through the house to make sure they saw nothing out of the ordinary. They didn't. In the den, the bags of gemstones lay on top of Tony's desk, undisturbed. They had not disappeared, not turned to shit, they were what they had always been: diamonds, rubies, emeralds, sapphire, topaz.

Helen refused to touch them. She turned back around, returned to the hallway. "Give them away," she said. "Throw them away."

She never wanted to see another jewel or gemstone again.

Tony nodded tiredly.

Neither of them seemed to know what to do next. It was late, they were exhausted, and they should probably clean up, tend to their wounds and go back to bed, but instead they stood there for several moments, leaning against the wall in the hallway. After awhile, Helen started to notice a distinct pressure in her abdomen, an uncomfortable yet very familiar urge. She looked at the clotting wounds on her arms, saw the sparkle of diamonds in the drying blood. Next to her, Tony shifted uneasily, pressing his legs together, bending forward slightly. She looked at him.

"I have to go to the bathroom," Tony admitted. "And I'm afraid to."

"Me, too." Helen felt a sharp cramping in her bowels, and wondered what was in there, what would come out.

"We have to go sometime."

Across from them was the bathroom. The light in there was on, but that did not lessen the ominous atmosphere. She thought that she would never forget the sight of those diamonds in the clear water, piled like a pyramid.

"I'll go first," Helen said. She walked over to the bathroom, stepped inside. Looking at the toilet, she felt a sharp cramp, then turned back toward Tony. "Wish me luck," she told him.

"Luck," he said softly.

She closed the door behind her.

FRANK

"It tastes like honey."

"Nuh-uh."

"It says so right here. 'His tongue slid into her moist opening, and he tasted her delicious golden nectar, the sweet honey of her love.' "

Chase shook his head. "My brother's *done* it. And he says it tastes like sweat."

Johnny and Frank looked at each other. "Ewwww," they said simultaneously.

"You guys're like a fucking cartoon show." Chase grabbed the book from Frank's hands and tossed it back into the closet with the others, covering up the pile with a load of dirty clothes.

Frank picked up his Coke from the floor and finished it off, tossing the can at the wastepaper basket and missing. That's what he liked about hanging out at Chase's house—the boy's parents were never home. They always had the place to themselves. They could do cool stuff like read porno books or go to chat rooms on the Internet or make prank phone calls. That wasn't possible at his and Johnny's houses. Johnny's mom didn't work, so she was always at home. His own mom did work and was gone, but since his dad worked at night, he was home all day. That was the worst.

But Chase's house was open range, they were free to do whatever they wanted, and it was almost like they weren't kids, like they were college students rooming together, grown-up buddies hanging out in their own pad.

"Why should we believe your brother?" Johnny said. "Maybe he's lying and the book's telling the truth."

"Because I know him. Because I caught him in his room with a babe once when my parents were gone. And because he doesn't just *talk* about things like you two dweebs. He actually does 'em."

"Us two dweebs?" Frank said, smiling.

"Yeah," Johnny said. "Between school and sleeping and hanging around with us, I don't see where you have a whole hell of a lot of extra time."

"All right, like *us*," Chase said, giving in. He finished his own Coke, threw the can in the air and karate kicked it across the room, where it hit the edge of a table and landed on the carpet. He looked from Frank to Johnny. "You know, we have a chance to change all that."

"All what?"

"I overheard my brother talking on the phone. He and his friend Paul are going to the shrine tonight. They're going to try to use it."

The shrine.

Frank glanced at Johnny, then looked quickly away. Neither of them had ever seen the shrine, but they'd known about it ever since they were in grammar school. It was in the backyard of that lady professor's house, next to Johnny's, and rumor had it that she was a witch. Such rumors were understandable. Her house looked like it ought to be condemned, which was weird for someone with a job like hers, and she was hugely fat. Hardly anyone ever saw her, and when they did, it was only very briefly as she got in or out of her car. She taught about ancient religions or something at the junior college, and supposedly she'd put up the shrine to worship her gods. According to Keri Armstrong, who'd moved in fifth grade but who used to live on the opposite side of the witch's house and was the only one of them brave enough to go into that overgrown backyard on a truth-or-dare, the shrine could grant wishes. If you wished the right way and said the right words and did the right things, it would give you what you wanted. A lot of kids had talked about using it over the years, but as far as he knew, none of them had ever been brave enough to go through with it.

"What are they going to do?" Johnny asked.

"They want money. Chaz has his eye on this old Charger that he said him and Paul can rebuild. They found it in *The Recycler*, even went down to look at it, but it's two grand and in shit shape, and they'll need another grand just to get it to work. So they're going to ask for three thousand."

Frank whistled.

"Yeah, I know."

"It's not gonna work."

"No." Chase flopped down on the couch. "You think that cow's really a witch?"

"There's no such thing as witches."

"I know that, dill weed. I mean, do you think *she* thinks she's a witch? Obviously she doesn't have magic powers or anything. Otherwise, she wouldn't be so fat and her house wouldn't be such a goddamn mess. But if she thinks she does, she might still do all those spells and potions and things, even if they don't work, just because it's part of her religion or whatever." He leaned forward conspiratorily. "Maybe she sacrifices cats or dogs on that altar."

"Or kids," Johnny said, putting into words what they'd all been thinking.

"Or kids," Chase agreed solemnly.

They considered that for a moment.

"So what's your plan?" Johnny asked excitedly.

They both knew Chase had a plan. He never suggested they do anything without having some detailed scheme in mind, and they knew he didn't want to just spy on his brother and his brother's friends. Frank feigned an enthusiasm he did not feel. "Yeah. What's the plan?"

Chase grinned. "We follow 'em out there, see what happens, see if they get their money. If they do, we ask for a hot chick for ourselves."

"You just said it wasn't going to work."

"It probably won't. And if it doesn't, we'll throw some rocks at 'em and scare 'em. They'll be just as freaked by that place as us and they'll probably crap their pants. If it *does* work . . ." He raised his eyebrows comically.

"But . . ." Johnny said. He thought for a moment. "The shrine. How does it . . . operate? Do you just pray to it or do you have to bring it something or what?"

27

"I'm not sure," Chase admitted.

Frank didn't like anything about this. He didn't believe in magical powers or the supernatural, but . . . still. "What if it's a Monkey's Paw–type deal? What if it gives you what you want but in some way that punishes you? Like your brother gets his money but it's because your parents die in a car crash and he inherits the cash? Or you ask for a babe and she's a corpse or something?"

"*I* ask for a babe? *We* ask for a babe."

"Whatever."

It was obvious that Chase had not thought through any of these possibilities, and though Frank hoped that he'd been able to scare his friend, that Chase might change his mind and cancel the whole thing, it was obvious from the expression on his face that the other boy gave such concerns only the briefest of considerations before deciding to go through with his original plan.

Since Chase didn't know exactly when his brother would be heading over to the shrine, only knew that it would be late and long after dark, he suggested they all meet in his side yard at nine sharp, next to the fence where they used to have their clubhouse.

Frank shuffled his feet and looked down at the ground, refusing to meet Chase's eyes. "I might not be able to make it," he said. "If I'm not there by nine, you guys go on without me."

"Whaddaya mean, you might not make it? It's Friday night, dude! What are you going to do, stay inside and watch TV with your mommy?"

The truth was, that sounded a whole hell of a lot better

than sneaking through the witch's backyard to spy on Chase's brother. But he didn't want to be tagged for life as a pussy and a momma's boy.

"Listen," Johnny said, "we'll tell our parents we're going to a movie." He looked at Frank. "I'll say that your mom's driving us; you tell your parents that my mom's taking us." It was tacitly acknowledged that Chase would have no problem getting out of his house.

Frank snorted. "You don't think my parents'll look out the window and notice that your parents' car's still in the driveway? You're two houses away! Jesus, what a stupid plan."

"Sneak out," Chase said. "I don't care how you do it; the details are up to you. Just make sure that you're there on time." He looked from Johnny to Frank. "You understand?"

Both boys nodded.

"Good. Because, trust me, there'll be hell to pay if you don't show."

They met at the appointed time in Chase's side yard, where Chase was keeping an eye on his brother's bedroom window. Chaz and Paul were still in there, and Chase said he thought they were waiting for another friend, but almost immediately after he said that, the bedroom light went out and a moment later the two older boys walked out the front door.

"The front door? I had to sneak out my window!" Johnny complained.

Frank had, too, although escape from the house had been much easier than he thought. It was the first time he'd ever done such a thing, and the only thing he was worried about was getting the screen back on the window when he returned.

"Come on!" Chase whispered. "Let's go!"

They followed Chaz and Paul as the older boys walked down the sidewalk, around the circle, the three of them keeping to the shadows, staying on lawns, darting from bush to bush. Chaz and Paul were acting casual, but they were acting *too* casual, and it was clear that they'd planned this thing out in advance. When they reached the witch's house, they walked past it, stopped, pretended to talk, then walked back in front of it again. They were obviously on the lookout, making sure they had not been spotted, and when they determined that the coast was clear, they ran into the overgrown front yard.

The darkness seemed to swallow them. Frank knew it was only the power of suggestion, a holdover from his younger days, when he'd been afraid to even look at that house and yard at night, but it seemed to him that illumination from the street-light in front of Johnny's died right at the edge of the witch's property line, that light was not allowed on that wild weedy stretch of ground.

"Hurry up!" Chase had brought a flashlight but he didn't want to use it, not unless he had to. He thought it would give them away, and he sped after his brother and Paul, darting from dead tree to dead bush, pushing through the high dry weeds toward the side of the house. When they were far enough back from the road and thought no one would be able to see, Chaz and Paul switched on their own flashlights, and from that point on it was easier to trail them.

They moved past a broken lawnmower and a discarded washing machine, a tree stump and a pile of buckets, and then they were in the backyard. There was no wall, no gate, no

30

barrier of any kind, and it was only by the position of the fence next door that they knew where they were. They passed behind the edge of the house, and back here, if possible, the yard was even more of a mess. Frank understood now why neighbors had gotten up petitions against the woman, trying to make her clean up her place. It *smelled*, for Christ's sake. Like her sewer had backed up or like she and all of the neighborhood cats and dogs had just taken a dump back here. Next to him he heard Johnny, the most squeamish member of their trio, gagging as though he were about to puke.

"Shhh!" Chase warned.

The debris and the foliage both grew thicker as they tried to follow the intermittant glow of the flashlight. This was a big yard, Frank thought, much bigger than any of theirs, and already he was lost, his sense of direction all screwed up. High bushes, and piles of wood and old rotting newspapers blocked the view of any of the adjoining yards, and even the black bulk of the house was lost from sight. They passed by a mountain of dead leaves, a bunch of scrap metal and chicken wire, and a pile of cardboard boxes filled with garbage. They seemed to be going in circles, and it occurred to him that Chaz and his friend didn't know where the shrine was either; they were just searching by trial-and-error.

Then they were there.

Chase, in the front, stopped and crouched down behind an upside-down birdbath. Frank and Johnny followed suit. Chaz trained his flashlight on the shrine. Frank wasn't sure what he thought it would look like, but it had been more like those things in the Chinese restaurant or in his friend Thanh's house:

31

a red alcove with a little plastic statue inside it and some gaudy Asian doodads hanging from the top, little pots sitting in the front with some burning sticks of incense.

This, though, was . . . different.

For one thing, it was big, as tall as he was, rather than a little box that came up to his knee. And it looked old. It was sort of an arch shape or a tombstone shape, and it was made out of mud or adobe or cheap cement that was all flaking off and crumbling. At the top was some sort of design, a squiggly spiral that was carved into the deteriorating material. Below that was a rounded alcove that was either painted black or went back far enough that light couldn't penetrate. It looked like the sort of space where there should be a statue of a saint or Jesus or Mary or something, but it was empty. On the short stone platform in front of it were fingernails and photographs, underwear and hats, stuff that appeared to have been left by previous visitors.

Frank had never known anyone brave enough to actually go to the shrine—until tonight—and he found himself wondering if maybe the people who had come here before were adults. The thought frightened him. He imagined Mr. Christensen or Mr. Wallace or maybe even Chase's mom sneaking out here in the middle of the night to ask for a raise or a baby or a new car.

Johnny's dad got a new car last year.

Frank didn't want to think about it. He focused his attention on Chaz and Paul. What the hell were they doing? Both boys were unbuckling their belts, pulling down their pants and pointing their already erect peckers at the shrine. They started stroking themselves.

32

"Your brother's a homo," Johnny whispered.

Chase elbowed him in the side.

"Ow!"

Frank held his breath, afraid his friend's outburst would give them away, but the older boys were too engrossed in their activity to pay attention. Neither of them spoke. Chaz had placed his flashlight on top of an upside-down garbage can, pointing the beam at that dark featureless alcove, and the light threw the two into clear relief. Frank could see their right arms moving in tandem, a rhythmic back and forth motion as they stroked themselves.

He wanted to go home. It was too dark to see his friends' expressions, but they had to be freaked by this, too. They were out of their depth here.

Suddenly Paul stiffened, and a beat later Chaz did the same. Their arm movements accelerated, reaching a fever pitch, and then stopped. Both boys' heads drooped, as if they were exhausted, and their arms hung limply at their sides.

Something moved out of the dark opening in the middle of the shrine, a small awkwardly waddling creature that looked like a burnt Barbie doll. It had a horrible, powerful stench, the reek of rotting vegetables, and in the middle of its blackened mouth was one single shiny ultra-white tooth. It squeaked when it moved, not the animal squeak of a mouse but more like the mechanical squeak of a rusty door hinge.

Frank had never been so scared in his life. This was something out of a nightmare, only it was far worse than any nightmare he had ever had. The blackened creature stepped directly into the flashlight beam, but that did not render its features any more clear or its appearance any less frightening. It stopped waddling, stood on a pile of clipped fingernails, and its squeaking intensified, speeding up, gaining in volume.

Paul suddenly dropped to his knees, while Chaz backed away in horror. It was as though the burnt figure had spoken to them and they had understood. Chase's brother, still facing the shrine, seemingly unable to look away, continued backing up until he hit a bush and could go no farther. Paul bowed down like a man about to be knighted, like a subject prostrating himself before his king, head and shoulders touching the ground. The figure reached out, caressed his hair, then bent forward, its single-toothed mouth pressing against Paul's ear. The squeaking subsided to a whisper.

And Paul started convulsing.

Only the bottom of the flashlight beam touched him, but it was enough for them to see the spastic vibrations assaulting his body. The burnt creature was still whispering, and beneath the sibilance Frank heard the sickening crunch of bone on stone as Paul's head jerked up and down, slamming repeatedly into the platform, knocking aside panties and baseball caps and photographs and fingernails. Blood black enough to be oil spread out from beneath the boy's smashed face and engulfed the personal items, and Frank suddenly realized that the creature's whispering had turned to hissing laughter.

Chaz ran.

The rest of them followed.

All of them were screaming. Chaz had left his flashlight and Chase hadn't turned his flashlight on, but somehow they got out of the backyard easier and faster than they'd gotten in. They ran through the tangled jungle of dead plants and debris that was the witch's front yard, and then they were on the sidewalk.

"Oh shit!" Frank said, looking ahead. He grabbed the back of Chase's collar, put his right arm out to block Johnny and forced his two friends into Johnny's yard.

His dad was walking Aarfy and was less than a house away!

What the hell was he doing out this late?

Chase's brother had seen him, too, and the older boy ran up shouting, "Mr. Marotta! Mr. Marotta!"

"That's your dad!" Johnny said.

"No shit, Sherlock." Frank ducked behind a camilla bush next to Johnny's front porch and dragged his friends with him. They watched as Chaz explained what had happened, gesticulating wildly. Then he took Aarfy and ran toward Frank's house, while Frank's dad hurried over to the witch's yard.

"Fuck!" Chase said. "Your dad's gonna get killed."

"No he's not!" Frank responded, but he wanted to jump up and leap out of the bushes and yell for his dad to *Stop! Turn around! Stay away from there!* An instinct for survival and self-preservation kept him mute, however, and he told himself that whatever had happened was over and his dad would be fine, and he made himself believe it.

Johnny stood. "I'm going inside. I'm through."

"But we gotta find out what happened to Paul!" Chase said.

"Your brother's going to get help, probably call the police. Frank's dad's over there now. There's nothing else we can do. I'm going to bed and I'm not waking up until the sun's out!"

"I'm going home, too," Frank said.

"Pussies," Chase said, but there was no meaning behind it. He was scared, also. It was his brother's friend who had been killed, but his brother was still alive, and like the rest of them

35

he probably wanted to go home and hide in the safety of his well-lighted house until this night was done.

"Later, guys," Frank said. He hurried back across Johnny's lawn to the sidewalk, looking toward the witch's place, half-hoping to see his dad, but the old man was nowhere in sight and the dilapidated house was completely dark.

The entire street seemed much more threatening than it had earlier this evening, the night not merely a darker version of the day but an entity unto itself. Glancing back periodically at the witch's house—

Why hadn't he shouted out to his dad?

—Frank jogged down the sidewalk toward home, humming a song to himself, trying to keep his fears at bay.

"hello?"

The voice was small, soft, barely audible. It was a girl's voice, and it came from up ahead, from behind the Millers' hedges.

"hello?"

Frank slowed, stopped. He thought for a moment, then walked into the street, making a big detour around the hedges. If something was hiding behind there, waiting for him, ready to jump out at him, he wasn't going to sit still for it and make the attacker's job easy. He walked out to the middle of the circle, then passed by the hedge boundary and looked back toward the Millers'.

It really was a girl.

And she was *naked!*

She was sitting on one of the decorative boulders that the Millers had in their Southwest-themed yard, and he could see everything! She didn't even seem to care! A streetlight in front of the house shone on her like a spotlight, and he saw her long blond hair, her small pointy breasts, the triangle of hair between her legs.

He felt like he'd died and gone to heaven, and he quickly looked to the right to see if Chase or Johnny were still around—though even if they were, he was not sure he'd invite them over. There was no sign of either of his friends, however, and Frank walked back over the asphalt to the sidewalk, stopping at the edge of the Millers' property, about five feet away from her.

She looked at him. Her eyes, he saw, were large and blue. "hello?" she said in that soft small voice.

"Hi," Frank responded. His own voice sounded much softer than he'd intended, and his throat felt dry.

She stood up from the boulder and walked carefully across the Millers' gravel toward him, the small rocks obviously hurting the soft bottoms of her bare feet. She grimaced as she stepped onto the sidewalk next to him. Her approach was so open and straightforward that he half-expected her to put her arms around his neck and kiss him—

Had Chase been wishing for a naked girl when they were crouched near the shrine? Had his wish been granted?

—but instead she said, "Where am I?"

Frank didn't know how to answer, didn't know what she was asking. "Uh, William Tell Circle," he said.

She nodded, looked around.

"Where are you from?" he asked her.

She shrugged. "I don't know."

"Well, where are your parents?"

She looked at him as if she didn't understand the question. "I don't know," she said finally.

They seemed to have reached the end of their conversation. She apparently had no more questions to ask, and despite the fact that she was a naked babe, maybe *because* she was a naked babe, he was a little freaked by her. He looked down the sidewalk toward his house, wishing he'd never sneaked out tonight. Behind him, though he couldn't see it, he was acutely aware of the dark tangled jungle that was the witch's house.

Where his dad was.

"I . . . I have to go home," he said.

The girl touched his arm. "My name's Sue," she said. "What's your name?"

He swallowed hard. "Frank," he told her. It was the first time any girl had touched him, let alone a naked girl, and he thought about the story he'd have to tell Chase and Johnny. Once more, he glanced toward their houses to see if they were out and watching what was going on. It was going to be impossible to make them believe this unless they saw it for themselves.

The girl, Sue, took her hand away, letting her fingers trail down his wrist, over the back of his hand.

"I have to go home," he said again, thinking about his dad and prodded by a vague sense of urgency.

She nodded, but when he started walking, she followed him. Like a puppy dog, he thought.

He stopped. She stopped.

He turned and asked the question he'd been wanting to ask since he saw her: "Where are your clothes?"

She smiled. "I don't have any."

"O-Kay." He stretched the word out, in that sarcastic way he'd heard high school kids do.

She kept smiling.

"Look, it's late at night, and I really do have to go home, all right?" He glanced over at the witch's house. No sign of movement. No sign of his father.

"All right," Sue said.

Not only did she follow him, but she took his hand, holding it in hers like they were boyfriend and girlfriend. He wanted to shake her off him, wanted to get the hell away from her. How was he going to explain this to his mom? But he also wanted to keep holding her hand, keep touching her, maybe touch her somewhere *else*, and he was beginning to think that he might be in love with her.

Was she in love with him?

It seemed so.

Together they walked back to his house and up the driveway.

He left her out front, in the patio between the garage and the house, while he went inside. He had a feeling it wasn't a good idea to spring a naked space cadet on his mom without warning her first. Luckily, Sue didn't ask any questions but acceded to his bluntly stated wishes.

His mom was in the family room. Alone. Eating an apple and watching an old Harrison Ford movie.

Frank frowned. "Where's Chaz?" he said. "Did you guys call the police?"

"What?"

He knew from his mother's tone of voice that Chaz had

39

never made it here, that she had no idea what had happened. He suddenly felt cold. "Where's Aarfy?" he asked.

"Oh, your dad took him for a walk." She squinted as she looked at him, seeming to notice for the first time that he was dressed and not in pajamas. She put on her Mom voice. "Where have you been?"

"That—" *witch's house,* he'd been about to say, but instead he said, "—lady professor's house. Chase's brother and his friend Paul were going back there to ask for three thousand dollars from the shrine to buy a car, only Paul got killed and Chaz ran into Dad and told him about it and Dad's back there now and Chaz was supposed to bring Aarfy back home and come here and tell you and call the police." It all spilled out in a confusing torrent—and he hadn't even gotten to the naked girl yet—but his mom seemed to understand his story even as she dismissed it.

"Chaz Pittman probably just scared himself—"

"We were there, mom. We saw it. Me and Chase and Johnny."

"hello?"

Great. Sue wandered into the living room, peeking tentatively around the corner before stepping forward in all her glory. This was all he needed.

"Dad could get killed!" he yelled. "Call the damn police!"

He had never sworn in front of either of his parents before, and that got her attention.

"*What* did you say?" She stood, put her apple down on the table and glared at him.

Frank felt like sobbing with frustration. "Chaz's friend Paul was killed in that woman's backyard. By a little burned monster. I saw it. Dad went back there to check up on it, and I should have stopped him but I didn't, and now he might get killed, too." He did start to cry. "Call the police."

Some of his fear must have translated because now anger and worry were battling it out on his mother's face, and she strode past the naked girl, opened the front door and scanned the street. "Gil?" she called. There was no answer, and she shouted his name again, louder. "Gil!"

"Call 'em," Frank said, crying.

She ran into the kitchen, where the nearest phone was, and he returned to the living room, slumping down gratefully in her chair. On TV, Harrison Ford was hiding in a barn from some bad guys who were trying to kill him. How nice that would be, he thought. You could get away from a person. You could hide, you could fight, you could win. But the thing that came out of that shrine . . .

He sat up suddenly. Where was Sue? She'd been standing there only a few minutes ago, and he'd expected her to follow him into the room, thought she'd probably sit herself down right next to him. And where was his mom? She should've been back in here by now. Or at least he should have been able to hear her voice. He picked up the remote control, pressed the Mute button.

The house was silent.

No.

Frank jumped up and ran to the kitchen. He should have sneaked over, should have approached carefully, but the last thing he was thinking about was his own safety—he wanted to

41

know if his mom was okay, and he wanted to know *now*—and he dashed through the entryway and swung around the side of the refrigerator until he could see the entire room.

His mom was not okay. She was lying on the floor just below the wall phone, the receiver dangling above her head, spinning on its spiral cord. Her eyes were open, staring at nothing, and blood dripped from her mouth in a thick mucus-like strand. There was blood on her back, too, deep animal-like scratches. Frank could see her back because Sue had ripped his mother's shirt off. The naked girl was kneeling on the floor behind her, trying to pull down her pants, humming a nursery-rhyme ditty that sounded suspiciously like *Here We Go 'Round the Mulberry Bush*. The girl's chest and stomach were smeared with blood, though there didn't appear to be a scratch on her.

Frank stood there for a moment, frozen, torn between wanting to rush at the little bitch, beat the shit out of her, give his mom mouth-to-mouth and save her life, and wanting to turn tail and run like hell away from that monster.

Fear won out. His mom's eyes were open, unblinking; it was obvious that she was dead and there was nothing he could do to bring her back. Sue had somehow murdered her in—what? four minutes?—and unless he got out of here quick, she'd be doing the same to him.

So he ran back out of the kitchen, through the entryway, out the front door, down the driveway and onto the sidewalk. He glanced quickly behind him, but Sue wasn't following, and he looked over at the witch's house. As he'd feared, as he'd known, there was no sign of his dad.

Frank dashed next door to the Boykins' house, but changed

his mind at the last minute and ran across their lawn to the Millers', leaping the small line of rose bushes in between. The Boykins' porch light was on, but he'd seen when he got closer that there was no light in their living room or kitchen, and he figured they were probably asleep. They were old, went to bed early, and he didn't want to spend ten minutes ringing their bell and pounding on their door while he waited for them to open up.

He might not have ten minutes.

That was the thought in the forefront of his mind, and he saw again his mom's dead staring eyes, her drool of thick blood, the deep scratches on her bare back.

The Millers' house was dark, too, and he swerved up their driveway and back onto the sidewalk, running next door. He knew he could just knock on Johnny's bedroom window and get his friend's attention, so he bypassed the front stoop and ran around the side of the house, rapping both fists on the windowglass. "Open up!" he yelled. "Hurry!" He looked over his shoulder, expecting to see Sue coming toward him, arms outstretched, covered in his mom's blood, but the coast was clear.

"Johnny!" he called.

The drapes did not part, no light shone between the cracks.

Frank kept pounding, his stomach sinking a little. "Johnny!"

No noise, no light.

He stopped rapping on the window and pressed his face against the glass, trying in vain to see something through the narrow breach where the curtains met. Behind him was the Millers' bedroom window. The two homes were close together,

43

and he half-hoped that his pounding and shouting had woken up either Mr. or Mrs. Miller, but when he looked over there, the house was dark.

He'd found Sue in front of the Millers' home.

Johnny's side yard suddenly didn't seem quite so safe. But this was his friend's place. He knew this house, knew these people, and he ran into the backyard, ready to take one last chance and pound the shit out of Johnny's parents' bedroom window.

Their window was open, though, as were their drapes. The light was off in the room, but a back porch lamp was on, and by that indirect illumination he could see their bodies naked and strewn across the blood-splattered bed. Between them was another naked form, a girl, a blond girl. It wasn't Sue, but there was definitely a resemblance, and she was on all fours, licking blood off Johnny's dad's face. He heard the lapping of the girl's tongue, smelled the horrid heavy stink of death, and he immediately started puking. Instinct and decorum dictated that he should bend over and remain in place until he finished regurgitating the contents of his stomach, but his brain knew that to do so would mean almost certain death and overrode that impulse. Still throwing up, the vomit splashing over his shirtfront and onto the ground, Frank fled, running back around the side yard the way he'd come.

Johnny's parents were dead.

That meant Johnny was dead, too.

He wanted to scream in terror, wanted to run straight down the street and not stop running until he hit the police station two miles away, but his dad was still at the witch's house, and though he doubted there was anything he could do to save his father if he was really in trouble, Frank knew he had to try. He was more frightened than he had ever been in his life, but he hurried without hesitation down the sidewalk toward the light-less black space that was the professor's yard. He was drawing on strength he didn't even know he possessed, and he thought it was probably like the resolve that sent firemen into burning buildings, that made soldiers run through gunfire to save their buddies in time of war.

He thought about those naked girls as he ran. What were they? They had something to do with the shrine, of that he was sure, but why were they going around the neighborhood killing people?

Had they gotten Chaz and Aarfy?

He'd forgotten about Chase's brother and the dog until now, and he wished he hadn't remembered. The two of them had obviously disappeared somewhere between the spot where they'd left his dad, and his home, where they were supposed to be headed. Even though that was only four houses away.

He kept running, acutely aware that at any second *he* might be attacked, that one of the naked girls or . . . something else might suddenly take him out and make him disappear. He glanced over at Chase's home, saw the porch light on, saw the flickering blue light of a television through the sheer curtains. Everything looked normal. But Chaz had disappeared, and for all Frank knew Chase and his parents lay slaughtered inside. He looked back at Johnny's place, at the Millers', at his own. The entire street looked normal, actually, a typical night in a typical suburban neighborhood, and it was scary how deceptive appearances could be.

Then he was running across the dark front yard of the

witch's house for the second time this night, and though his heart was pounding with terror, though his feet wanted to veer back toward the street, he turned around the side of the building and ran past the lawnmower, the washing machine, the tree stump, the buckets, into the backyard.

The moon was up now, and he could see better than he could before, but the backyard still seemed darker, filled with horrors he could not see and not imagine. He remembered that burnt waddling doll-like thing and the terrible squeaking it made, and his blood felt like ice water. He could not continue to run back here, it was too crowded. He stopped, looked around. He didn't want to draw attention to himself, didn't want anyone or any*thing* to know he was here, but he had to find his father. "Dad!" he called out, searching the darkness for signs of movement. "Dad!"

As he'd expected, as he'd feared, there was no answer, but he refused to give up, refused to let himself believe that his dad was dead.

He pressed on, moved farther into the backyard. "Dad!" he called, but he did not shout as loudly this time.

"Dad?" Volume falling.

"Dad." A low rough whisper.

Something about this place discouraged loudness, intimidated him into silence. He didn't want to go anywhere near the shrine, but he knew that was exactly where he needed to go if he really wanted to know what had happened to his father. He walked around a tangled dead stickerbush, then down the narrow path that he seemed to remember leading to the shrine.

"Dad," he said—

—and tripped over something in the dirt.

46

There wasn't time to break his fall. He tumbled forward, sprawling, and his forehead hit something soft and smelly that he thought was a rotten watermelon. One hand and arm scraped the hard dirt ground while the other twisted beneath him but luckily did not break. His knees and legs fell on what felt like a sack of sand, and he immediately pulled himself forward, lurching to his feet.

It wasn't a sack of sand. It was a dead body.

It was Chase.

He was on his back, facing up. His face had been chewed on, and over his forehead and what remained of his cheeks scurried big black beetles that in the moonlight appeared to be the same shade of pitch as the burnt creature in the shrine.

Frank screamed once, an instinctive reaction of shock and horror, but he immediately stopped and shut up. Whatever did this was still out there, and he couldn't let it know he was here, couldn't give away his location.

Ahead was the shrine, but he could not continue on. He was in way over his head here, and it was time to call in the cops. For all he knew, everyone in the neighborhood was dead, so he couldn't count on being able to rouse a neighbor. He didn't even want to take a chance with someone on the next street over. He would go to the Arco station over on Washington. Even if the gas station was closed, it had a pay phone out front, and he was pretty sure you could dial 911 from a pay phone without having to put in money. If not, there was a Circle K farther down that was open twenty-four hours.

He stepped carefully over Chase's body, not looking down, then hurried up the path the way he'd come.

A light went on in the house.

Frank ducked behind a half-collapsed pile of old bricks, trying to not even breathe, afraid the witch would know he was here and come after him. He didn't know for sure that the light had been turned on by the professor or that she was really a witch or that she had anything to do with what had gone on tonight, but he was not willing to take that chance, and he crouched lower. Spiderwebs tickled his face and arms—he even thought he felt the quick scurrying legs of the spider itself on the back of his wrist—but he remained in place, silent, unmoving, hoping and praying that the light would go off and she would go away.

The light did not go off. Another light went on. And a creaky door opened.

"i'm scared."

The girl's voice was right next to him, soft and frightened, and his heart started thumping hard. *Sue,* he thought. But it wasn't Sue. This girl was dark-haired and dressed, wearing what looked like a Catholic school uniform: white blouse, blue skirt. She also looked vaguely familiar, and Frank thought that he had seen her before at the library or the park or the grocery store.

Had she been there the whole time? It was possible, but he had the feeling that she had crept over here from somewhere else, somewhere close, her own hiding place.

"i'm scared."

"Shhh," he told her, and the two of them remained quiet, waiting, but there was no further sound, no indication that anyone had come out of the house into the backyard.

His right leg was starting to cramp, and his left wrist still hurt from where he'd fallen on it. He shifted position until he was facing the girl and no longer had to turn his head to see her. Tears were streaming down her cheeks, shiny like snail trails in the moonlight.

"What are you doing here?" he whispered.

She'd been sobbing quietly, but she pulled herself together, sniffled. "I just came here with two friends of mine. I didn't even want to. They wanted to. They were going to . . . ask the shrine for . . . something. But they're gone. I think they're dead."

Frank ignored the hair bristling on his arms. "What makes you think that?"

"There was this little burned doll. It was alive. And it . . . it . . ." She started sobbing again.

"What's your name?" He thought if he could distract her, maybe she'd stop crying and start talking and he'd be able to find out some information.

"Cass," she said.

"I'm Frank."

They were still whispering, still very much afraid of being overheard and found out, and the whispering made everything seem so much more . . . intimate. It was a strange word to be using in such a time and place, but that's how he felt. He'd never been so near to a girl before—

except Sue

—and despite the circumstances, or maybe because of them, there was something strangely exciting and exhilarating about their close quarters conversation.

"I go to John Adams," he said.

She wiped her eyes, her nose. "Me, too."

"I thought you looked familiar. What grade are you?"

"Seventh."

"I'm in eighth." Frank looked over her shoulder. He couldn't see all of the house through the bushes, but he could see that both lights were still on. He heard no one else out here, though, no other sounds save their own breathing and whispers.

He didn't know what else to say, and she obviously didn't feel like talking, so they crouched there in silence. Cass shifted position, her fingers accidentally brushing the back of his hand, a touch that felt electric. He wanted to reach out, take her hand in his, hold it.

He shouldn't be thinking of her like this. His mom had been killed, his dad was probably dead, Chase's body was lying on the ground less than five feet away, Johnny and his parents had been murdered, and *her* friends were missing and probably dead. What the hell was wrong with him?

The door of the house creaked again—someone coming out? someone going back in?—and they both froze. Once more, there were no other sounds, no sign of activity, but they remained in place for a long time afterward, not speaking, afraid to move.

Cass was no longer crying, no longer sniffling, and after what seemed like an hour of doing absolutely nothing but the minimum amount of breathing necessary to stay alive, Frank forced himself to relax a little. "Hey," he whispered.

"Hey," she said back.

"So what happened to your friends? Did you see it?"

Silence. At first he thought she was going to start crying again, then he thought she wasn't going to answer, then finally she said softly, "I saw part of it."

When it became clear that she wasn't going to say any more,

he decided to try a different tack. "What were they going to ask for?"

"I don't know," she said quickly, embarrassed.

"Come on."

"What were *your* friends going to ask for?"

"I asked you first."

Even in the blue illumination of the moonlight, he thought he could see her redden. "A guy."

Frank laughed. It was the first funny thing he had heard all night. She punched his shoulder. "So? What about you?"

"Two of us were just along for the ride. But our friend—
Chase

—was going to ask for—" Now it was his turn to redden. "—a girl."

"Looks like we both got our wish, huh?"

He couldn't see her face, she'd leaned back into the shadow, and he wasn't sure how to take that. In his mind, she'd been smiling sadly, but maybe she had a different kind of expression on her face. Against his will, he felt himself responding, felt a stirring in his lap.

Again? Jesus. His mom was dead, his friends were dead, half the neighborhood was dead, and his dad was missing. How could he even think about such a thing at a time like this?

"Maybe we should try to get out of here," he suggested. "Try to get some help."

She nodded.

"You think we can make it? You think anyone's out there?"

"Stay there. I'll check." She suddenly stood up to take a look around, and he could see up her skirt.

51

She wasn't wearing any underwear.

Now he was completely aroused. It was too dark to see anything clearly, anything specific, but he saw darkness, saw hair, and it was the most exciting sight he had ever laid eyes on.

She quickly crouched back down again. "Let's wait a minute," she told him.

Frank looked at her, not sure if she was genuinely worried that they might not make it out of the witch's backyard or if she merely wanted to remain here and spend more time with him. Did she know he could see up her skirt? Had she wanted him to look?

As if in answer, she moved a little closer. "I took off my underwear before I left the house," she said. "We all did."

He looked at her, saying nothing.

She knew he'd seen, she'd wanted him to see.

"We heard you and your friends talking," she admitted. "You were wondering what it would taste like to . . . to . . . you know." She glanced shyly away, nervously licked her lips. "Are you still curious?"

He didn't know what to say, didn't know how to respond. This was like a porno book. Or one of Chase's lies about his brother.

"It's okay if you—" she said quickly.

He swallowed hard. "Yes," he managed to croak out.

Now it was her turn to be tongue-tied.

"I didn't mean . . . I wasn't trying to . . ." He let the thought trail off, not sure how to finish it.

Cass took a deep breath. "I wouldn't mind if you . . . you know . . . did that."

They looked at each other, both unsure of what to say next or how to proceed. He was the boy, he supposed he should be the one to take the initiative, so he reached up tentatively, put his arms around her waist, drawing her closer. She didn't object, and slowly, he moved his head up under her skirt.

He kissed her there, stuck out his tongue, pressed it in.

She couldn't have heard them talking, he realized. They hadn't talked about that here. They'd talked about it in Chase's house earlier in the afternoon.

His skin erupted in goosebumps.

She was one of them.

He should have known it. Nothing about this made any sense, scenes like this just didn't happen in real life, and it was his own fault that he fell for it, that he went along with it. His friends and family were dead, and here he was indulging in some *Penthouse Forum* fantasy in the filthy backyard of a witch.

But why hadn't she killed him yet? What did she want? What was she waiting for?

He couldn't let her know he knew. Surprise was his only chance. So he wiggled his tongue around that area, kept licking. She'd been talking, saying something, and though he hadn't been paying attention, he noticed now that she was no longer saying words. Her voice had turned into a mechanical squeak, the same sort of noise that the burned thing in the shrine had made. From the direction of the shrine came a pounding, an echoing boom that superceded all other sound.

It was now or never.

He tried to pull away, tried to slowly and unobtrusively move back, in preparation for a mad dash to get the hell out of here . . . but he could not. His lips were sealed to her genitals, and he felt something *moving* over his lips, creeping outward over the skin of his cheeks and chin and up by his nostrils. It was like a new skin was growing, fusing the two of them together, joining his lips to her vagina.

He and his friends would've joked about this, would've laughed if they'd read about it or heard it from someone else. "The dude musta died with a smile on his face," he could imagine Chase saying. But it was real, it was here, and there was nothing funny about it.

He tried to yank his head away, but that produced only a sharp sensation of pain as the movement threatened to pull off the skin from the lower half of his face. He started punching her in the stomach as hard as he could, hoping it would get her to release him, wondering even as he did so whether she had any control of what was going on between her legs.

The punches seemed to have no effect, and that creeping skin was starting to cover up his nostrils, cutting off his air, so he felt blindly around until his fingers curled around one of the piled bricks. He gripped it tightly, then brought it up and slammed it against her side. There was no reaction, no response, not even any blood. The brick hit her skin and did no damage. She was squeaking loudly now, like a rusted train being pulled down unused tracks, and as her wet skin sealed shut his nostrils, fusing with his face, he knew that he was about to die.

Her skin tightened on his own, squeezing his head. Cartilage in his nose broke, splintered into fragments. The bones in his cheek shattered. He swallowed two teeth that popped out, held two others loose in his mouth. He was getting weak from the lack of oxygen. He dropped the brick, unable to hold it any longer, and his arms and legs dangled loosely, uselessly, as though his body were already dead and only his brain was still alive. He was being held up, suspended by their fused skin. And then . . .

And then . . .

He was let go. The skin of his face was his skin again, he was no longer connected to her, and he fell back onto the ground, the back of his head hitting the brick that he'd dropped. He felt a warm gush of blood. He wanted to sit up, wanted to roll away, but he could not move. He was too weak, and he realized with horror that although he was free from her, he had not been saved. He had been too hurt, had been without oxygen for too long, was losing too much blood. He was still dying, and unless he got to a hospital pretty damn quick, he was not going to make it.

Dad?

He could barely see, could not smell at all, and his right ear was filled with blood, making all sound muffled, but he was filled with the certainty that his father was here, nearby, and that he was okay, that he had not been harmed. A sense of relief flooded over him, and for the first time since that burned thing had killed Paul, he had the feeling that everything was going to be all right.

Above him, Cass was still standing, and as he watched she faded away, disappearing into the shadows, into the night, the most devastating expression on her face that he had ever seen, a look not only of the purest physical agony but of a knowledge so horrible that he could not even imagine what it might be.

He was fading himself, dying, his eyelids getting heavier, his vision more blurry, his strength ebbing. He thought he heard his father's voice, somewhere close, saying "Take that" and he wanted to call out, tried to call out, knowing that if he could get his father's attention, if his dad could just find him and speed him over to the hospital, all would be well.

But no sound emerged from his mouth, and he found that he could not even move his lips.

His eyes were completely closed now, permanently shut, and he knew finally and with certainty that he was not going to make it. He heard his dad's voice fading away, heard everything fading away. On his tongue, he could still taste the girl, still taste her sex.

It did taste like honey, he thought.

It did.

It did.

GIL

I don't know why I didn't go to work. I don't know what made me stay home. Part of it was that I hated the swing shift. I'd been transferred over from graveyard the week before, and while most people think graveyard's a bitch, it's a cakewalk compared to swing. Now, I've never been one of those guys to use sick days to attend my kid's baseball game or band concert or school play. Hell, I don't even use them when I'm really sick. But somehow the prospect of another night of swing, combined with the fact that it was Friday and yesterday I'd been denied a vacation in October that corresponded with Lynn's . . . well, let's just say that the decision to play hooky wasn't a tough one to make.

I called the plant and told them I wouldn't be coming in.

Luckily, I didn't have to talk to a real person. I don't think I could've gone through with it if I did; I'm not a very good liar. But I got Human Resources's answering machine—maybe a lot of other people were calling in sick, too—and I quickly left my message and then took the phone off the hook so they wouldn't be able to call me back.

Home free.

Even though it wasn't a school night, Lynn made Frank go to bed at eight. He'd done something he wasn't supposed to before dinner, and while she'd told me about it, I'd only half been paying attention and didn't really know what it was. Still, I automatically supported her, and when he appealed to me for clemency, I said, "You heard your mother."

Afterward, the two of us sat on the couch in the living room, snuggling together, watching TV, and it was just like the old times before we had Frank. I was even thinking that I might get lucky. Her pants were unbuttoned, the way they often were after a full dinner, and when I slipped my hand inside them she didn't object like she usually did and push me away, looking over her shoulder to make sure Frank wasn't creeping up on us. She let my hand stay there, my fingers pressed against her crotch, and it was nice.

Then Aarfy started barking. That stupid dog was howling up a storm, desperate to go out, and I realized that no one had taken him for a walk after dinner. I'd thought it was Frank's turn; he'd obviously thought it was mine, so even though it was late, already after nine, I got up off the couch, leashed him up and took him once around the block.

We were almost home when it happened. Aarfy was making one last pit stop at the fire hydrant in front of the Millers' when

I heard screams. It sounded like a bunch of kids, but when I looked up I saw only one guy running toward me.

"Mr. Marotta! Mr. Marotta!"

It was one of the Pittman kids, the older one (I could never remember his name), speeding down the sidewalk, waving his arms. There was panic in his voice, and when he got closer I could see that his shirt was torn. There was a big dark stain on it, and while I didn't know what it was, my first thought was: *blood.*

Then he reached me, and I saw that it was one of those shirts that was supposed to be torn and the dark stain was a picture of a monster or something. Still, he was panicked, terrified, and I held up my hand. "Slow down there, bud, slow down. What seems to be the problem?"

I thought it might be a dog that got hit by a car, or maybe even that his mom had a heart attack or had been beaten by his dad. But I wasn't prepared for the story he told me. It came in confused bits and pieces. He was too rattled to think straight, but I was able to jigsaw fit his frightened disjointed utterances, and what he said seemed unbelievable. He and his friend Paul had snuck into the backyard of the pig sty next to Ed Christensen's house because there was supposed to be a shrine hidden there that could grant wishes if you approached it in the right way and were willing to pay the price it asked. They hadn't even gotten around to asking, though, when a monster that looked like a burned-up doll came creeping out of a hole in the middle of the shrine. The Pittman kid was afraid of it, but his friend Paul had a weird reaction and bowed down before it like he was worshiping a god. Then the monster touched Paul and whispered in his ear, and he started having some sort of spastic fit, slamming his own head down on the ground until he'd split it open and was dead.

I wasn't sure how much of this I actually believed, but I believed it more than I usually would have just because of the kid's panic. He was terrified, he'd seen something that scared the living shit out of him, and whether he'd added or embellished or exaggerated, I thought the crux of his story was true. Something bad had happened in the backyard of that house and now his friend was dead.

I'd never seen the woman who lived in the house at the end of the cul de sac. In fact, I only knew that a woman lived there because Ed had told me about her, although I'm not sure he'd ever seen her either. She was supposed to be a teacher at the JC, some sort of physics or philosophy professor. Her house was a mess, the front yard a jungle of dead trees and overgrown weeds, the backyard even worse, and Ed and Tony and some of the other neighborhood neatniks had circulated a petition to have the city crack down on what they said were health code violations. I'd been tempted not to sign it just on general principles. A person's house wasn't a democracy. Neighbors didn't get to vote on how it looked. It was a dictatorship. And the owner had the complete and total right to do whatever he wanted with his house and his land.

Or hers.

But the truth was that the damn place smelled like a catbox. Santa Ana winds hit just right, and the foul stench of that yard even made it over to my house. I could imagine what it was like for Ed and Tony. Not to mention the fact that Frank sometimes played over at his friend Johnny's house next door. I didn't like the idea of my boy being exposed to germs and rats and who-knows-what-all over there.

So I'd signed the petition, but nothing came of it. Ed said the city sent someone down, some inspector, but that the old lady was never home. He was trying to get them to go to the junior college and hit her up where she worked, serve her with a subpeona or some sort of notice ordering her to clean up her yard, but they weren't willing to go that far. So there it sat.

I'd never heard of this shrine before, and I don't know why I believed it was really there, but I did. I remembered neighborhood legends and secrets from when I was a kid, things that parents didn't know existed but that we'd seen or sometimes even built with our own hands. There was a whole separate world that parents didn't know about, and I'm sure the same thing was true today.

Aarfy was barking, straining at his leash, getting anxious. "Here," I said to the Pittman boy, handing him the leash. "Take my dog home. Tell my wife what happened, and call 911. I'm going to go over there and check—"

"Don't, Mr. Marotta! That monster's still there! It's small but it's . . . Jesus Christ! I've never seen anything like it!"

The monster was the one part of his story I definitely didn't believe.

"Look, I'll be fine. Get to my house, tell my wife, call 911. I'm going over there now." What had just occurred to me was that his friend Paul might still be alive and in need of emergency medical attention. I didn't know CPR, not exactly, but I'd seen it in movies and on TV and figured I knew enough to keep the kid alive until police or paramedics came by.

The boy stood there stupidly, holding on to the leash.

"Go!" I told him.

He ran off toward my house, Aarfy leading the way, and I hurried away in the opposite direction. All the homes on the circle had backlit curtains and porch lights on, but the professor's house was totally dark. With the bushy trees around and behind it, all individual features obscured, it looked like a giant amoeba, like The Blob or something, but I pushed that thought away. I didn't want to let that kid's fear and paranoia get to me, and the last thing I needed to do was start thinking about monster movies.

I thought of knocking on the door first, but it looked pretty unlikely that the professor was home, so I cut across her driveway and ran by her front window toward the side of the house, nearly tripping over a rock or some other hard object half-buried in the ground.

I slowed down when I reached the side yard. It was just too damn dirty and crowded to go running through. I didn't want to slam my shin against something or cut myself on a rusty piece of metal. Besides, I was almost out of breath just from running across the street to get here.

I walked carefully through the rubbish and into the back-yard. This was a corner lot—if there *could* be corner lots on a circle—and was bigger than most of the other backyards. Bigger than mine, that's for sure. It was also a bona fide health hazard, filled with more junk and garbage than I had ever seen before. It looked like a fucking dump. Not "dump" as in ratty place but "dump" as in landfill. It literally looked like four or five garbage trucks had tilted their backs over her fence and deposited all their contents on her dead lawn. There were a lot of trees and bushes here, but there were even more garbage cans and moldy cardboard boxes and pieces of rusted scrap metal. I walked past a garage door opener propped against a drawerless wooden dresser, the hood of a white car piled high with broken clay pots and bags of charcoal.

I made my way down a narrow path through the debris. There, between a collapsed playhouse and a sticker bush that appeared to have overgrown a rotted woodpile, was the shrine. I knew what it was immediately, and the sight of it sent a shiver through my bones. It was the creepiest thing I'd ever seen, and I wished I'd thought to bring a flashlight. Hell, I wished I'd stopped by the Christensens' house, gotten Ed off his dead ass and made him come back here with me. I might be an adult, but this place was spooky, and it wouldn't've hurt to have someone else along for the ride.

The shrine was a Catholic-looking adobe thing, like one of those old altars in a Mexican village or something. But there was no saint in its alcove, only a black empty space. It wasn't like the statue of a saint had been stolen or anything, it was more like that black space itself was the thing being worshiped. I can't explain it any better than that, but that's how I felt and it scared me.

There was no dead body, though, no little fire-roasted monster, nothing that would indicate that the Pittman boy (what *was* his name?) had been telling the truth. I'm not sure why I thought it would be otherwise, but I'd honestly expected to find the dead corpse of a teenager laying there and some sort of doll-sized monster eating his flesh.

This place encouraged that kind of thinking.

I turned to look back at the house. It occurred to me that

the woman who lived there might not know about the shrine. Her yard was so overgrown, was so densely packed with crap, that someone could hide or even live in it without her knowing. So maybe she didn't know it was back here, maybe someone else had snuck into this fucking pig sty and set up this altar for . . . what? Witchcraft? To perform satanic services?

Whatever it was, it was nasty, wrong, and even if there was nothing here now, I knew the Pittman kid was telling the truth. His friend *had* died in this spot. I didn't know where the body was now, but it had been here earlier. I was sure of that.

I took a step forward. No one had built this thing recently. It was old. It had been here a long time. I bent down and saw underpants and caps and photos. People had been coming here for years, making pilgrimages to this place. But who? Neighborhood children? The thought terrified me. Had Frank been here? Did he know about this place? Was he involved in a cult or some sort of *River's Edge* thing? I didn't think so, but you could never tell. Parents were always the last people in the world to find out what their kids were really like. I *did* know that Lynn and I kept a close watch on what he did and monitored him pretty closely. He wasn't allowed out at night unless we knew exactly where he was going and with whom. I didn't know what had happened here tonight, but thank God Frank was home right now, in bed, not roaming around like the Pittman kid and his friend.

I looked closer. There were also little white snippets of stuff that looked like fingernails and beneath the fingernails a folded piece of paper that looked familiar—the petition we'd signed to have the health department investigate this place.

I didn't like that. As far as I knew, Ed had sent the petition to the city and had kept the only copy for himself. What it was doing here was a mystery. Although since the Pittman boy had said they'd come out here tonight to ask the shrine for money, I couldn't help but think that someone had left the petition here and asked the shrine for something else. What that something else could be, I had no idea.

An icy cold passed through me.

I stood, glanced around the darkness. There was no reason for me to stay. I'd checked what I'd come to check and nothing was there. No dead body, no monster. Now I was trespassing pure and simple. But the certainty that something very bad *had* happened here, all appearances to the contrary, made me decide that I needed to confront the woman who owned the house. Either she had no clue what was going on in her backyard and needed to be told, or she did know and needed to be questioned. Whatever the case, I knew I had to talk to her.

I walked away from the shrine without looking behind me, and made my way back down the path and through the side yard, then across the dead lawn to the front porch. I knocked on the door, waited, knocked on the door, waited, knocked, waited. I must have done this for five full minutes, but there was no answer and I heard no noise from inside the home. A car was in the driveway, an old Ford Torino, and though she could have walked somewhere, could have gone someplace in someone else's car, I didn't think that was the case. She was in there. And she might be in trouble.

I felt suspicious and more than a little scared, and a practical part of me said to get my ass home and call the cops. But another part of me said the Pittman kid had already called the cops, who would be here shortly, and they could rescue me if I failed to rescue the professor.

After only a moment's hesitation, I walked around back again and then up the rickety wooden steps that led to a screened-in porch. Not only was the door unlocked, it was open, and a primitive superstitious part of my brain thought that it looked like someone or something was inviting me in. I thought about walking back down the stairs and rooting through that trashy yard for a pipe or some sort of weapon, but I was already at the top and decided just to go in.

The porch was as filthy as the backyard, piled high with old furniture and boxes. "Hello?" I called out. "Anybody home?"

If anybody was, they weren't talking, so I walked a little ways down the porch to where the door to the house itself was. This door was open, too, and the hair on the back of my neck prickled. I almost turned around then and there, but some mule-headed bit of stubbornness refused to let me be frightened off like a nervous little girl, and instead of leaving I stepped into the darkened house.

"Hello?" I called.

There was no answer, and I felt around on the wall next to me for a light switch. I found one and flipped it on.

I didn't know where in the house I thought I was. Some sort of foyer, I suppose. Or a laundry room. I was in a bedroom, though. It was empty, but the bed looked like it had been slept in recently—or else it always looked that way because the professor never made it. That I could believe. The bedroom was as messy as the porch, with books and newspapers strewn all over the hardwood floor, thick black strings of cobwebs that had collapsed in on themselves hanging from the stucco ceiling. The room smelled of must, dust, old sweat and dried urine, and hanging over an antique chair with ripped upholstery was a nightgown stained with fresh blood.

I wished I had brought a weapon, but it was too late now, and I stuck my hand in my pocket, grabbed my keys and held them in my fist for a makeshift set of brass knuckles. I walked into the next room, another bedroom.

And there she was, sitting in front of a vanity mirror, combing her hair.

"Oh Jesus," I said, and my voice was a whisper that felt like it was going to turn into a scream. "Oh Jesus."

The fat woman's skin was transparent. I remembered hearing a story from a guy at the plant that in pre-war Vietnam, the upper class used to breed rats, force feeding them nothing but ginger root. They'd do this for several generations, and somewhere down the line, when the female rats gave birth, the babies would be transparent and the Vietnamese would eat them as a delicacy because of the subtle ginger flavor that permeated their meat. That's what this reminded me of. Only this was a person not a rat, and I was pretty sure that she had not been born this way; she'd *become* this way.

It was the professor, I assumed, and from the books piled on the bed, it looked like she was a philosophy not physics instructor. I don't know why I noticed that; it had nothing to do with anything.

She was still seated in front of her vanity, but she'd turned away from the mirror and was staring at me. There was a sly smile on her lips, and I could see the white fat of her cheeks through her clear skin, the orangish muscles that worked her mouth. "Which one are you?" she said.

I turned tail and ran. It would have been shorter, probably, to continue on through the house and speed out the front door, but I had no idea what awaited me in other rooms, and my sole thought was to get the hell out of there as quickly as possible. I ran back through that first bedroom, down the length of porch, then leaped the steps and hauled ass around the corner of the house.

I ran next door to Ed's. I thought about going home to call the cops, but I didn't want to upset Lynn any more than she was already or let Frank know anything about this at all, so I opted for Ed's instead. I guess I could've gone to the Pittmans' house and gotten Bill to come with us—it was his kid who'd started this, after all—but I didn't know Bill Pittman that well and didn't like him much and, to be honest, didn't think he'd be much help. He was kind of a dilfy little guy, a scrawny wannabe redneck who was drunk more often than not, and I doubted he'd bring much to the table. Ed, though, was an ex-Marine, a big strapping guy, and while he worked now as a salesman for a drug company, there was still nothing soft about him. He was a good man and a good friend, and while he was a little anal retentive sometimes and a little too by-the-book, he was exactly the type of person I'd want watching my back if I got in a jam.

Ed and his wife were night owls, and I was glad to see that their front door was open. That meant they hadn't gone to sleep yet. But my relief lasted only a few seconds. Because when I reached the screen door, I knew something was wrong immediately. Ed made sure his wife kept their home spotless, but I could see through the screen that the living room was a mess. It looked like a tornado had torn through there.

It looked like the professor's house.

With a sinking feeling in my gut, I opened the door and walked in.

They were on the couch in front of the television, Ed and Judy, and they'd been burned beyond recognition. If it weren't for the fact that they were sitting in their own house on their own sofa and Ed was nearly a foot taller than his wife, I would have had no idea who they were. Their clothes and hair were gone, their faces little more than charred skulls, their bodies blackened bone. The couch itself was not singed, only the bodies, and it looked like they had been killed elsewhere and posed there. I thought of what the Pittman kid had told me about the little burned monster at the shrine, and I knew this was connected. It made no sense, at least not to me, but somehow it did to someone somewhere, and though these were the bodies of my friends, I kept waiting for them to move and start coming after me.

I felt overwhelmed, not knowing what to do or where to turn. Where were the police? Shouldn't they have been here by now? I glanced at the television set, thought of how I'd left Lynn sitting on the couch, watching a movie. What if something had gotten into my own house, what if something had happened to Lynn or Frank?

I turned, started back out, and saw through the screen a slim shape leaning against the wall at the edge of Ed's garage, a silhouette of cascading hair.

Lynn?

68

I opened the screen, and the figure walked casually around the edge of the garage toward me.

The hair was Lynn's, but the long thin face beneath it was like nothing I had ever seen. Huge eyebrows jutted across sleepy baggy eyes, and strange lumps protruded from the skin of the cheeks and forehead. The mouth was open but not smiling, revealing stained rectangular teeth behind an oversized upper lip.

But it was the way this creature walked that scared the living fuck out of me. Because it wasn't marching purposefully toward me, wasn't trying to chase me and catch me. It simply was strolling over. As though it knew me. As though we were friends.

I didn't know what it was and didn't want to know. Ed's garage and house were close together, only a couple of steps apart, and the thing was already at the doorway. There was no way I'd be able to get by it. I slammed the front door shut, locked it and ran through the house to the back door. I was in the laundry room when I heard the front door unlock, open and close and the sound of casual footsteps on the hardwood floor of the living room.

Ed and Judy had triple-locked the back door—knob, deadbolt, chain—and it took me a moment to get them all unlatched. Then I was outside and flying. I ran around the dark side of the house, terrified and out of breath, sure that at any second that long-haired travesty of a woman was going to grab me. But nothing did, and I made it safely around the front. I looked across the circle at my house, saw Lynn standing in the open doorway, looking through our screen, as though investigating a noise she'd heard outside.

Or was it Lynn?

Of course it was. Yes, this was a silhouette, too, but I couldn't be fooled twice. I knew my own wife, goddamn it. I was about to shout out to her that she should close the door, lock it and stay inside, when she did exactly that. In the stillness of the neighborhood, I heard the door slam, and a feeling of relief washed over me. She was safe, she was fine.

But for how long?

I was on the sidewalk now and was going to run home and call the cops, but I thought about that long-haired thing following me and knew I didn't dare let it know where I lived. I had no idea what it was or what it could do, and I wanted to keep it as far away from my family as possible. I looked over my shoulder at the side of the house, but it was still not there, still not coming.

It would be, though.

At its own pace.

In its own way.

It was the shrine that was at the center of all this. I had no idea if it was sitting on some sacred spot and getting its energy from that, or if it had been granted power from some sort of spell, or even if it had been built in such a way that its architecture made it what it was. But I knew it had to be destroyed, knew that if all this was going to stop, I would have to demolish it.

I suddenly thought of a plan.

My friend was coming around the corner, still sauntering in that relaxed unhurried manner. She was far enough away that I couldn't see the specifics of her strange and terrible face, but I'd seen it once and that was enough. I'd never forget it, and

70

when I saw that long cascading hair, my flesh erupted in goose bumps. My gut instinct was to run, to get as far away from her as quickly as possible, but I needed tools, needed weapons, and I ran up the driveway to the garage.

For once, I was grateful for Ed's Felix Unger tendencies. In my own garage, I usually had to dig around for ten minutes to find the tools I needed, but Ed kept everything neatly organized. I had no problem picking out an ax, a crowbar and a hammer. I didn't know exactly what I would need, but I wanted to be prepared, and I quickly carried all three back out.

She was coming.

She was already walking around the side of the garage. This close, her face not in shadow but illuminated by the full glow of the porchlight, I could see those enormous hairy eyebrows over her still-sleepy eyes, those strange protruding lumps on her skin. She hadn't been smiling before, but she was smiling now with those stained rectangular teeth, a loose casual grin akin to the amiable nonchalance of her walk, and it was all I could do to force myself to drop the crowbar and hammer and grip the ax with both hands.

I'm not a hardass. I've never been in the military, and I'd certainly never killed anyone before. But I felt no qualms as I lifted the ax and swung it at that impossibly deformed head. She—it—saw me but made no effort to stop or run or move out of the way, and I hate to admit it but I felt a sort of grim satisfaction as the blade chopped through cheek and nose and embedded itself in skull. *This is for Ed,* I thought. *This is for Judy.*

I'd been half-afraid that she would keep walking, that nothing would be able to stop her, but she crumpled on the spot, nearly pulling me down with her until, at the last second, the ax blade was freed from her skull with a sickening squeak of bone. There was no blood, no slime, no liquid of any kind that spilled from the gaping wound, and I waited there for a moment but she didn't move.

Now I was in a hard spot. In movies, this was where the hero walks away while, behind his back, the supposedly dead monster gets up and comes back to life. I didn't want to make that mistake, but I didn't have the stomach for chopping her up.

What were my choices, though? I could reach down and see if I could feel a pulse or a breath to see if she was still alive—but maybe she'd never had a pulse, maybe she'd never been alive, and maybe that was when she would suddenly grab my hand and pull me on top of her.

I stood there for a moment, then stepped back and gathered up my courage and prodded her with the blunt edge of the ax blade. No movement, no reaction. Still, I couldn't be sure she wouldn't spring up and attack, and though the fire was gone from my belly and I no longer had any desire for violence, I picked up the ax and chopped off her head. It wasn't just one whack, like you see in the movies. My first swing went halfway through, exposing corded muscle and a segment of white spine. No blood still, but at least the interior of the neck looked the way it was supposed to. I pulled the ax out and up, did it again, and this time it went nearly all the way through. There was only a little bit of flattened skin at the bottom that was connecting the head to the body, but one more chop took care of that, and I used the ax to push the head away.

I picked up the crowbar and the hammer. It was time to put an end to all this.

I hurried next door. On the other side of the professor's house, I saw darkness moving over the roof and walls of Tony and Helen's place. It looked at first like it was being engulfed by some sort of monstrous shadow, but when I got closer I saw that it was a tidal wave of black bugs that were swarming over their home. Whatever it was, I was certain that it was connected to the shrine, and the sight of it spurred me onward, made me run faster. Or as fast as I could while carrying the tools. This time, I didn't care if I bumped into objects on the way, and I dashed through the side yard, not slowing down when I reached the back. I slammed into a unseen tree stump, nearly tripped over a hose and a rake, but I stumbled and stabilized and kept going.

Lights in the professor's house were on, I noticed. I thought of that transparent woman strolling through those filthy rooms, and the image of it chilled me to the bone. For the first time that evening, I saw this as though it was happening to someone else. I was in a fucking horror movie. I'd just been lurching from one thing to another since the Pittman kid (what the *hell* was his name?) first ran up to me on the street, but now I realized how much had happened, the extent of the power I was up against. I pushed the thought away, not wanting to be intimidated by what I was about to face.

I reached the shrine.

It looked even spookier to me than before, but I didn't give myself time to think about it. I dropped the ax, shifted the hammer to my left hand and swung the crowbar with my right.

The adobe was already old and crumbling, and my blow chipped off a large piece at the top. There was a shape carved into that rounded section of the shrine, a strange-looking spiral, and the second that it was cut in half by my crowbar, I thought I felt and heard a deep rumble, almost like a sonic boom, but maybe it was just my imagination.

That was it, though.

I guess I'd expected some sort of . . . defense. I thought the shrine or whatever sentient power lurked within the black space of that deep alcove might make an effort to protect itself. But nothing tried to stop me as I went at it with both hands, crowbar in the right, hammer in the left. I felt like John Henry or something, a superhuman man, and the shrine broke into pieces before my furious onslaught, chipping away bit by bit until only the alcove itself was left standing. I kicked away the photos and the fingernails and the petition and tried to tear apart the rounded alcove, but that thing was tough. It was not adobe like the rest of the shrine, but it was not metal or wood or cement, either. I couldn't tell what it was made of. All I knew was that my blows were having little or no effect on it, and I was feeling increasingly uneasy standing in front of that black open space.

I dropped the hammer and moved around behind the alcove, stepping over the rotted boards of the collapsed playhouse and balancing on a cobweb-covered log that had rolled off the woodpile some time ago. The alcove was black in back, too, only there were symbols written on it. Symbols and what looked like words in a foreign alphabet. They were almost as dark as the dome-like structure itself, and I probably wouldn't have noticed them if they hadn't reflected the moonlight. I wondered if they were written in blood.

I remembered what had happened when I broke off that symbol at the top of the shrine, and whether that sonic boom was in my imagination or not, I had no other ideas or plans, and I used the crowbar to start chipping away at the squiggly characters. This worked better. The metal crowbar smashed into and smudged a strange triangle-looking symbol, and all of a sudden a crack appeared in the top of the alcove. I hit one of those foreign words, and a piece of its backing flaked off, spiraling to the ground. I smelled shit and rotten eggs, and I thought that *this* was the alcove's defense mechanism. Like a skunk, it was trying to chase me away with foul odors, and that made me work even harder. I started *wailing* on that sucker, and was rewarded with almost immediate results. With each letter or symbol that splintered off or was scraped away, the alcove seemed to weaken and buckle until finally it collapsed in on itself with a noise that sounded more like the scream of a woman than the crack-clunk-thump of shattered stone hitting the ground.

I leaped out of the way, the log rolling beneath my feet, and stumbled through the rotten wood of the playhouse until I was once again in front of the structure. Or what used to be the structure. There was nothing left but what looked like a pile of jagged black rocks. In the rubble, I saw what appeared to be a burnt Barbie on top of a wiggly slice of cheesecake. I don't know if it was alive, but it was moving, twisting around in slow motion like it was doing tai chi, making a sound like a rusty hinge. I couldn't see any eyes, couldn't see any facial features, but I could tell that it was looking up at me, and that gave me the eeriest feeling I'd ever had. I shivered. The doll smiled at me, and in the moonlight I saw one bright white tooth.

I batted that fucker to Kingdom Come. The crowbar hit its midsection, and it flew apart, body cracking in half, legs breaking against black stone rubble, arms shattering into pieces, split head flying off into the dark. The cheesecake beneath it splattered everywhichway, and left in the center, on a small piece of crust, was a nasty black beetle with furiously snapping pincers. I smashed it with the crowbar, then smeared its guts around to make sure it was gone for good.

I looked down at my feet. The photos and fingernails had scattered, but the petition, oddly enough, had been blown back onto the little flat slab of adobe that used to stick out in front of the alcove and was now the only thing left standing. I raised my crowbar high and brought it down on that small slab, grateful to see it shatter.

The shrine was gone.

"Take that," I said.

I was out of breath and breathing like a mother, but I backtracked up the path and walked up the steps into the house, just to make sure it was all over. I wasn't afraid anymore, in fact I half-expected to find the transparent woman dead and dissolved, but she was in that first filthy bedroom and very much alive, and she attacked me the instant I stepped through the doorway. She was wearing the bloody nightgown that had been thrown over the chair, and she jumped me, knocking me to the ground. The light was on, so I could see her clearly, and she wasn't wielding any type of weapon, so I instinctively let go of the crowbar and reached up to grab her wrist.

Big mistake.

She was off me and rolling, surprisingly fast for someone so large. She grabbed the crowbar off the floor and ran with it to the bed, moving expertly around all the books and newspapers and magazines on the stained carpet. She turned around and swung, the crowbar whistling as it cut through the air, and I could see that she was crying. Her tears were invisible on that transparent skin, but the redness of her eyes and the quivering of her lips gave it away.

"Which one are you?" she demanded.

I shook my head.

"Which one *are* you?"

"I'm Gil Marotta," I said.

She backed around the bed until she was in the corner, sobbing, feebly swinging the crowbar, holding it in both hands. I could have rushed her and taken it from her. I could have killed her. But I decided to leave her alone and call the cops when I got home.

I turned to go, and a book hit me in the back of the head. A big book. It knocked me forward, stunned me, and another one followed immediately after, this one hitting at an angle and drawing blood. I whirled around, arms up to protect myself, ready to fend off another book or even a full-frontal assault if I had to, but she wasn't throwing books at me anymore and she wasn't rushing me with the crowbar. Instead, she'd fallen forward onto the bed, the crowbar on the mattress next to her but no longer in her hands. I ran forward, grabbed it, backed away.

She lay there unmoving.

Was she dead? I didn't know. I didn't think so, but I was not about to check.

I kept backing up, moving slowly so I didn't trip over any of the crap she'd left on the floor of that pigsty.

Power had a cost, and while I would never know for sure, I was willing to bet that was what had happened to her, that was why she had become transparent. Whether she provided the shrine with its power and was drained of it herself, or whether she had worshiped at that black empty space and a sacrifice had been demanded of her, the two were connected.

She moaned, lifted her head, looked at me.

I left the room, walked onto the porch, walked down the steps. It was over, it was finished. I'd call the cops from home, I decided, let them take care of her.

I felt exhausted, as though my body had been put through a wringer, but I thought about Lynn and Frank and smiled to myself. At least they were safe, at least they were all right.

I trudged across the circle to my house.

And my family.

PYRE

by Christopher Golden

1

On the morning Samantha Finnin's father was buried, she had no tears to cry. Though she would never have admitted it, especially to her mother, Samantha had not wept for her father at all. She felt as though she ought to, but there was a pain in her chest, a kind of cotton thickness in her throat, that seemed to prevent it. Her eyes burned, but she figured that was lack of sleep rather than grief. Somewhere, buried down inside her, she knew there must be sorrow, even despair, but in the days since the early morning call from her mother that announced her father's death, she had felt only anger and bitterness and resentment.

The limo rolled down Concord Street at the sluggish pace that was traditional for funeral processions. Samantha did not turn around, but she knew that if she had she would have seen that all the cars had their headlights on. The world seemed to have slowed down around them, this somber parade of mourners gathered to remember a man they all had loved in spite of himself.

It was the first week of May and the morning had brought crisp, crystal blue skies and a soft breeze that rustled the leaves on the trees with that sort of hush that whispered the secrets of angels. The air was redolent with the scent of blossoming flowers and the rich earth odors of fresh-cut grass. But in the limousine Samantha felt like a prisoner, deprived of all that. The tinted windows cast a pall upon the sky when she gazed out from within, and the atmosphere inside that vehicle was laden with the trace smells of the cologne and perfume and hairspray of mourners who had ridden in it before them.

Or maybe that's just Mom and David.

Samantha frowned and glanced over at the others riding in the limousine with her. Her mother, Tricia, had divorced her father more than a decade before. As far as Samantha was concerned, it was the best thing that had ever happened to the woman. Mom had found herself then, and five years later had met David Rusticio, who owned his own construction company north of Boston. Though ten years older than Tricia's fifty-one, David was in many ways not quite as "old" as his wife. Samantha got along with her stepfather fairly well, but she had been in college by the time her mother married him, and so the truth was they did not know one another that well. She certainly had never considered him her father. Some might have suggested that was because her biological father had still been alive, but that wasn't it. Carl Finnin had never been much of a father to her either.

And now he was dead.

Samantha tried to hold her breath for a while, but eventually she surrendered and reached out to hit the button that operated the window. It retracted into the door with an electric whine and the spring breeze rushed into the back seat, whipping her long white-blond hair around her head and across her face.

"Samantha!" her mother said quickly. "Please, honey, close that."

With a frown, Samantha gazed back at her. "I need some fresh air, Mom."

Tricia reached both hands up to her tightly coiffed hair, done very early that morning at Salon Trebbiano in Andover. Peter Trebbiano had gone in at seven A.M. to prepare her for her ex-husband's funeral mass. He had been doing Tricia's hair for as long as Samantha could remember.

"Samantha," her mother said sternly. There was a look on the woman's face that made her feel ten years old again. "I know how hard this must be for you, honey, but let's try to keep our composure for a little longer."

She spoke so sweetly Samantha did not have the heart to utter any of the responses that came into her head. Not the one that included an indictment involving her mother's concern being more about her hair than about composure, nor the simple query as to why they ought to keep their composure in the first place. Her father was dead. Was anyone going to care if she lost it, went absolutely bugfuck out of her mind, dropped down on her knees screaming to God for an explanation, or better yet an apology?

Not that she would, mind you. Hell, she couldn't even cry.

It hurt, that part. More than anything else, in fact. Samantha knew she ought to cry and the truth of it was, deny it as she might, she *wanted* to cry. She simply could not summon the moisture to her eyes. Partially, she thought, because she had not been with her father when he died. Yes, she had visited him in the hospital during his chemotherapy and yes, she had seen the husk of him, the hollow shell of him, at the wake just last night, but the two things seemed somehow unrelated without her having witnessed the moment in between when her father—smiling, flirtatious, self-deprecating Carl Finnin—had become a corpse.

It was partially that which kept her from crying.

But, far more than that, it was that her father had been capable of being an utter and complete asshole, an immature son of a bitch with no apparent recognition of the ways in which his behavior had wounded and scarred his only daughter.

"*Sam,*" her stepfather said kindly, cautiously, as the limo rolled painfully slow through the streets of Boxford.

"Samantha, what is wrong with you?" her mother snapped, ignoring David as though unaware of him.

With her eyes closed, Samantha let the breeze wash over her face, whipping her hair back. She breathed deeply of the spring air and felt the warmth of the sun on her face. When she let her eyes flicker open, she saw the gates of Ashgrove Cemetery ahead. Reluctantly, she turned from the open window and sat back against the leather upholstery.

"I'm twenty-three years old, Mom," Samantha said without even looking at Tricia. "Please don't talk to me like I'm a child. Not today."

At length she turned to find her mother staring at her. She was still a beautiful woman and in some way that made the dampness of her eyes that much worse. They were rimmed with moisture and shot through with red; even after all the shit he had put her through and the years that had passed, she had still loved her ex-husband. The breeze through the open window ruffled her hair.

Samantha reached out and clasped her mother's hand in her own, even as the limousine came to a halt behind the hearse that held her father's coffin and a dozen or more extravagant floral arrangements.

"You were always the strong one," Tricia said, lips pressed together.

It wasn't strength, of course, but how could Samantha explain it to her mother? Even after all that Carl Finnin had done to her—the philandering, the boozing, the financial mess that had cost her their house—she could still cry for him.

Samantha stepped out of the limo first. Her mother and David got out on the other side and walked around to stand nearby. They all watched as the men from the funeral home rolled Carl's casket out onto a wheeled metal stand like a giant TV table or a hospital gurney. A hand landed on Sam's shoulder and she glanced up at Father Corcoran from St. Andrew's and smiled thinly, hugging herself in her severe black jacket and skirt.

Cold. Samantha felt very cold.

Whatever solace she had taken from the breeze and the cloudless blue sky and the new growth of spring was gone now. The wind was cold, the late morning rich with color but devoid of compassion for the true emotions in her heart. She watched them roll her father's casket toward the gravesite and lift it off, moving it to the mechanism that would later lower it into the earth. It occurred to her that they'd arrived too quickly, that in the past when she had attended funerals, the casket was already in place when mourners reached the cemetery.

"Bastard," she whispered under her breath, biting her lip, glancing sidelong at her mother to see if Tricia had heard.

Mom was crying, David holding her, understanding. How could he be so understanding? He was her husband, but here she was, crying silently over the guy she was married to before he came along. Samantha supposed that was maturity in action. It seemed foreign to her.

Carl Finnin had rarely been home during her childhood, but when he had been, Samantha had loved him desperately, gazed up at him with wide-eyed adoration that can only be given by a daughter to her father. He burned with the electricity of natural charisma and changed the dynamic of every room he entered. The truth was, as a girl, whenever her father had taken her with him on an errand or to the office, she had never felt for a moment that she was a burden. Stuck in a corner, drawing with crayons and stationery, she was just happy to be with Daddy. When he spoke to her, it was like she was the only girl in the world.

Only as an adult did she realize that was the way he talked to *all* the girls. That she had mattered to him more than anything when she was right in front of him, but when she was out of the room, more than likely he forgot he even had a daughter. Out of sight, out of mind. That old saying applied to Carl Finnin very well. And so much for child-support payments after the divorce, or regular visits of any kind, for that matter.

When it occurred to him, Carl would show up and take Samantha off to dinner or a movie, usually in conjunction with some date he had set up or because he happened to be in the area doing something else. And Christmas. He usually showed up on Christmas, his gifts generic and thoughtless. The sweatshirt or doll or little bracelet might have been for anyone. Like he was buying them for someone else's daughter, a distant cousin. Samantha had often thought that might be truer than she wanted to admit. Carl might well have bought a dozen of each gift he had ever given her, and presented the others to nieces and the daughters of his girlfriends.

Samantha knew that she had to let go of the bitterness in her heart, but it wasn't that simple.

She had loved her father. Adored him still, though they rarely spoke. Even after college she had not been immune to his charm, to his easy smile and generous laughter. In part because of that love—and in even greater part due to her fear of his answer—she had never asked him *why*. Why he had behaved as he did, how he could have treated his only daughter that way, if it ever hurt him to know that they had only the past and their common blood to connect them.

Why?

Car doors slammed, the sound echoing across the grounds of the cemetery, off the gleaming marble facades and weathered granite faces of the true grove in Ashgrove Cemetery. The orchard of the dead.

Mourners began to swarm around her and Sam's mother moved in close by her now. Aunt Evelyn, her father's sister, gathered her own family around. Samantha's cousins were appropriately solemn, but Aunt Evelyn offered her a sweet, sympathetic smile. Her husband, Uncle Ken, stepped over to Samantha and wordlessly kissed her on the top of the head. The people swept in and crowded around the hole in the ground, keeping a uniform distance away from it and the casket suspended above. The flowers had been arranged quickly and expertly by the men from the funeral home, and it occurred to Samantha how mundane they must think all of this. They did it every day; the carrying of the dead, the positioning of the flowers.

Father Corcoran cleared his throat and began to address the congregation around the grave. The stone was there already, FINNIN written across the front, engraved deeply and ornate. Samantha had never known her father's parents, both of whom were buried here, but they had bought a plot large enough for themselves and their children, and their children's spouses and their children.

A place for me, Samantha thought, grim and cynical. *Such a comfort to know.*

The priest spoke, but she did not hear him. His voice was like a low buzz in her ears. Instead she heard the rustle of stiff, starched suits and skirts, the sound of soft weeping, the low cough of Uncle Ken, getting over a cold. The grass rippled with the breeze and Samantha stared at the casket.

Why? she asked again, fully aware that it was a question that could never be answered. Her temples hurt, a dull ache that seemed to pulse all through her head. Her left hand fluttered up to her still-burning eyes and came away moist.

Only then did she realize she was crying. And she had no idea when the tears had begun.

Suddenly she was even angrier with her father. *Bastard,* she thought as she glared at the cherrywood box draped in flowers and an American flag to mark his service during the Vietnam

War. He didn't deserve these tears, but she could not stop herself from giving them to him.

Father Corcoran droned on and Samantha wept freely, jaws clenched tightly together, staring at flowers and headstones and the ground, but not at faces. Her stepfather slipped an arm around her and Aunt Evelyn reached out to take her hand, which only made her cry harder.

Through her tears the perfect blue day seemed stormy and gray.

At last, breathing deeply and trying to calm herself, Samantha wiped at her eyes and glanced around at the mourners. So many faces, friends and colleagues of her father and mother, relatives both close and only slightly familiar, her own friends from high school and college.

And Brian.

Samantha stopped, swallowed hard and tasted the salt of her tears, and stared a moment at Brian Knapp. He wore dark, round sunglasses and his hair was cut almost too short. His suit was gray with thin stripes and he did not look at all comfortable in it. Brian gazed at her from behind those Secret Service–man glasses, face etched with shared sorrow and compassion, and yet the edges of his mouth ticked upward in the hint of a smile, no more. Just a moment of reassurance for her.

It helped. Samantha took a long breath and let it out, and she returned that glimmer of a smile he had given her.

She had not seen Brian in five years, not since the summer after they had graduated high school. Not since Scottie's house in Biddeford Pool and the ghost games and Monument Island.

The island.

Sam's face went slack and what little color she had retained drained from her face. Pieces of memory like shards of broken glass tumbled out of the past.

2

It's the end of June, officially summer by a handful of days, and eighteen-year-old Samantha has a fine buzz on thanks to a quartet of rum & Cokes made with Captain Morgan, which she has just discovered and likes far too well. They're on the beach, or the little stretch of sand that passes for beach there in Biddeford Pool.

Freshly graduated from Boxford High School, Scottie has himself the ultimate graduation present: the keys to his parents' beach house for a long weekend without any adult interference. Samantha thinks it's almost funny. They've got to know that the place is going to be a party for four days straight; if they don't they're either painfully naïve or complete morons. But they go for it anyway.

It crosses her mind that maybe the Guilfords just figure Scottie's eighteen now, a high school graduate, and he's going to have to start making his own decisions and taking the consequences as they come. Sam's given this some thought since graduation, actually. It's pretty liberating. It's also terrifying.

On the other hand, she's staggered past buzzed now and is well nigh on to shitfaced. Not quite hammered. She'd rather not get too hammered, actually, because then there's the vomiting and the hanging on people and saying things that will embarrass her later. She's witnessed that one too many times, and done it a few as well. It's never good.

So no more alcohol for Samantha tonight.

None.

Dan and Traci run far ahead, bare feet kicking up sand behind them. They laugh and Dan starts tickling her, trying to prod her toward the water as if he's going to throw her in. Traci gets serious, wags a finger at him. Don't you fucking dare, Daniel. He gives her that trademark grin and throws up his hands. As soon as she drops her guard he tackles her on the sand and they roll around and a second later they're all over each other yet again.

Samantha gets a mental image that makes her want to laugh and makes her a little nauseated at the same time—last night Traci and Dan took off down the beach to fool around. Drunk off her ass, she started to give him a blowjob only to gag and throw up all over him. This morning Traci had hardly blushed telling Samantha and the twins the story—she thought it was a riot. At the time, Samantha had thought it disgusting, but in retrospect, it's pretty fucking funny.

Seeing them tussling on the sand like that gets her giggling to herself. The twins, Kara and Kat, are walking on either side of her and they shoot her matching inquisitive looks. Samantha makes a low gagging noise and pretends to throw up, and the other two girls begin to giggle uncontrollably.

Scottie frowns at them like they're out of their minds. He and Tim stop and sit on the sand, stretching out. Brian joins them, putting down the boom box he's carrying. Sheryl Crow's sexy voice rasps on the radio. The waves roll in with a soft, constant hiss that Samantha can feel inside her. The ocean breeze blows through her too-short blond hair and it's chilly all of a sudden. Colder than it should be. Hell, it's summer now, after all, and it had been plenty hot that day.

But the chill isn't an illusion and it's not brought on by the Captain Morgan either. Beneath the fabric of her lime-green bikini top her nipples harden and she wishes she had worn a sweatshirt.

"Fucking cold out here," she murmurs.

"Sit down, I'll warm you up." This from Tim, who has wanted to get in her pants since the first day of high school. Not that this puts her into any special category, for the same could be said of most of the girls at Boxford High.

Tonight, though, Samantha chooses to ignore the lascivious tone of his words. She plops down on the sand beside him and lets him slip an arm around her, and she's grateful for the warmth. For his part, Tim is the perfect gentleman, just as she knew he would be. He's all talk, or almost all. A good guy, underneath all that horniness. And not half bad looking, with pitch-black hair a little too long, just like her own latest cut was a little too short.

Brian sets down a six-pack of cold Coronas in their midst. They're all carrying drinks already except for Samantha and she glances nervously at the other houses on the beach. Little cottages really. Some of them are lit inside, mostly older couples according to Scottie, but the only other people they see on this stretch of beach are a pair of fortyish women jogging.

He glances at her, indicates the beer. She shakes her head, but she smiles sweetly at him. Brian is her best friend, bar none. She can't talk to him the way she does to her girlfriends; but then she can't talk to them the way she talks to Brian, either. There have been times in the past four years where knowing she had him to talk to, to hold her when she cried, was the only thing that got her through without completely losing her mind.

Every heartbreak, Brian was there. When her parents' divorce was final, Brian was there. When she was in the hospital with mono, Brian was there. When she embarrassed herself after too many drinks and threw up in the bushes in the twins' backyard, Brian held her hair away from her face. He knew her better than anyone. Samantha likes to think she has been that kind of friend to Brian as well.

She watches him now as he slips up beside Kat and puts an arm around her waist. Kat smiles and kisses him quickly. Kara turns around and puts her hands on her narrow hips and stares out at the surf crashing on the sand and the streak of moonlight that cascades across the water.

The moon seems cold to Samantha. It isn't like the sun. It doesn't warm her. Like a ball of ice in the night sky, it seems to glow with a halo of frost.

"Look at all the gulls," Kara says. "They're so gross."

Samantha frowns and glances up to where Kara's pointing. A small egg-shaped island stands perhaps two hundred yards from shore. Its coast is rocky and jagged, not at all inviting despite the woods that sprout from the island farther inland. Kara's right about the seagulls, too. Samantha has seen pictures of St. Mark's Square in Venice and all the pigeons there. This is far worse than that. Seagulls soar and turn and glide on the wind above those trees, but there are only a few in the air at a time. The rest of them are spread out across the jagged, inhospitable face of the island, roosting on every rock and tree Samantha can see.

"There must be thousands of them," Kara adds.

Samantha shudders. Kara said they were gross, but she thinks they're also pretty creepy, so many of them just sitting there.

"That's Monument Island," Scottie says as he uses his key chain to pop the cap off a Corona. "Supposedly there's an old monument out there. My father says it must be Native American, but Mom told me she'd read it's supposed to be left there by the Vikings."

"That'd be sort of cool to see," Brian says. "The Vikings were here way before any other European settlers, but there isn't a lot of evidence of it."

Tim laughs. "Yeah, all right, Indiana Jones. We'll check it out first thing in the morning. For now, just shut up and drink, motherfucker. Jesus." He rubs Sam's shoulder and though she likes the contact, something in his laugh makes her wince.

"Can't," Scottie says.

Brian and Tim glance at him. Samantha does, too. She realizes that they're all looking at him now.

Scottie shrugs. "You can try if you want. It's pretty shallow at low tide. But I've gone out there a couple of times and those fucking birds won't let you within ten feet of the shore. They're brutal, man. Peck your goddamn eyes out."

"Get the fuck out of here!" Tim snorts.

"Come on, Scott," Kat says, hugging herself as she comes over to take a Corona and sit down next to Sam.

Even Traci and Dan sit up now. Her tank top is twisted

around and she's smiling mischievously as she reaches up under it and snaps her bra back into place, but she's paying attention.

"Serious," Scottie tells them. "I've seen it. I shit you not, I swear. They're maniacs, all of those birds. Probably their nesting grounds or something, but they won't let anybody on the island. I saw some bird-watching asshole get his arms all torn up last summer. He ended up having to dive into the water. One of the damn gulls even took his hat."

Samantha can't help laughing. It's a deep laugh, and she snorts. "They took his hat?"

Scottie laughs, too. "You had to see it." Then he pushes his fingers through his brown hair, blue eyes glistening in the moonlight, and he smiles. "My mother said the story was that the Vikings lost so many warriors or sailors or whatever to disease and battles with the Indians and shit that they had to build a monument to them. They'd take them out to the island and build a big . . . what do you call that, the bonfire when they put the corpse on it?"

Brian doesn't even smile. "A funeral pyre."

Scottie snaps his fingers. "Exactly. So they burned the bodies on these bonfires and the fates or the Valkyries or whatever would come and get them."

Samantha shudders as she stares out at the island. "So it's like a cemetery out there?"

"No, you're missing the point," Scottie says. "They burned them. Maybe there's bones out there, but the way my mother tells it from what she read, probably not even that. The Vikings believed that the remains of their warriors were purified in the fire and then they were brought back to life, returned to the battlefields from heaven."

93

"Valhalla," Brian corrects him, turning now to stare out at the island. "They would have been taken to Valhalla, the hall of dead heroes and warriors, before being returned to battle."

"How is it you spend so much time in the library and still have time to party with us?" Tim teases him.

Brian shrugs, smiling. He had glasses for a long time, but he wears contacts now and his blue eyes are sparkling. He's always been a big guy, a little too doughy maybe, but in the last year he's slimmed down and now he's just tall and broad-shouldered, enough so that he might intimidate someone who didn't know him.

Kat kisses his cheek. "Don't worry, babe. Being smart might be considered uncool in high school, but college starts in a couple of months. Smart is sexy now."

"Yeah, you better watch it, Kat," Kara said. "The girls are gonna be all over Bri the first week."

Samantha thinks they might both be right, but not just because Brian's smart. He doesn't look like the old Brian anymore. In his way, he's the best looking among the guys in their group; only she's never really noticed it before. He looks more like a man, and the other guys, well, they're just the guys. Kids, still.

Just like me, she thinks.

But then her gaze drifts toward the island again and she thinks of bodies burning and she trembles.

"Jeez," Tim says quietly, kindly, beside her. "You really are cold. You want my shirt?"

Samantha smiles. "No. I'm good, thanks."

"What you need is a beer," Tim assures her.

"Only if you want me to totally retch all over you," Samantha replies without thinking. Then, realizing what she has said, she glances over at Dan and Traci and starts laughing again, a hand fluttering up to her mouth trying to stifle it.

They all start to laugh, then, except Dan, who stares at Traci with his mouth hanging down. He looks pretty comical.

Kara leans against Sam, sighing as her giggles subside. "All right, since we're in spooky mode, you guys want to do that 'light as a feather' game?"

Samantha knows this game. One of them is on the ground and the others gather around and pretend that person is dead. Then using only two fingers of each hand at strategic points, they try to lift the corpse up as high as they can. It shouldn't work, but she's done it before. She knows it does. Brian tells her it all has to do with leverage and mathematics, but he's never really explained it to her satisfaction and so Samantha still thinks it's pretty freaky.

"I'll pass," she announces.

But the others don't. Everyone except Brian agrees to play and so he comes to sit by her while Tim is on the ground with his arms crossed over his chest and his eyes closed. Samantha doesn't even want to look at him, the image is so disturbing.

"You want to go for a walk?" she asks Brian.

He smiles and stands up, brushes the sand off his ass and offers her his hand. She takes it and he hauls her to her feet. There are catcalls and taunts about their cowardice, but Brian and Samantha are together in this and when they're together they can put up with just about any amount of shit. It just feels different to her when Brian's with her.

Kara hushes them all and silence falls upon the beach, save for the caw of distant gulls and the rush of the surf. For the moment, Samantha and Brian stay to watch.

"This is Tim," Kara says. She is kneeling by his head, two fingers beneath his skull. The others are lined up around him and they echo her words.

"This is Tim."

"Tim is driving home late. He's been drinking," Kara says, and the circle repeats her words. Samantha is surprised that there are no jokes, no chuckles. "Too fast, he rounds a corner. There is an oncoming truck, taking up too much of the road."

Again they repeat her words.

"They collide."

"They collide."

"Tim is dead."

"Tim is dead."

Samantha shivers, reaches for Brian's hand and they turn together to walk away. Behind them, the group begins to chant, insisting to the spirits or the gods or just the darkness around them that Tim is both light as a feather and stiff as a board, repeating the words over and over. Soon, Samantha and Brian have walked far enough that they cannot hear the chanting anymore, only the surf, and the rumble of car engines passing on the shore road beyond the row of beach houses.

It's dark enough that when they pause and look back, they can barely see their friends.

"I hate that stuff," Samantha says.

"I know."

There's something in Brian's voice that makes her pause, then glance up at him in concern. He has wide, beautiful tur-

96

quoise eyes that are bright and shining when he's laughing, but dark and troubled when he's not. There's a cast to his eyes now that sends a chill through Sam, as though he bears some wound she cannot see and that he hopes to hide.

Brian glances away, feeling her scrutiny upon him.

"What?" she asks, slightly urgently, worried for him.

His smile is shy, and a little sad. "Nothing."

Samantha pokes him hard in the chest, grinning. "What?" she demands.

"Just gonna miss you, that's all," he replies, shrugging. "We're going to be so far away from each other. I mean, I know we have to go. This is life, right? But I've been thinking about it a lot."

A sweet warmth spreads through her, melting away the chill she had felt before. "You big goof. We've got the rest of the summer. And then, even after, we'll run up ridiculous phone bills and we'll see each other during breaks and holidays."

He draws his palm across his chin and it rasps on the stubble there. Brian hasn't shaved all weekend. Samantha frowns; her levity is not having its desired effect.

"Hey," she says softly, touching his arm.

"I'm such an asshole," Brian mutters. He takes a deep breath and as he shakes his head and at last meets her gaze, an ironic smile crosses his face. "I've been in love with you practically since the day we met. A million times I wanted to tell you, but I just couldn't get up the guts. I was afraid if you didn't feel the same way I'd lose you completely."

It's like all the air has been sucked out of Sam's lungs. Her mouth is open just a little and for a few seconds she thinks absolutely nothing at all. Her mind hasn't even begun to con-

97

front his feelings, to turn them over and attempt to interpret them with her own heart.

And then he lifts her chin and he kisses her, soft and light, sweet and perfect, and Samantha breathes in quickly, a tiny gasp with which she inhales his warm breath. She feels weak suddenly, and she is about to kiss him back hungrily, all thoughts of Kat gone from her mind. But then Brian breaks off the kiss and pulls back, searching her eyes for reassurance.

Samantha breathes deeply, takes a step back. She can't smile, but she wants to. Her thoughts are scattered and she wants to put them together, but she starts to shake her head out of disbelief. Brian sees it and she can tell from his expression that he has assumed rejection. Samantha panics; she needs time to digest it, that's all.

She's about to tell him that when a scream tears the darkness around them, echoes out across the waves and along the beach. They turn together and stare back the way they've come.

"That's Kat," Brian says, breathless.

They begin to run, kicking up sand. There are more shouts of panic and alarm as they rush toward their friends, who are all still gathered there on the shore. Scottie kneels by Tim, one ear against his chest, and it looks really silly and profoundly unnerving all at once. A gag. It's got to be a gag.

But it isn't.

Samantha and Brian reach the circle and the others are freaking out. Scottie shouts at Dan and Traci to run back to the house, to call an ambulance. They take off, Traci crying and Dan whispering "Jesus" over and over, somehow half-prayer and half-curse.

"Come on, Timmy!" Scott snarls as he begins to perform CPR. He breathes into Tim's mouth, then presses on his chest. "Fuck! Breathe, you motherfucker!"

"What happened?" Brian asks as Kat clings to him fearfully. "How the hell did it happen?"

Kara is hugging herself, staring down at Tim's too-still form with haunted eyes, and suddenly Samantha knows they are not kidding around. This isn't a gag. Tim is dying. Maybe he's dead already.

Scottie keeps up the CPR, but he's losing it a little bit, cussing like a lunatic. Samantha doesn't blame him. The houses around them are silent. The moonlight casts a yellow glaze over their faces, so that each of them looks just as still and dead as Tim does right now, like his body is the hard plastic of a department store mannequin, not the jock who'd been trying to get her in bed for the last four years.

"Oh my God," Samantha whispers, her voice so small and frail that the words are almost unborn, nearly stolen away by the wind and the crash of the surf.

She can't look at Tim a second longer and so her eyes move up and away from him, to the houses again, up the beach to where Dan and Traci have run, wondering how long it will take for them to call, for EMTs to arrive. Then she glances out across the waves and she sees the island.

A fire is burning.

Back from the cruel, rocky shore, up on the hill in the midst of the woods on the island, the glow of fire burns high and swirls with black smoke. It is bright and fierce and Samantha stares at it in stunned silence. How can it be, with all the gulls there? And the gulls themselves have not moved. Some still swoop above, but most of them roost on the stones, unruffled by the blaze at the peak of the island.

Then Samantha sees the women. Three of them, draped in red, beautiful things with skin like alabaster and hair raven black. They stand on the shore of the island, their arms spread wide, palms up, and flames dance upon their open hands.

Samantha cannot breathe.

The women begin to walk out across the water.

Someone shouts, "Yes!"

Shuddering with fear and a bone-deep chill, Samantha glances over to see Scottie grinning, nodding to himself. Then she sees why. Tim's eyes are open. He's breathing again, awake, still pale but very much alive. The smile of relief that washes over Sam's face is fleeting; she turns to look back out at the island.

The fire is gone.

The women are gone.

In denial, she shakes her head. This isn't her imagination. They weren't illusions or phantoms or some crazy shit like that. She saw them, saw that fire. Quickly, she turns to the others and notices that Brian is also staring out across the water, gazing at that island with an expression that is part dread and part disbelief.

Brian saw them, too.

3

"Are you trying to tell me that you don't remember *any* of that?"

Brian smiled. "Well, obviously I remember the part where you broke my heart."

He said it off the cuff, just two old friends razzing each other after too long apart, but Samantha knew he meant it. There were a million arguments she could have made, a million ways she might have tried to explain, but she had given up feeling like it was her fault years ago.

"Hey, you were with Kat, and you can't blame me because you didn't have the balls to speak up before that night." Samantha arched an eyebrow, daring him to argue. "Things got crazy after that and there just never seemed to be a chance to—"

"Whoa! Whoa, Sam. Hold on," Brian replied, leaning back in the booth and raising both hands. "I still love you. Maybe we haven't seen each other in forever, but you were my best friend for a lot of years. I'll always love you. But I'm over it. No worries."

Samantha smiled sheepishly. She was warmed by his admission of affection even after all the time they'd been apart. But in the back of her mind, his words echoed. *I'm over it.* The tragedy of that was, she did not think *she* was.

All those old emotions charged the air between them, still alive, still electric. But that was not what she wanted to talk to him about. That was not what she needed him to remember.

*   *   *

The day had been one long series of hugs and handshakes, staring at vaguely familiar faces obscured by the curtain of her own tears. Unable to cry at first she had found herself incapable of stopping once she had begun. After the graveside service, Aunt Evelyn and Uncle Ken had invited mourners back to their home in Andover. Relatives had besieged Samantha with memories of her father; most of them charming, some of them funny, and some tragic. Those three adjectives had pretty much summed up his life.

Brian had spent that time circulating through the room, speaking to her relatives and family friends who had known him in the high school years when he and Samantha had been best friends. None of them had seen him since that time, but truth be told most of them hadn't really seen Samantha much either. The people who recognized him treated Brian like a long-lost cousin.

Several times Samantha spotted him, but both of them were constantly engaged in conversation. It was not until the afternoon had worn on and most of the people had left that she stumbled into the kitchen looking for a quiet place to sit down and found Brian and Aunt Evelyn talking, with Brian doing the dishes. He had stopped midsentence, a tea saucer suspended in midair, and stared at Samantha. No smile, no welcome, just a sort of sadness to his features that she knew must mirror her own.

Aunt Evelyn might have left the room then, but Samantha did not even notice. Later when she thought about it, she could not recall at what point her aunt had departed.

"Hey," Brian had said, his voice lower, raspier than she remembered. But that might just have been emotion.

Samantha opened her mouth to respond. A simple "hey" would do it, just the way he'd said it. It was the way they had always greeted each other back when, in person or on the phone. The word would not come out. She was incapable of producing that single syllable. Samantha bit her lower lip, fresh tears springing to her eyes. Silently she damned them, for she had thought the crying over. Then she moved into his embrace, though perhaps fell would be more accurate.

Brian crushed her to him and she sobbed against his chest. He shushed her and whispered nonsense words that spoke to her heart only. Trite, hollow words that reminded her how incapable human beings were of eloquence in such moments. And yet it wasn't the words themselves that soothed her, but merely his voice, his touch, and the knowledge that he was willing to bear some of her pain.

"I miss him," she whispered, her voice choked with grief.

"Ssshhh, honey, I know you do."

"I fucking hate him," she snarled, not at all concerned that someone might overhear.

Brian stiffened but held her just a little tighter. Samantha bit her lip as though that could hold her anger back, but it came spilling out of her.

"Why didn't he love me, Brian?"

"He did love you," Brian replied, voice hitching. "He was your dad, Sam. He was proud of you."

"But he never told me that. And after he left us it was like he didn't care if I was ever in his life again. I hate him for leaving before I could make him say he was sorry."

There were no words after that. Her tears dried. Brian held her for several more minutes until Aunt Evelyn came back into the kitchen to ask if Samantha was all right and to tell her that her mother was looking for her. It was time to go.

Samantha glanced at Brian, saw the reluctance in his eyes and felt it in herself.

"I'll take you home later if you don't want to go now," he offered. "Maybe we could get a cup of coffee."

So here they were, sitting in a booth in the back of Java Man in Newburyport. Samantha watched through the plate-glass windows as the early evening sidewalks of the eccentric little seaside town churned with people who had not spent the morning at a funeral and the afternoon pretending not to grieve. They spilled out of offices or emerged from cars to trek toward trendy restaurants and quaint shops.

The world moved on. But there was a stone in her heart that would trouble her forever if she did not find a way to remove it, to stop the pain it caused. Its sharp edges cut her on the inside, where the wounds would not show.

The moment she had seen Brian at the cemetery, the memory of that night up in Maine had come flooding back in painful, breathtakingly precise detail. She could even recall how the salt air had tasted on her tongue. The image of that fire and the spectral women across the waves was etched finely in her mind's eye. That night on the beach she had spoken to Brian about it, and he had admitted that he too had seen that fire, that burning funeral pyre, and those women. Even so, she had done her best over the years to convince herself it had been imagination or inebriation, and then forced herself to forget.

In the time they had spent together this afternoon she and Brian had caught up on each other's lives, talking like weeks had passed instead of years, happy just to be in each other's presence again. But now she stared at him, shaking her head.

"You're really saying this," Samantha said, voice soft. "Don't do this to me, Brian."

The apology in his eyes never made it to his lips. "I don't know what else to tell you, Sam. I remember that stupid game and the thing with Tim. Scott gave him CPR and got him breathing again. It was scary and, yeah, a little freaky, but this thing with the island—"

"Can I get you folks anything else?"

They both looked up at the waitress and Samantha wondered how the woman had appeared beside them without either of them noticing. Her name tag identified her as "Juliette" and with her apron and the peach-colored uniform Java Man made her wear, she looked very much as though she had just arrived through a time warp from a 1950s diner. Even the coffeepot clutched in her right hand had a sort of antique quality about it.

"I'd love another cup," Brian told Juliette.

The waitress topped off Brian's cup and turned to Samantha.

"I'm good, thanks."

Without another word, Juliette did a half-pirouette and sauntered off as though pouring coffee were her greatest ambition in life. And maybe it was. Samantha smiled to herself at the thought. It would have been nice if her own life were that simple.

The echo of her conversation with Brian seemed to whisper in her ear then and a chill swept over her. She wished she had not sent Juliette away. Some hot tea would have been welcome.

Samantha cast a glance at Brian, her expression grave. He added cream to his coffee and stirred it, but he seemed uneasy under her gaze and in that instant, Samantha understood.

"You're afraid," she said.

Brian blinked, his mouth open in a little circle. His nostrils flared and he shook his head. "Don't do this, Sam. Think about what you're saying. It's completely outrageous." He squirmed as he said it, tapping the edge of his mug with his spoon. When he raised the mug and blew steam off the top, he watched her over the rim as he took the first sip.

Her heart ached. She knew it had been a very long time since they had last seen each other, but she still cared deeply for Brian and she had believed him when he said he still loved her. But now he was lying to her, and, she thought, to himself as well.

"Don't bullshit me, Brian," she said. "It's not fair. Don't do that to me."

Slowly he began to nod. He set the mug of coffee down and did not look at it again. His gaze met hers steadily and suddenly all her memories of the high school boy he had been were sloughed off and replaced by this man she felt as though she was noticing for the first time. This handsome, rugged-looking man with wide, kind eyes. Those, at least, had not changed.

"All right, Sam. Let's say I saw something. For the sake of argument, of course."

"Of course," she agreed.

"Why does it matter? Why do you care if I remember?"

Her lip was ragged from all the times she had bitten it that day, but she gnawed it gently again. When she spoke, she glanced away.

"He's dead, Brian. The rest of my life, I'll have it hanging over my head. I'll be fucking haunted 'cause I never got to make him talk to me."

Slowly, as though he was about to pass out, Brian's head tilted backward until he was staring at her down the line of his nose. He took a deep breath and shook his head, letting his chin drop again.

"Jesus, Sam—"

"I can't do it alone, Brian."

"No, Sam, holy shit, come on!"

"Even if I managed to not get arrested, I'd never be able to get him out of the ground."

He still shook his head back and forth in denial, but the movements were tiny, almost imperceptible. "Sam," he warned.

She steeled herself and reached out to take his hand, silently daring him to look away.

"I need you, Brian. You saw it that night, I know you did. And besides . . . I don't have anyone else."

He closed his eyes. "Oh, fuck."

4

"Are you sure you want to do this?" Brian stared at her, enshrouded in the darkness inside the van.

Samantha would not answer him. She sat in the passenger seat and stared out her window across the moonlit fields. If she were to turn, the view would change. Through the windshield, she would see the aging, decrepit, chain-link fence that marked the border between the Applecrest Farm and the Ashgrove Cemetery and she could not look at that fence just now. Not yet.

"Sammie."

There was an uncomfortable tension in Brian's voice unlike anything she remembered from their childhood together. She had to keep reminding herself that no matter what she felt this was not the old Brian. As familiar as everything seemed, as comfortable as she felt with him, five years had passed, many hundreds of days that had flowed by for each of them. She wanted to tell him not to call her "Sammie," that nobody called her that anymore.

"*Sam,*" he said, insistent.

His voice pressed at her to look into his eyes again. There was not even the dashboard light to see by. Only the moon. And even that was veiled behind a thin cover of clouds.

She had rented the van that evening for just shy of thirty bucks. Applecrest Farm was so enormous and so quiet this time of year that with the headlights off there was very little risk of them being discovered. They had waited until there was nobody else on Grove Street and then turned right on the dirt tractor road that wound up the hill among the rows of apple trees. No headlights, engine running quiet.

Now they were parked on the other side of the hill's crest, out of sight of the farmhouse and barns where the owners had a bakery shop that sold gifts and the products of the farm.

Brian stared at her now and it felt to Samantha like a dream. Not a nightmare, exactly, but a terrible, weighted, surreal moment that could only have come to her mind during the help-lessness of sleep.

"Fuck, Samantha, come on!" Brian rasped.

It wasn't a dream. Samantha knew that. She was not some sickly, flighty heroine from a tragic Italian opera. The seat beneath her, the cool glass beside her, even the chilly air that pushed through the slightly open window to rustle her hair—all were tangible things, even Brian's presence and the scent of his aftershave.

"Don't ask me again if I'm sure," she told him. "I don't think I can do this without you, but we're here now, so if you're not coming I'm going to have to try to do it alone."

Samantha got out of the van, making sure to be quiet with the door, cursing the dome light as it went on. The hill was not terribly steep, but she knew that with the weight of the burden she hoped they would be carrying back, it would seem like a mountain. She marched downward toward the ravaged, rusty fence. Beyond it was a small wood and she knew just past that were the first rows of headstones, the oldest in the cemetery. She could see them in her mind's eye and silently she cursed her father for the cold heart that had led her here.

Brian caught up with her just as she reached one of the many openings that had been cut and torn in the chain link over the years. She slipped through easily with only a soft chinking of metal as she pushed the fence aside to allow her passage. They moved quietly through the wood—really little more than a copse of trees—until they came to the small cluster of ancient headstones that dated back to Colonial times. Thin slabs of granite, brittle, some of them cracked and broken. The grass needed trimming, for there were no surviving loved ones, nor even descendants, to keep after the groundskeeper about their care.

The cemetery was vast, with winding paths and roads. Many of the more recent stones were beautiful marble, carved and ornate, more akin to monuments than gravestones. There were several dozen crypts as well, scattered far and wide across the lawns. Fortunately the land flattened out, so that they would not be trudging uphill the entire walk back.

Not once had Samantha turned to confirm that Brian was following, nor had she offered to help him carry the tools that they would need. She reached their destination, the rose-tinted marble yet to be etched with record of the most recent burial there.

Her eyes burned with the threat of new tears, but Samantha ignored them, would not allow them. She turned away, looked out across the stone gardens for a night watchman or the groundskeeper, but there was no sign that anyone else was about, not even a light burning in the window of the small brick building near the front gate.

Samantha could smell the fresh-turned earth of her father's grave. The dirt was still soft there. She thanked God it hadn't rained. Brian stepped up beside her, handed her one of the shovels, and they set to work.

From the moment this course of action had occurred to her, Samantha had somehow managed to gather up her grief and pain and regret and used it to push down within her any sense of the enormity of what she had proposed, the sheer grotesque horror of it. Now as she began to dig, it flooded in. Yet once begun she found it was a task she could not abandon. And as the digging went on, hours in which she and Brian sometimes shared the effort and sometimes alternated, she found herself becoming numbed by the monotony of the labor and the chill of the cold spring night.

They worked together in silence save for the call of night birds and the chink of metal shovel on the occasional stone in soft, turned earth. Though she had somehow walled herself away, dulled her mind from the reality of what precisely she was uncovering, more and more her mind turned to Brian. Twisted as her thought process had become, she could not imagine how he could justify to himself participating in this act.

What must he be feeling, she wondered, what emotions snaking through his heart enabled him to aid her this night? Despite the time since they'd last seen one another it felt to her in so many ways—as she now realized it must also feel to him—that those years had come and gone almost unnoticed. They had been inseparable, the closest of friends. She would have died for him. Brian had loved her, and maybe, just maybe she had loved him as well.

For Sam, that love had faded over time, perhaps buried in a grave of its own so that she would never have to wonder what might have been. Perhaps Brian had put his own feelings six feet under as well, but now they had been unearthed or else why was he there at all?

She watched him digging down in the hole they had made, carving out the long rectangular shape that the gravediggers had obscured that same morning. Brian worked for perhaps ten minutes more, then wordlessly climbed out and let Samantha replace him. She dropped carefully into the hole, not wanting to pack the earth down any further.

On the third thrust of her shovel she struck wood.

The impact reverberated up her arms and she froze there, wide-eyed, staring at the ground. A fresh surge of nausea roiled in her gut. It was as though despite the burning of the muscles in her shoulders and back from her labor, none of this had been real until the shovel struck her father's coffin through the loosened soil.

The cemetery fell silent save for the whistle of cold wind past her ears and the hush of rustling leaves in the trees above. Brian said not a word. The night birds were quiet. There came not even the sound of an engine from the road.

"Oh, Jesus, Daddy," Samantha whispered, and the shovel fell from her hands.

Her knees were weak, but she did not collapse, slumping instead against the cold, damp earthen walls inside her father's grave. She covered her mouth to keep from screaming. As though it might shelter her from that sound, that feeling in her arms, she turned her face toward a corner of that hole, the scent of moist earth enveloping her completely.

A dry voice rasped her name. "Samantha."

She started, jolted by the sound, and spun around, nearly stumbling over the handle of the shovel.

Brian crouched at the graveside above her, his form silhouetted against the indigo sky, a shadow upon a shadow.

"It's okay," he said. "I understand. You had to do this. But we should go now. Come on, I'll take you home." He reached his hand down as if to hoist her up out of the hole.

Eyes stinging, dirt on her lips, Samantha bent and picked up her shovel, then turned back to the work at hand. In a soft voice layered with grim emotion Brian asked her to stop. She realized that he had never imagined she would go through with this. Looking back now, Samantha was not sure herself if she had intended to see it through.

She bent low and began to scrape shovelfuls of dirt from the top of her father's casket. Brian said nothing more but after a few minutes he dropped into the grave with her. It took another twenty minutes for them to clear away the earth around the coffin, to free it completely from the ground.

They moved on either side of it, squeezing down between the walls of the grave and the casket, and took hold of the steel handles on either side. As they tried to lift it, Sam's already aching shoulders screamed in protest. In her head, macabre math calculations: her father's weight while he was alive, the amount of blood in the human body, the size of organs removed during preparation for burial. A corpse had to be much lighter than the deceased had been in life. So it had to be the casket.

"Try just the top," she told Brian. "Tilt it up."

Together they grabbed the handles at the head of the wooden box. It was still unimaginably heavy, like shimmying some enormous bureau, drawers full, across the carpet. But somehow they managed to raise that front end, to drag the bottom across the dirt, to lean the casket against the wall of that hole in the ground.

Awkward weight shifted and thumped inside the coffin. Samantha winced but tried not to think about it.

"Get up there," Brian told her.

Samantha climbed out of the hole, reached down and grabbed hold of one of the steel handles. Brian crouched behind the casket and put his fingers beneath its bottom edge.

"On three," he said.

Then he counted, and they pulled. The casket rose perhaps

two feet from the bottom of the grave. Brian's face reddened, his eyes wide, veins standing out on his neck.

"Shit!" he muttered. "I've gotta drop it."

He backed off and let it crash down to the earth again. It rocked forward, nearly falling upon him, but he pushed it back, bumping it against the wall of the grave. Brian rested with one arm on the casket, chest rising and falling. His eyes looked haunted and Samantha wondered if he had made himself as numb as she was.

When he stared at her, she knew what he was going to say.

"There's no way we're getting this thing out of here without help."

"We don't have any help," she reminded him.

"Unless you've got a cable long enough to tie to the bumper of the van that would reach all the way down here and drag this thing out of the ground . . . maybe a winch and a pulley . . . we're done here. It's time to go home."

He gazed at her. "This is crazy and you know it. There are other ways to work out what you need to work out."

"Not really," she replied, pressing her lips together so hard they hurt. "Maybe there are ways for me to find out how to live with it. But there's no other way for me to resolve it. I need to know. I need to hear his voice and look him in the eye."

Brian's expression hardened. "He doesn't *have* eyes anymore, Samantha. And his lips are sewn shut. He can't say anything to you. He's *dead*."

Samantha began to breathe in short gasps like a child about to have a tantrum. She glared at him.

"Brian, look at me, right now. *You* look me in the eye and tell me that you didn't see what I saw that night up at Scottie's."

For a long moment he met her furious gaze; then he dropped his eyes and looked away. Samantha swallowed, her throat dry, her breathing slowing.

"Open it," she said.

His head snapped up. "You're out of your fucking mind."

"Open it, Brian. You help me get him out of the hole and I'll carry him the rest of the way. You don't even have to come with me after that if you don't want to."

He swore through gritted teeth, stomped about a little down in the grave. Then he grabbed the shovel.

"How?" he asked. "How do you open it?"

"I don't know. There's got to be a way to do it from outside. Otherwise funeral directors would constantly be locking them shut by accident."

"Maybe," Brian whispered. "But Sam, I don't know the first thing about caskets and I don't want to."

"Open it."

His lips pressed together as though the ghoulish reality of their chore had finally struck home to him. "Fine," he muttered. "Jesus Christ, I can't believe we're doing this."

Brian lifted the shovel and managed to get its tip lodged in the crease between the lid and the base on the upper part of the coffin, where the head would be. He set one foot against the wall of the grave. Earth showered down around his ankle. Then he pulled, using his leverage, groaning as he pried open the coffin with a shriek of a wood and a snapping of locks.

It opened.

Samantha watched her father's corpse tumble out at Brian's feet.

Something shut down inside her. She stood frozen at the

edge of the grave. The way the body had struck the earth the skin on the corpse's face was pulled taut. Whatever stuffing had been packed behind his lids to replace his eyes pushed now against the thin skin. His lips were slightly parted, thread visible where they had been sewn together.

She should have screamed. Samantha knew that. She should have screamed and turned and run away and prayed to God to forgive her. But her breath came easily and her eyes were dry. Her skin was cold, but that might have been just the air.

Brian stood immobile, muttering the name of the Lord again and again under his breath. "Jesus Christ, oh Jesus, what the hell are we doing? Oh, Jesus!"

"Pick him up, Brian."

He looked up and she saw that he was crying. "Sam, come on! Oh, Jesus."

"It's too much now," she said. "Too far. You know why we're doing this. Where we're going. You know what I think is going to happen there. Help me, Brian. Pick him up."

Brian sucked in a breath and nodded silently. He moved around the corpse, slightly crouched, his hands searching the air as though trying to find a place where he could pick it up and not be touching something dead. At last he grabbed her father's body under the arms and began to lift.

"God, it's heavy. I didn't think it would be this heavy." He squatted down, got his weight under it and grunted as he drove upward, pistoning his legs, forcing the corpse with its awkward, flailing limbs up onto the edge of the grave. Samantha bent and grabbed the back of her father's suit jacket in both fists. The fabric scrunched up in her hands as she hauled it forward, this dead thing, this hollow shell. Brian pushed the legs up from

116

behind and they succeeded in rolling it onto the lawn of the cemetery.

"We're going to need something to carry him," Brian said, his voice small and tight. "We can manage now, but if we're going up to Biddeford, we're going to need something to carry him in."

Samantha knelt and rolled her father's body onto its back. "Then we'll stop on the way."

She reached out a hand to her father's face. His skin was cold to the touch but it did not feel human; more like rubber, dry and without the oil and elasticity it would have had in life. The face of the dead man was contorted into a horrid Halloween mask expression.

Father Corcoran had consecrated the grave, had given this dead thing over to God.

But God would just have to understand.

"Come on."

Samantha slid a hand beneath the armpit of the corpse and Brian did the same on the other side. Together they hoisted him up.

"We're just going to drag him?" Brian asked.

For the first time since the corpse had been unearthed, Samantha met his gaze, searched his eyes. They were glazed over, wide with a numb sort of fear almost like surprise and she thought of some human-shaped animal caught in the headlights of a speeding car. There was still time for Brian to get out of the way, but like that deer or raccoon, he was so stunned by his circumstances that it really was too late for him. He had surrendered himself to the devastating collision with the grille of that oncoming car.

"Wouldn't it be easier to carry him?" Brian asked.

"It's just as easy to drag him," she said. "We'll have to carry him later. Might as well wait until we don't have a choice."

So they began, moving back across the cemetery among the trees and headstones, trailing the dead man across the neatly cut grass that was green in some places and brown and ragged in others. A chilly wind moved through the trees, a quiet rustle that seemed almost respectful but was perhaps merely cautious.

The hill began to slope upward and the way became more difficult. Samantha kept her eyes forward, determined now. Every few moments Brian glanced anxiously around as though some unknown predator lurked nearby. When they again passed those Colonial-era gravestones, he paused and Samantha stumbled, nearly fell.

"What the fuck, Brian?"

But he was staring back along the path they had followed. "Sam, his shoes," he rasped.

They had been hauling the corpse along by its arms, its feet trailing along the ground. Now she saw that it had no shoes. Somewhere along the way the dragging had pulled them off, left them on the grass back behind them in the dark.

"Forget it," she said.

"But—"

"Brian, they're going to notice the *hole*. Never mind the shoes."

They started again and in a few minutes they were working their way through the fence. Together they dragged her father's corpse back to the rented van. Brian worked the rear doors open and Samantha took the legs as they lifted the body into the back. They closed the doors with a quiet double click.

The moon cast its yellow gleam down upon the orchard and a strange pattern of shadows and ghostly light played upon Brian's face. He looked haunted.

The hell with him, Samantha thought. *It's me who's haunted.*

And then she realized maybe that wasn't true. Maybe he had been haunted all along—by her.

"What if it doesn't work, Sam?" he asked, staring at her.

Ignoring him, she turned and climbed into the passenger seat of the van. Brian slipped into the driver's side and put the key into the ignition. He paused with one hand on the wheel and the other on the key, but he did not look at her. Instead he stared straight out the windshield at the fence and the graveyard beyond.

"Jesus," he said again, this time in a whisper. "What if it does?"

5

It was midnight.

Though Samantha had been aware of the passage of time she'd had no idea it had taken them so long at the cemetery. The only things open at this hour were a couple of twenty-four-hour pharmacies and all-night gas stations. But there was no way that they were driving all the way up to Maine with a dead man in the back of the van without covering him up with something. After a brief debate on the subject Samantha agreed that they ought to return to her apartment.

Brian waited in the van, just in case.

Now she stood in the middle of her living room and it

seemed as though worlds were crashing together. Whatever woman it was, whatever daughter it was, who could do something like this, she didn't live in this apartment. This was a whole different world—a world of cookbooks and art prints and a Chinese fighting fish named Leo, of bills that needed to be paid and books half read, of Sting and Nelly Furtado battling it out on the CD player.

For the first time in her life, Samantha felt like an intruder in her own home. She gazed stupidly about the room at these things that belonged to her and yet belonged to someone else entirely. There was a ton of leftover Chinese food in the refrigerator and she felt suddenly hungry at the thought of it. Her stomach rumbled.

Quietly, like some peculiar prowler in her own home, she went along the hall to the linen closet and hauled out an old bedspread covered in a design of pastel clouds that had been hers in college. Across her mind flashed the faces of friends who had slept beneath it on the couch here in this apartment and lovers who had shared it with her during her days at Rutgers.

Now it was a death shroud.

She stepped gingerly back through the hallway toward the kitchen as though afraid she might wake her other self, the girl to whom this evening's actions would seem an abomination. Samantha grabbed a plastic grocery bag from the narrow hollow between the refrigerator and the cabinets, opened the fridge and stuffed it with leftover Chinese food and several bottles of spring water, then grabbed two forks from the drawer.

After a moment's hesitation, she took a box of matches and sealed them in a plastic sandwich bag and stuck the bag in her pocket. There was a plastic gas can in the back of the van, but they had forgotten matches. It would all have been for nothing if they couldn't get the gas to burn.

When she went to leave, Samantha froze just inside the door, feeling the apartment at her back and the darkest of nights ahead of her. Her skin crawled, flesh tingling with the oppressive weight of the air in the apartment crushing her as if it wanted to drive her down, pull her back, prevent her from going. But she wasn't that woman tonight.

This girl she was did not belong here.

Back down at the van she rapped sharply on the passenger window and Brian jumped, startled. He had been staring straight out the windshield as if unable to look back at what they were transporting. Now he stared at her dumbly a moment and then, as if snapping awake, jumped out of the van and went around to the back.

Brian hesitated at the open rear doors.

"I'll do it," she told him. "Just shut me in and get back behind the wheel."

A look of relief washed over his face. This small task, this one thing he did not have to worry about. Samantha understood completely, but she still wanted to crack her fist across his face.

Samantha climbed into the back and Brian closed the doors behind her. When he was back in the driver's seat, she slid the bag from her kitchen between the seats at the front of the van and dropped the bedspread on the floor in the back. For a long moment she only stared down at her father's body, at the thread eternally tugging his lips into a horrid rictus grin. She heard the rustling of the plastic bag as Brian looked inside.

"What the hell is this?" he muttered, more to himself than to her. Then he spoke up. "Sam? What *is* this?"

As if she had not heard, she picked up the bedspread and laid it over the corpse. She tucked it beneath him on one side and then rolled the body over so that she could press it under. As horrible as that preserved face had been, in some ways the blank, shrouded shape of his features beneath the spread was worse. Samantha rolled the body over and shoved it against the wall of the van so that it looked more like a carpet swathed in blankets than anything else. She tucked the gas can up against it.

When she was done she scrambled back into her seat, grabbed her seat belt and strapped in. Brian was still staring at her. She rocked forward a couple of times as if her own motion might get the van rolling.

"Let's go," she urged.

"What's with the Chinese food?"

"What do you think?" she replied, although suddenly any hunger pangs she had felt were gone. The very thought of eating anything made her stomach clench. The water was there, though, and that was good.

Neither of them mentioned the food again and neither touched the bag for the entire ride.

At first they were confined to back roads where stoplights made them pause frequently, exacerbating their anxiety and impatience. As quickly as they could without the risk of being pulled over by the police, they made their way to Route 495 and headed north. Biddeford was off Old Route One on the southern coast of Maine. It didn't have the wealth or cache of Kennebunkport or Cape Porpoise or even Ogunquit, but anywhere along that shoreline was beautiful.

The summer homes and cottages in Biddeford were stacked practically on top of one another. With the exception of a single phone call her sophomore year of college, Samantha had not talked to Scottie since the summer after high school graduation. She did not even know if his parents still owned the place. Somehow, though, she managed to navigate well enough to find Biddeford Pool and thread their way into the oceanside neighborhood where they had spent that weekend five years ago. Brian had been there as well, but he was useless. When Samantha pointed out a convenience store that she was sure had been there the last time they were up this way, he only shrugged and gazed blankly at the building.

"Take this left," she instructed.

After a period of trial and error, Samantha told Brian to drive down a narrow lane that led to the beach. She stepped out and walked out to the sand to gaze up and down the sand. Off to the south, she saw the island.

Once she had an idea of its location it was a time-consuming but simple enough matter to maneuver through the intricate network of tiny roads and beach houses. They drove down a short road that looked familiar to her and passed a cottage she thought might have been the one. Samantha remembered it as yellow, but it was green now; though, of course, it probably had been painted in the meantime. A fuchsia Mazda four-by-four flatbed sat in the driveway.

"That it?" Brian asked.

"I think so. Obviously we won't be parking here."

Ahead the road began to turn west, away from the beach.

At the next left Brian turned and a moment later the ocean came into view again. When they reached the end of the narrow road there was a small parking lot, sand blowing across the cracked pavement. A large white sign proclaimed it as BEACH PARKING and announced a list of activities that were prohibited. Among them was overnight parking.

"Shit," Samantha whispered.

But then that particular dilemma was forgotten as they drove into the lot and saw another car parked there.

"What the hell is this?" Brian muttered. "It's the middle of the night."

"Pull up right next to them," Samantha said.

The van rolled up beside the car and Samantha looked down at it, saw that its windows were steamy. People were moving inside, pale limbs flailing. The arrival of the van had set things in motion inside that car. There were shouts and laughter as the people behind that filmy window scrambled to pull their clothes on.

After a few moments the driver's window rolled down and the face of a guy not more than twenty poked out.

"What the fuck is wrong with you?" he barked. "Freak!"

Whatever amusement or excitement had been fostered in the couple by the interruption was now overridden by their anger at not being able to finish what they had started. Samantha did not smile, did not even reply. The guy gave her the finger as he backed out of his spot. Tires spun on the loose sand as they drove away.

Brian killed the engine and they sat in the van a minute.

"You know, we're probably gonna get towed."

Samantha spun and gaped at him as though he was the one

124

who had lost his mind. Then, after a moment, her grim expression cracked into a smile and she started to laugh. Brian gazed at her oddly for a moment and then he began to laugh as well. The lunacy of what they were doing had caught up with them. Samantha knew that they were just venting the tension of the moment, but it felt good.

Then the gravity of it all swept back into her and she wiped at her eyes, which had begun to water with her laughter.

"Doesn't much matter if we get towed, but I think we'll just get a ticket. As long as we don't get stopped before we get out to the island."

She did not want to say it any clearer, didn't want to say that what was really important was that nobody caught them with a corpse in the back of the van.

Brian blew out air and turned to look at her. "Guess we'd better hurry then, before someone comes."

6

The tide was coming in.

Biddeford Pool wasn't much different now than it had been the last time she was here. The formation of the Maine coastline at that spot created a zone of complacent waters. At low tide, you could walk out to Monument Island. If you were particularly tall, the water would rise only chest high. Shorter people might have to swim a little when the waves came. But even now, with the tide coming in, the waves weren't very high.

Even with the ache in her shoulders and back Samantha had been able to help Brian carry the corpse in its bedspread sling out of the back of the van and quickly out onto the beach. They dragged it to the sand and into the water. In an instant the spread became saturated and it clung unsettlingly to her father's familiar features. Then the corpse began to sink.

Samantha groaned as the weight of it tugged at her and had to adjust her grip to keep the body from being dragged out of her hands by its own heaviness and the gentle rhythm of the tide. Something popped in the back of her neck and she hissed air in through her teeth.

"I thought it . . . I thought he would float," she whispered, words barely audible over the soft wash of the ocean on the shore. "Aren't there supposed to be gases or something?"

Brian stared at her. "What the fuck you asking me for? Besides, he's been . . ."—his voice lowered so she could barely make out the word *dead*—". . . for days. If there's supposed to be something inside to make him float, I'm guessing it's been gone a while. And he's . . ." *embalmed*—"so I've got a feeling that might let the air out of the tires."

A ripple of anger and unease went through her at the sheer inappropriateness of his words and Samantha turned to glare at him.

"Have a little respect," she warned.

Brian shot her a hard look that let her know exactly how crazy he thought she was. She didn't remind him that he was out here with her, and that his reasons weren't as simple as him still having feelings for her, or wanting to get into her pants to consummate something they'd flirted at a long time ago.

"I just thought this part was going to be easier," she said. Then she glanced past him at the dark cottages that lined the beach both north and south as far as she could see. Most were empty or sleeping, the only light or life within the gleam of moonlight on blank windows. But there were several that had deck lights on and windows that glowed from within.

"Just hurry," Samantha said.

The strange umbilical that connected them now grew charged with both bitterness and determination. Their joint purpose compelled an uneasy cooperation, but it was enough. One hand wrapped in the end of the bedspread and the other gripping it tightly, Samantha held on to her end of the burden and slipped deeper into the water. Her jeans and her sweatshirt were soaked through by increments as they moved farther from shore, and by the time she was immersed up to her thighs, the waves lapping at her waist, she realized how frigid the ocean was.

And she thought of fire. Looked forward to the pyre. She wondered if, saturated with seawater, her father's corpse was going to be difficult to burn. Her gaze ticked toward the plastic gas can, only a third full, that bobbed along behind Brian, tied to his belt with a bungee cord from his car.

A wave rose high enough to soak her top and sweatshirt around her navel, and Sam's teeth began to chatter. Brian was holding on tight as well and now they were halfway out to the island and she began to feel at last as though they had arrived at their destination. No alarms had been raised from the shoreline; no blue police lights strafed the cottages.

The farther from the shore they moved, the more distant the hush of the surf. But as Samantha edged backward, glancing over her shoulder now and then to navigate, new sounds reached her ears. The surf again, but now a slap against hard earth and stone rather than the soft rasp of water over sand. And other sounds, the shifting flutter of wings and a throaty choral trilling that Samantha would have thought of as cooing if it had come from more elegant birds.

But these were scavengers. They were gulls.

Anxious, she renewed her grip on the bedspread, wrapping her hands in it, and then glanced over her shoulder again. The action twisted their burden around so that they were approaching the island at an angle now. Samantha could see it looming there in the dark, its stony, rough-hewn shore forbidding and farther up, not far from where the thick brush grew up, the gulls; a carpet of gulls that undulated as if the ocean tides formed waves in their ranks as well as the swells of the sea. Their feathers reflected the starlight with a queer iridescence.

She hated them. Always had. Filthy animals not much better than pigeons. But the gulls on Monument Island were not like any others she had ever seen. There were hundreds of them by conservative count, more likely thousands, though she did not want to admit that to herself.

Thousands.

Some of them in the sky, some sitting on the waves the way gulls often did . . . but none on the shore. These were scavenger birds, but not one of them fluttered down to land on the beach and scrounge for bits of discarded food. In her mind, Samantha saw images of seagulls stealing cookies from beach blankets, digging in the sand for a melon rind or a crust of sandwich, trying to eat anything they could find, including plastic candy wrappers and lipstick-stained cigarette butts.

Not these. The legions of gulls on Monument Island circled their territory, but they did not leave it.

"Hey," Brian whispered. "What's up with the—"

"Shush."

128

A wave crested high enough to wash over her breasts. It took a moment for the cold water to saturate her layers, but when the frigid water soaked through to her nipples Samantha gritted her teeth and shivered violently. Her left hand lost its grip on the bedspread and the corpse began to shift and slide in its hammock-shroud. Samantha stopped and bent to catch the edge of the fabric again, pulled it up tight, and as she did so, another wave washed over her back, so cold that it made her bones ache, a pain subtler and more profound than the burning of her overtaxed muscles.

I'm going to get pneumonia and die out here, she thought, and chuckled softly. That was pretty funny.

Again she glanced at the floating gas can, rising on the waves, eddying with the light current that swirled around Brian's chest. The tide was coming in, but it was still low enough that Samantha realized the water was already becoming shallower. She turned to look at the island again.

A pair of gulls floated on the water nearby. Black eyes stared at her. She tore her gaze away and shot a preemptive glance at Brian. *Don't say a word,* she thought. *Just keep quiet.* She had no idea if he understood, but he remained silent regardless, his eyes ticking sideways to stare past her at the floating gulls.

With a slap of wings against the air, a third gull came down from the night sky and settled upon the waves. Three others followed in quick succession and shortly there were half a dozen of the creatures floating on the surface of the ocean staring blackly at them. Samantha took a step forward and felt a tug on the bedspread. She glanced back sharply to see that Brian had paused. She gave a light pull on their burden to get his attention and when he tore his gaze from the gulls, he stared at her with an expression of even greater reluctance than he had worn at her father's grave.

Unwilling to speak a single word, Samantha only tugged on the spread again, the fabric straining, the weight of her father's corpse like an anchor between them, mooring them to this spot.

At length, Brian nodded and they continued on.

They walked the gauntlet. More gulls swept down to join the others and a new kind of cold not born of the water or the air settled into her bones as they opened a path for her to pass through. On each side of her, the black-eyed birds kept baleful watch, but soon the waves were lapping around her thighs again and then her knees, and the cotton-draped corpse was dragging along the rocky bottom.

Samantha glanced up at the island, at the trees and the thick brush, at the rocky shore just ahead, and she remembered with utter clarity that night five years before. The women—*three of them, draped in red, beautiful things with skin like alabaster and hair raven black. They stand at the shore of the island just at the water's edge, their arms spread wide, palms up, and flames dance upon their open hands.*

With a start she blinked and saw only the dark ocean around her, the island ominous ahead, felt the weight of the dead man they were carrying. In that instant the memory had been so rich and real as if she had been seeing it all again. That night with all the talk of death and of Viking warriors and Valhalla and . . .

Samantha frowned and glanced back at Brian. So smart, his mind filled with retained knowledge from a thousand books. She had forgotten, really, how smart he was. That night he had told them more than any of them would have known about the myths of the Norsemen who legend said had settled here for a time. Samantha wondered if that had made what they had both seen that night harder for him to accept, or easier. Scottie had started to tell them about the legends and about the gulls keeping people away.

The gulls.

The birds were still staring at her. Samantha did not want to look into their eyes and so she kept her gaze forward. But she remembered what Scottie had said. The gulls wouldn't let anyone get within ten feet of the island. They'd peck your eyes out.

Samantha was perhaps two feet from shore, only a white froth around her ankles, the corpse dragging behind her. She paused and stared at the place where the waves slapped the rocks. They would have to heft the waterlogged corpse up onto the land and then drag it through the brush. Maybe they could rest for a while; now that they were here, another ten minutes seemed very little to ask. Not here on the shore, where someone with keen vision looking out from the cottage might spot them, but there in the brush . . . past the roosting gulls.

She wondered if it was their nesting place and if that was why the legions of sea birds clustered so tightly together there, where the rocks met the undergrowth. The trilling of the birds continued, an almost orchestral sound, though the ones floating nearby were silent.

Samantha glanced back at Brian, who nodded grimly. She wrapped the spread around her arm and together they lifted it out of the water and carried it onto the shore.

The moment her foot touched dry land, the trilling stopped.

It was replaced almost immediately by a deafening flurry of wings beating air and then the gulls began to scream.

A cloud of birds rose from their roosts on shore and moved toward her and Brian like a tornado. Others had been circling above and dropped down at them now as though they had forgotten to fly and were concerned only with attack. Those in the water flew the several feet that separated them, wingtips slapping the surf.

Brian shouted as a gull slammed into his chest.

Samantha screamed as tiny talons tugged at her hair and a bird struck her face, wings battering her. It pecked her cheek, cutting her, and the salt air stung the wound as blood dripped down her face. Talons raked her arm through her thick sweat-shirt and the birds swarmed like insects around her.

In a frenzy, she shouted and cried out and covered her eyes with her arms. She screamed at them and beat the air, and felt the satisfying connection as her left hand batted a gull from the sky. She kicked something near her cold-numbed foot that pecked at her leg.

"Sam!" Brian called from behind her. "Back into the water! Get back into the water!"

"No!" she roared, blood streaming like tears down her face. When she screamed again, the words were for the gulls, for whatever power suffused the monument that gave the island its name, whatever presence lingered in that altar and the ground beneath it.

"Fuck you!" she screamed hysterically.

Eyes still closed, birds scratching and pecking at her, Samantha bent down and scrambled until her hands closed on the sodden bedspread. Her exhaustion forgotten now, she pulled up on her end and she ran up the rocky shore, not slowing when she twisted her ankle on the difficult terrain. The birds flew right into her now, struck her, and she staggered back. Again she screamed but the words were unintelligible now.

With another surge of energy she pushed forward again and the bedspread snagged on the rocky shore. Samantha pulled it sideways, stumbled beneath the onslaught of the birds. The fingers of her left hand loosened and the spread slipped loose and it opened and the wet, pale, gleaming corpse of Carl Finnin rolled out and flopped onto the rocks.

Despair overtook Sam's frenzy and she dropped into a crouch beside her father and threw her hands over her head to wait for the birds to drive her down onto the ground. They could tear her apart, but she was not leaving him here.

A flutter of wings.

A curious trilling.

The onslaught ceased as suddenly as it had begun. Slowly, Samantha looked up, wincing at the pain in her face and hands where they had injured her the worst. Dozens of gulls had alighted upon the ground near the dead man. Like solemn mourners at a wake they filed past the hideous corpse with its sewn-up grin, stuffing leaking out from behind one torn eyelid.

Brian stood perhaps ten feet off shore, his neck a bloody mess and a pair of long, deep scratches on his left cheek. He stared wide-eyed at the birds and then looked slowly up at Sam.

Even as he did, the gulls began to drift off in ones and twos, some floating again on the water, others taking to the sky, and the largest mass hopping back to roost on that strange zone between rock and brush.

133

But where there had been an unbroken, rustling carpet of the birds stretching across their intended path before, now there was a ten-foot swath of bird shit dappling the ground, a gap among the roosting gulls.

Almost like an invitation.

7

There was no path. Subconsciously, Samantha had expected that when they reached the thick brush that led up the steep hill that made the bulk of the small island, there would be some narrow way by which they could travel inward toward the altar. But there was no path.

Of course there was no path.

The gulls had kept tourists and curiosity seekers away. If she were to believe the legends—and oh how she believed— the last people to visit this small isle with any regularity were Vikings who had set up a trading outpost on the rocky coast of Maine. A path would have required the tread of human feet to wear it down over time.

Another time she might have felt a sense of wonder about being the first person to intrude upon this wild spot in so very many years. But Samantha was wounded, scratched and bleed- ing; exhaustion had partially numbed the muscles in her shoul- ders and neck and arms, but not completely. So rather than wonder she felt only dull anger at the lack of a clear trail. Brian suggested, his voice muffled as though he were in a daze, that they might try to circle around and see if there was an easier way inward and upward.

Samantha crouched, pulled the edges of the bedspread in both hands and turned around so that she held it over her shoulder like some mighty sack—a macabre, grotesque Santa Claus. She waited then, for if Brian did not pick up his end, the corpse would just slide out onto the ground again. Seconds ticked by. She did not look back at him.

Finally, she felt the shifting of her burden as he hefted it off the ground. Then she started forward. The low brush was not difficult, mainly a matter of being careful where she set her feet down, as each step might have caused her to stumble. The going was steep and so she bent into it, her calves prickling with needles of pain from the exertion, tendons and ligaments protesting. But Brian had the bulk of the weight, coming up behind her, and he made no complaint so she felt the need to stifle any groan or curse she might otherwise have uttered.

The way became even more difficult as they pressed on through the small trees that populated the interior of the island. It was spring and the leaves had started to return, but each branch remained a skeletal claw that threatened to add to the damage the gulls had done.

Samantha kept her head down, her elbows joined in front of her face, her hands clasped over her right shoulder gripping the bedspread. And they pressed on.

After several minutes, the trees and the very air itself seemed to darken around them. She frowned and glanced upward. The night sky was still relatively clear, the moon and stars still there, but somehow they suddenly seemed far more distant than ever before, as if they had retreated farther from the world. Or as though Monument Island was trying to hide itself away from their view.

The terrain flattened out and Samantha paused, then stumbled forward as Brian took two more steps before realizing she had done so. When they were both standing still, they looked around and realized they had come to a sort of plateau. Perhaps one hundred feet ahead, the island continued upward toward its highest point, but here it had flattened out and the trees were taller and more sparse, mostly full-sized oak and ash trees. Samantha was relieved. The going would be much simpler now.

With a deep breath, she set her body again to transport their burden, and continued. She had not gone a dozen steps before she saw it there, off to the left, in a barren clearing on that plateau. No trees grew around it; rather there was a kind of rough circle of large rocks jutting from the ground there. Each was as tall as she was, some narrow, as if slivers had been driven up out of the earth, and others as much as ten feet across. But that image in her mind of them being driven up from the earth was what struck her right away. She had read about stone circles before. Stonehenge was perhaps the most famous, and she had seen pictures of that. Slabs of granite erected on a plain so that they created a pattern, a circle, a place of worship. But very much man-made.

This wasn't like that at all. Though there were other rocks that protruded from the ground on this plateau—and it was a craggy island, so that was normal enough—this circle seemed to have formed naturally. Which was impossible, of course. Samantha knew that. And the Vikings who had come here must have known that, too. Almost certainly, the extraordinary nature of that spot was what had led them to build their altar at the center of the circle.

136

For the altar was all the stone circle was not. It was the same stone, of course, the sort of flinty ledge that comprised most of the rock on the island. A geologist could have told her what it was called, but Samantha had been seeing the stuff all her life and so in her mind it was simply rock. Brown and gray and stratified.

Once upon a time, someone had broken it away from the hillside, this enormous piece of stone that must have measured five feet by ten. They had chipped and sanded away at one side to flatten it and laid it upon a foundation of half a dozen much smaller stones that functioned as its legs. The elements had smoothed it over the ages.

"Do you hear that?"

Samantha glanced behind her to find Brian staring back the way they had come. She followed his gaze but saw only the trees and brush, the ocean beyond them, and a few cottages that had lights in the windows. The sea breeze seemed to wash over everything, but Samantha heard nothing out of the ordinary. When Brian turned to look curiously at her, she shrugged.

"I don't—"

"Singing," he said. A nervous smile flickered across his features. "Listen."

Again she scanned the slope of the island behind her and the surface of the ocean. The hush of wind and surf was omnipresent, static white noise that was inaudible unless you tried to pay attention to it. For a long moment, Samantha could hear nothing else. Then she wrinkled her brow as another sound came to her, a sweet, high melody. As suddenly as it had become audible to her, so did it stop almost immediately.

Samantha shook her head. "It's nothing," she said. "Music from one of the cottages. Maybe just the wind on the rocks. If it finds a crevice or something, the wind can whistle."

Brian looked at her as though she were crazy and shook his head slowly. "That's not the wind."

A flash of anger went through her and Samantha gritted her teeth. What the fuck was wrong with him, letting himself get all freaked out now, after everything they'd been through today.

"It's almost over," Samantha told him. "Try to keep your shit together for a few more minutes, okay?"

He winced as if she had slapped him and Samantha did not blame him. The edge she heard in her own voice was disturbing, but she refused to let him see that it bothered her as well. Earlier that day as they caught up over coffee, everything had seemed so much clearer and more tangible. It had made sense to her then that Brian had showed up at her father's funeral. Seeing his face had triggered her memories of Monument Island and the ghost fire and the legends Scottie had told them about.

There was something fateful about that. In the back of her mind it had even occurred to her that there was a whole lot of destiny at work here, not merely that life had put her together again with the only person in the world who might have helped her do this thing, but that there might be a second chance for them. It had been years since Samantha had spent any time with a guy she really cared about whom she felt reciprocated. The idea that fate had thrown her together with Brian again with some determined purpose—a way to discover the love they had once shared—had not seemed terribly far-fetched at all. Particularly not given the other things crowding in her mind at that time.

Now he was just getting on her nerves.

"You've changed," he said glumly, eyes on her.

Samantha frowned. "Yeah?" Then she nodded. "Yeah. I guess I have. You, too. Life will do that to you."

A sadness seemed to flow through him and his eyes to cloud over. Then Brian fixed his grip more firmly on his end of the bedspread and nodded to urge her on. He said nothing more about what he had heard, but Samantha found herself listening more carefully to the wind and the surf and glancing anxiously at the deeper shadows in the places where the trees grew closer together.

With a deep breath, Samantha lugged her father's body in its linen-closet shroud to the stone circle, slipped among the obelisks that jutted from the ground and rested the corpse upon the altar there. Brian approached to set his end down as well and the body folded awkwardly under the bedspread, limbs poking the sodden fabric as though the corpse were moving of its own accord.

"Take the spread off," Brian said. "He'll never burn otherwise."

Samantha was bent over with her hands on her knees, catching her breath, and she blinked in surprise at his tone. His gaze had grown hard and he looked not at her but at the dead man upon that slab of rock. The plastic gas can still hung tethered to his belt, sliding against his soaked jeans. Now Brian reached down to grasp the can by its handle and he investigated it to make sure it had not opened during their crossing, that no seawater had gotten in. When he was through, he regarded her at last.

"Go on," he said. "I'll start gathering wood."

Without another word he moved between the standing stones in the circle and was gone. Samantha edged sideways to try to see him and caught just a glimpse of his silhouette in the darkness, gray shadow against black night. For a long moment she peered through the gap between two stones and found herself hoping he would cross her field of vision again, but he did not. As if entranced, she gazed at the snatch of clearing she could see between the stone and the budding branches that scratched at the sky with each gust of wind. It was as though the stone circle were a cage.

Something rustled behind her and Samantha felt the hairs on the back of her neck stand up. Spooked, she spun to see that the wind was blowing back the bedspread. It flapped heavily, still soaked, but it pulled back enough to reveal the feet of the corpse on the stone slab. Water dripped from the toes of her father's black socks and suddenly it seemed awful, even shameful to her that she had left his shoes back in the cemetery.

Daddy.

When she could see his face—that monstrous death mask—it was easy to distance herself from the cold, dead thing. But as she stared at those black socks clinging to lifeless feet, an image forced its way into her head of her father wading into the frigid water of Ogunquit Beach with her. Samantha might have been ten or eleven, certainly no more. The salt spray had a flavor she could taste on the air and the beach was packed with people flying colorful kites and Quebecois women who had come down from Montreal and wore bathing suits that required a remarkable and wonderful shamelessness that made her eyes go wide with something very like admiration.

Yet there was her father, that late spring afternoon, stepping into the water with his hands up, moving so tentatively, almost daintily despite all the people around him who might think he looked silly. And he had looked silly, but Carl Finnin hadn't cared at all. When his daughter had giggled and covered her mouth, already waist deep, he had given her a scowl that hid a smile beneath.

"You're lucky you're a girl," he had said. "The cold water does a job on guys."

Then a wave had come and washed over him high enough to reach his navel and her dad had hissed air in through his teeth and pulled his legs tight together, bringing his hands down to shield his groin. Samantha had giggled even more loudly at this little dance her father had done, for he looked as though he had to go to the bathroom.

With a small groan he had dived into the water and come up seconds later to let out a small shout, something about the cold. When he saw his daughter's grin, Carl Finnin had splashed her and then swum closer to her, humming an ominous tune.

"You're in trouble now, Sammie," he had said. "Watch out, 'cause the shark's coming and he eats little girls for breakfast, lunch and dinner."

She had shrieked with giddy pleasure and turned to run for shore, but it was too late. Her father had lifted her up above the waves and then, over her protests, he had hurled her into the water. Sam's eyes had widened with astonishment and she held her breath, stunned that he had actually done it. Her heart had gone wild and she'd squeezed her eyes tightly closed as she hit the water and went under. Part of her was furious, part of her terrified and part of her would never, ever be more in love.

When she surfaced, it was to wipe the stinging salt water away from her eyes and then she had lowered herself into the water and began to hum the shark music, headed for her father.

The grin on his face was full of mischief and joy.

How was it that she had forgotten that grin?

Freezing cold, her lower half soaked to the skin, Samantha shivered and gazed blankly at the unmoving feet clad in those black socks. The wind gusted again and she hugged herself. Despite the circle of stones, it blew the bedspread back farther and revealed her father's legs. His suit pants had several strands of seaweed stuck to them. Samantha had no idea how they had gotten there, inside the spread, but it seemed very wrong to her and so she went to the sodden corpse and carefully plucked the stray seaweed from the fabric, then wiped her fingers on her sweatshirt near her shoulder where it was still dry.

Snap!

With a sharp intake of breath, Samantha glanced quickly around. Her heart hammered in her chest and she tried to peer between the stones again. A moment later she belatedly recognized the sound as the cracking of wood and realized that it must be Brian gathering kindling for the pyre.

The pyre, she thought. Breathing evenly, she turned back to the altar. Slowly she went to the corpse again and began gingerly to unwrap it, to disentangle her father from the shroud that clung to him. When she was through she shifted him carefully, as though to keep from waking him, and removed the bedspread altogether.

She brushed damp strands of hair away from his pale face.

Something shifted behind her and Samantha turned to find Brian standing between two stones, arms piled high with splintered tree branches.

"You'll have to put him on the ground while we lay the wood out. Then we can lift him back up."

Samantha nodded and shifted her father's corpse so that Brian could put down the armload of branches and sticks on the altar. They lowered the dead man to the ground together and then she helped him go back and forth to the pile he had made beyond the circle, carrying in more kindling and laying it out on the stone table. It took only a few minutes, and then they raised the body again, hefting it higher so that they could place it on top of the wood, which cracked and shifted under this new weight.

Brian took a respectful step back. The wind seemed to die then. Either that or it had shifted so that the stone circle protected them from its chill.

Samantha did not want to look at the dead man anymore. There were too many images in her head and feelings in her heart. She had to know how he had gone from being that man at the beach with her to some distant, hollow creature.

Abruptly she stepped over to Brian, who flinched at her approach as though she might strike him. She reached down and grabbed the gas can that knocked against his leg and untied it from his belt.

"I can do that," he offered.

"Thanks," she said. But she knew that the offer was only half-genuine. Even if he was willing, they both knew that she had to do it.

Samantha unscrewed the cap and heard gas sloshing inside, smelled the fumes that rose from within. The plastic container was maybe one-third full, but it was heavy nevertheless. She raised it high over her father's corpse and carefully spilled it out in splashes that began at those black socks, lingered at his chest where the wet layers of clothing would need the most help burning, and then finished at his face. The pale dead flesh took on an oily sheen as the gasoline dripped from it onto the dry branches below.

The gas can dropped from her hand. Samantha plunged her fingers into her wet pocket and retrieved a small plastic baggy. In the light from the moon and stars she held it up and peered at it. Within the plastic was a second bag, and inside of that, a box of matches from the Hardcover Restaurant. The plastic was wet on the outside, but when she opened both bags she found that the matchbox had been kept dry.

Samantha stuffed the plastic bags into her pocket and then opened the box of matches and took one out. She struck it, and tossed it onto her father's chest, where it landed, smoldering, beside a black button on his suit coat. The suit was soaked with more seawater than gasoline, but it caught fire instantly, on just that one match.

Almost as though it wanted to burn.

The fire spread quickly and in seconds Samantha and Brian had to back away from the pyre so that their backs were nearly to the stones. Oily black smoke rose from the burning gas and Samantha watched as her father's socks caught fire. His face began to char a moment later, the skin blackening, stretching until it tore, a sudden, growling rush of fire erupting above his head as his hair caught and blazed up.

The stink of burning flesh was like nothing Samantha had ever smelled before.

Brian did not leave the circle, but he turned away, unwilling to watch the body burn. Samantha did not look away. Not once. But though her gaze remained constant, watching the branches blaze up and the limbs and digits and face shrivel and be consumed by the fire, her eyes saw other things as well. She saw inward, and she remembered every time he had brushed her off or forgotten she was there, every birthday that had passed without notice, every opportunity that had come where he might have expressed even the most remote fondness for her, his only child, his little girl.

Her eyes were dry as she watched her father's body burn.

8

For long minutes she waited breathlessly, feeling the skin on her face tighten with the heat from the pyre. It seemed to her that the fire blazed higher than it ought to have, and that its color was unnaturally red, with streaks of orange that were too bright. She recalled the flickering glow in the sky above the island that night five years ago and the ethereal women who floated on the waves.

It was real.

It was true.

It had to be. Samantha had not been the only one to see the fire and those women. Brian had seen them as well. It had to be true. Samantha stood within that stone circle with Brian at her side and the acrid stink of charred meat in her nostrils, and she stared at the pyre with an acidic churning in her gut. If it wasn't true . . . she would never meet him face to face again, never be able to confront him. She had defiled her father's grave for nothing.

Minutes whispered by on the wind and the burning branches cracked and popped and flared, and soon the rage of the flame began to diminish. Slowly, Samantha slid her back down the rock and sat heavily at its base. Though she had not eaten any of the Chinese food in the van, she suddenly remembered it and the smell of it, and she turned to her right and threw up on the hard ground. Her stomach convulsed as though she might be sick a second time, but after a moment it subsided and she was able to sit upright again. Disgusted, she wiped her mouth with the back of her left hand and then dragged it along the ground to clean it, as though she were wiping dog shit off the sole of her shoe.

Without a word Brian sat down beside her. Samantha could not look at him; she had just begun to understand what it must have cost him in his own mind to do this with her tonight. *What the hell are you doing here?* she thought to herself, but still she did not look at him. The guilt she felt in those moments was as powerful as the grief and anger that had been warring within her since her father's passing.

The fire smoldered. Through the flames she could see that the corpse was a withered, blackened thing, most of its mass burned away in the pyre. Branches had become little more than embers. Gusts of wind carried them off like the glowing ashes on the tip of a cigarette. It would be miraculous if they didn't catch some of the trees outside the circle on fire.

Miraculous. Samantha tried to laugh but it came out a silent sneer. That was funny. There were no miracles on Monument Island tonight.

Her right hand slipped into Brian's and though he caught his breath, he did not pull back. Samantha put her head on his shoulder and watched the fire burn down. Though her clothes were dry in the front now, they were still damp beneath her and at her back, and the combination of that chill and the warmth of the dying fire was uncomfortable. Still, that did not keep her from succumbing to the heat on her face and her near complete exhaustion. Samantha's eyes began to close.

A gentle nudge awakened her, and a raspy voice spoke her name. Somewhere lost in her mind she had been dreaming, but the dream was already gone. Even as her eyes fluttered open pieces of the day's puzzle came back to her and she had a tiny spark of hope that it was her father nudging her.

"Sam," Brian said again.

She gazed into his eyes. They were red and puffy, for he was just as exhausted as she was.

"It's going to be light in a few hours. We should get out of here."

The will to argue had left her. She glanced at the altar, saw that the fire was completely out now save for a few embers that gleamed like red eyes from the darkness. Nothing. For an instant her mind began to follow the thread of this fact out to its natural conclusion, to the heartbreak her father's family would feel, the horror in her mother's eyes, when they all learned what had happened at his grave and had to wonder what had become of his remains.

Her lips quivered and she squeezed her eyes shut to hold back tears, her face contorted in a snarl of grief and self-loathing.

Then Brian reached up to gently stroke her face, to push her hair away from her eyes and all the emotion drained out of her. Weak and empty, Samantha took his hand and let him help her up. Brian slipped an arm around her and they walked out of the circle.

It felt wrong to her to be returning without the burden they had transported up there, but the way was much easier going down through the trees and the thick undergrowth. Branches tugged at her clothes, but Samantha barely noticed. She let Brian lead her and tried to think about nothing, numb to the cold and the world. The sound of the waves made her want to sleep some more, but she kept walking, one foot after the other, the simple motion a rhythm she could lose herself in.

"Brian, I—"

"Ssshhh. Don't, Sam. Really," he said, pausing in a tangle of trees to meet her gaze. "We'll be okay. Let's just get through the night. In the morning we can talk all you want."

After a moment's hesitation she nodded and they kept on. When they emerged from the trees and only the thick brush was left, Samantha saw the gulls' roost. The path that had opened to allow them to pass was gone. The trilling of the birds and the rustle of their feathers seemed to fill the air as though the sounds were all around her, too close. Their white and gray feathers had a ghostly sheen and, if possible, there seemed to be even more of them now.

Past the gulls there was less of the rocky island shore now that the tide was in. The water would still be shallow most of the way, but they would have to swim part of the distance to the beach.

The beach.

Samantha blinked and peered into the night. For a moment it seemed as if the whole world had just fallen away into nothingness and only the island and the ocean were left. But then dark, squat shapes resolved themselves—the cottages that lined the coast of Biddeford Pool. The night was at its deepest, perhaps even beginning to wane, and all the lights were off in those dwellings. It was as though she were seeing the world through a dark gauze . . . or a shroud.

Brian stepped on a bush and its brittle branches snapped. The sound seemed unimaginably loud.

He froze. Samantha nearly collided with him. She glanced up at him with only a dull curiosity, but when he turned toward her, eyes filled with dread, she felt a new stirring of fear within her.

"Wha—"

He put a finger to his lips and then pointed to the gulls. Samantha frowned and stared at them, not understanding at first. It took her a moment to notice the silence. No trilling, nor even the slightest ruffle of wings. They were completely still. And they were watching her.

"I don't—" she began.

The gulls took flight with a bombardment of noise, a sound like a thousand flags snapping in high wind, but they did not caw. Samantha gaped at the birds as they flocked toward her.

Brian clutched her arm, dragged her backward, shouting at her to run. He propelled her back along the way they had come, up the hill and into the thicket of trees. Branches crashed as some tried to follow. Samantha glanced behind her to see that many of them had veered off. Yet she felt them there, above the trees, pacing her. She could taste the bile in her mouth

149

from earlier and now her throat was dry and ragged and her pants were stiff with salt from their ocean crossing, which made it horribly difficult to run.

Her heart thundered in her own ears. She stumbled and began to fall behind. Brian grabbed her and pulled her forward again, nearly crashing into a tree himself before slipping around it. Limbs like skeletal fingers scratched at their faces and then the gulls were there. One of them tangled its talons in her hair and Samantha batted it away. She swung her arms wildly, snagging her sweatshirt on a tree and snapping a branch as she bulled her way through.

With an anguished scream she shook her head and slapped at them. A beak tore the flesh of her left hand. Her chest hurt, lungs burning. As she tried to catch a breath, a gull came from ahead of her, flew right at her face and tore a gash in her forehead. Blood flowed into her eyes.

Samantha screamed.

"Brian! Get them off me! Jesus Christ, get them off!"

But Brian was stumbling just ahead of her. He slammed into a tree trunk to scrape a gull off his back even as he tore one from his neck. Samantha wiped blood from her eyes and couldn't breathe as she watched him, ran to him, helped him to fight off a gull even as another tangled in her own hair. The sounds of them in the branches above her head chilled her to the bone. They were maddening, those flapping, rustling noises.

"Jesus Christ," she whimpered again. "Oh my God, please."

Samantha had no idea if it was truly God she was praying to, or something else, some strange essence that lingered on this malevolent island rock. But if it was God to whom she whispered, she feared he would turn a deaf ear. She had been faithless. And yet she had nowhere else to turn.

Off to her right now, crashing through the trees, Brian roared in pain and rage. Despair claimed Samantha and she stumbled. The gulls were going to drive her down. They might only hurt her, but she was not a fool. If they kept at it, well, there were so many of them that the gulls might kill her.

She lunged forward and dove onto the ground, bent to cover her head with her arms. On her knees on that unforgiving ground she pleaded for mercy to whatever power might listen.

Nearby she heard Brian muttering but could not make out the words. The thunder of gull wings filled the air still, yet it was receding. Slowly, cautiously, Samantha uncovered her head and lifted her eyes.

There were perhaps a dozen gulls circling high above and many more roosting in the trees behind her, but she and Brian had stumbled back into the clearing with the stone circle and the gulls would not follow.

"Oh, God," she sighed. "Oh, my God, thank you."

With a kind of joy she went to Brian, who was curled into a ball on the ground, and helped him up. His face was slashed and one of his eyes was swollen shut, though she could not see if the eye was damaged or just the flesh around it. He shuddered and she did not think it was from the cold. She also did not think he was going to stop.

"They went away," she said, hearing how small her voice sounded.

Brian kept shuddering and stared at her with his one good eye. "How do we get out of here?" he demanded flatly. "How do we get back?"

Wiping again at the blood that stung her eyes, Samantha looked around the sparsely wooded clearing. Her gaze settled upon the stone circle again and all the breath rushed from her body.

Within the circle of stones, above the altar, the air was glowing red and orange.

But the fire was out, she thought. *I saw it. It was nothing but embers.*

Then another thought struck her and she gasped. *Daddy.*

Samantha ignored Brian then, staggering toward the stone circle. He reached for her and grabbed her arm but, she shook him off, so exhausted and drained from her injuries that she nearly fell with the effort.

"Daddy," she whispered.

"No, Samantha," Brian growled behind her. "Stop it. This isn't right, don't you get it? Whatever this place is, it wasn't meant for this, for what we did. It's . . . it was a holy place. They burned their warriors here, purified them. Maybe they brought them back, maybe not. But there's nothing pure about what you want out of this. That's not what it's for. What we did . . . I think it's blasphemy."

But her mind was closed to him. The words barely registered as she moved toward the stone circle. Her stomach ached and she could not swallow, and all the bitterness and disappointment and pain that her relationship with her father had caused her seemed as nothing compared to the idea that she would be able to see him again, to look into his eyes and *ask* him to love her or explain why he would not.

A tall, broad figure appeared between two of the stones. The glow of fire inside the circle cast it into sharp silhouette so that it looked as though it were being born of the flame and the darkness. A spark of her old anger returned along with a flicker of hope.

At last, she thought.

The figure emerged from the circle and Samantha faltered. He was huge and had a thick blond beard. The sword that was gripped in his right hand was crusted with old gore and dripped with fresh blood as though he had just stepped from the battlefield. Yellow eyes burned beneath a dented iron helmet with metal horns jutting from it. He wore heavy boots and clothes made of leather and fur and thick cloth.

This was not her father.

A second warrior appeared from another opening in the stone circle, axe gleaming red in the moonlight, eyes a sickly burning orange. Then a third and a fourth.

"Daddy?" Samantha asked the night.

No answer came in return.

She peered into the circle, searching the dark and the fiery glow for some sign that he had returned. The terror that raced through her at the sight of these ghostly things, these revenants or specters, was laced with wonder. If they existed, if these were the dead men who had been burned here only to live again, where was Carl Finnin? Where was her father?

"Where is he?" she shrieked at the silent warriors who stood just outside the circle and glared balefully at her with burning eyes. "Give me back my father!"

Her anguished cry tore from her throat and echoed across the island, but the specters remained still. Her emotions in chaos, unleashed, drove her forward. She raced at the nearest, the first one she had seen.

"Sam, stop!" Brian screamed behind her.

"Give him to me, God damn you! I want him back!"

Samantha raised her fists. She would force them to listen, force them to answer. The warrior with the horned, dented helmet stood motionless, as though he had been carved from these very stones. She ran at him, shrilly screaming, all conscious thought set aside. Samantha Finnin had gone berserk. She struck out at the revenant and it was solid enough. The thing's eyes flared more brightly, but it did not so much as flinch as she balled her fists tighter and struck it again and again, screaming for the miracle for which she had sacrificed much of her sanity.

She did not even notice when the dead warrior began to raise his sword.

Brian tackled her from the side, drove her to the ground. Samantha hit her head and blackness swam at the edges of her vision. He was shouting at her, but the words meant nothing. She could not even hear them, could only see the contours of his face shaded by the glow of ethereal flame within that circle.

In there, she thought. She had to go inside the circle. *They're keeping him from me.*

"I told you!" Brian screamed down at her, his face close enough that spittle flew from his mouth and struck her, close enough that she could smell his stale breath. "We've got to go!"

Two dead warriors loomed behind him, outlined against the moon. Samantha's eyes widened in horror as the one with the horned helmet raised his bloody sword. Brian must have seen the terror in her eyes for he reared up and began to turn.

Soundlessly, the sword scythed across the night in a gleaming sweep. The blade hacked into Brian's throat, cleaving flesh

154

and cracking bone, and blood sprayed Samantha's hair and face and clothing as his head struck the hard ground nearby and bounced several times before coming to rest against the trunk of a tree.

Brian, who had been her best friend. Brian, who had loved her. Brian, whom she had dragged back into her life only to give him a nightmare in return for all he had given her.

Her mouth was open, but her throat whistled with a thin, reedy slip of air. No scream would come out. Samantha scrabbled backward away from the dead warriors. The others had remained still, but now they stepped away from the stone circle and started toward her as well. Leather scraped against leather. Weapons clanked. Their eyes burned with all the colors of the unearthly pyre that had consumed her father's corpse.

Blasphemy. Brian had been right. Whatever gods the people who had built this place believed in, it was holy to them. She had defiled it.

With the taste of Brian's blood mingling with her own upon her lips, Samantha rocketed to her feet. She could not run through the trees for the gulls awaited her that way and she was sure they would block her passage. But the other side of the island? It was possible that they did not guard the entire shoreline.

Two of the revenants, armed with double-edged battle-axes, stopped by Brian's headless corpse and began to hack him apart. A flurry of wings announced the arrival of a small flock of gulls, which settled down to peck at Brian, tearing chunks of his flesh away in their beaks.

Samantha ran through the clearing away from the dead warriors, away from the stone circle, away from Biddeford Pool. She was headed out to sea, scrambling to keep her feet beneath her as her momentum carried her to the edge of the clearing and into some thicker woods.

She cast a final glance over her shoulder and saw the red and silver gleam of bloodstained weapons as the dead men followed her. They had begun slowly but now they ran faster, grunting like animals. The sound snaked under her skin and Samantha felt something snap in her mind; she wondered if it was what remained of her sanity.

They were twenty feet away.

Past them was the stone circle, ghost fire burning within. She would never see inside it, never know if *he* was in there, waiting for her, waiting for that conversation that would never come.

And then, just as she slipped deeper into the trees and the ground sloped downward beneath her, roots and rocks under her feet, Samantha saw a final figure stepping from inside that circle. A tall man, though not so tall as the others. A dark silhouette in a suit with wide pinstripes and no shoes on his feet.

It should have drawn her back or at least given her pause, or so Samantha thought. Instead the sight of this last revenant snapped her head around, pushed her gaze away, and she ran through the trees, down the hill toward the rear of the island, holding her breath until it hurt and then beginning to hyperventilate, her chest rising and falling in tiny bursts.

Dead men crashed through the trees behind her. The branches that whipped at her face did not seem to slow them. She ran blindly, knowing that she must go down and down and that the path would take her to the ocean. But then the trees thinned out enough that she could see the waves below her and her chest tightened; shock and denial warred inside her but her eyes had not deceived her. She had been descending at an angle, still headed toward the shoreline but not directly.

Samantha corrected her path, pulled her arms in tight and lowered her face as she pushed through a tight clutch of trees and then she was out of the woods. Brush scraped at her jeans, snagged the denim, but she forged ahead, hope sparking in her as she saw the surf crashing on the rocky edge of the island sixty or seventy yards away. There were no gulls to block her way. Not one. She ran down the rocky overgrown slope at a wild pace she could not hope to control, barely keeping her feet under her.

Off to her right, death crashed through the trees and out onto the rough terrain—the warrior with the dented, horned helmet was first to appear, moonlight dull on the tarnished iron headpiece. The others followed, some farther along the tree line, but others closer. Too close. Samantha glanced over her shoulder with wide eyes and screamed with the collision of terror and fury and hope in her. The water was so close. The ocean crashing on the rocks. If she could just get off the island she would be safe.

Or would she?

The idea that this might not be true had never occurred to her. Even as it did, as the waves below lost the aura of safety they'd held under her gaze, Samantha heard a grunt and shot a glance at the warriors cutting across the downward slope toward her. The nearest had eyes that glowed with copper fire.

Beneath a thick red beard his dead lips were pale and gray and they curled back in a sneer. The warrior raised his axe and he hurled it at her.

Samantha spun away, lost her footing, and then—in a frenzied effort to avoid being caught—she leaped out away from the hillside. In a fraction of an eyeblink she pictured it all in her head. Her momentum would drive her out and down, she would hit the rocks and brush and she would tuck and roll and let it carry her downward until she could get up again and then she would rush the last few yards to the ocean.

As she dove forward she flung her arms out.

The axe whickered through the air, spinning around, and its razor-sharp blade caught the tips of the last two fingers on her left hand, shearing them off above the top joint.

In her mind the image of her landing splintered. Shrieking in shock and pain she fell to the ground in a long arc. Samantha struck hard, the air knocked out of her, and she tumbled rather than rolled out of the brush to the rocky ledge at the shore of the island and she struck her head again.

Blinking back the streaks of white that erupted across her vision like fireworks, she reached out her left hand for leverage so that she could stand. The bleeding, severed tips of her fingers touched the ground and she sucked air into her lungs through clenched teeth, blackness seeping in around the edges of her vision. The arm snapped back against her breasts and she held it there as she rose onto her knees, got one leg under her, and began to stand.

A rough and stinking hand grabbed her by the hair and hauled her to her feet. Samantha stared in horror at the dead thing in its horned helmet that held her, strands of hair tearing free of her scalp. Her mind screamed, but her voice was silent now. Her heart thundered, but her legs would simply not work any longer. The revenant's burning eyes studied her, its rotten teeth bared like an animal's. Beneath leather and fur its muscles were massive. It held her effortlessly by the hair like some filthy rag doll about to be discarded. The others gathered around her.

The warrior in whose grip she dangled raised his blood-encrusted sword in his free hand. Samantha barely noticed. Her gaze was locked upon his, searching for something alive in his eyes and finding only cold fire and bloodlust.

Nearby, the waves crashed against the rocks. The wind drove the surf higher and the trees upon the island swayed under its power. In her mind's eye she could see Brian being hacked apart, food for the gulls, his flesh tearing under their beaks. The urge to close her eyes, to accept the blade, was heavy upon her. But she resisted it. Instead she stared at the dead thing and she fought her exhaustion to stand straighter.

"I had to know," she whispered weakly. It was not an apology, merely an explanation.

The sword gleamed redly as it whickered through the air, its edge slashing toward her neck. A shadow moved among the dead men and some of the warriors were shunted aside. A hand shot in front of Samantha and grabbed the blade, stopping the sword with a wet slice and a jarring crunch of bone. The horned helmet turned, the warrior snarling as he glared at the intruder. But he lowered his sword.

Samantha stared into the face of her father.

Carl Finnin stood among them, salt-and-pepper hair and mustache perfectly groomed. Though he wore the clothes he had been dressed in for his funeral, this was not the face of a

159

dead man. The thread that had been used to sew his eyelids and lips shut was gone. He gazed at her with his own eyes, not the stuffing that had replaced them in the coffin.

The dead warriors, the resurrected corpses of Norsemen who had traveled to these shores centuries earlier, brandished their weapons, menace flowing from them with every agitated motion. Their eyes burned and they edged a little closer to Samantha and her father. A dead man, just as they were, but somehow returned from Valhalla despite the blasphemy of his burning on that pyre. The one with the horned helmet laid the flat of his sword against her father's chest to keep her from him. Carl Finnin slapped the blade carelessly away with a scowl that matched the Viking's own. And why not? They were all dead already.

"Daddy?" Samantha said, voice and heart breaking.

All the words rushed into her mind, all the questions she wanted to ask him, all her bitterness and love and every wish she had ever made that he would just love her. Something sparked in his eyes then and she knew that somehow he had read her mind, or simply seen in her all the pain, all those questions.

Her father slapped her hard across the face.

When he spoke, fetid spittle flew from the dead man's mouth and his eyes narrowed with contempt.

"You stupid, selfish girl," he rasped in a voice like the whisper of burning kindling. *"It was never about you. I never thought about you or anyone else, only what I needed. Me, Carl Finnin. And look. Look what you've done. You've grown up just like me."*

His words cut into her and Samantha could not breathe.

How could it be as simple as that, as brutally real? Whatever good had been part of him, at his core he had been callous and selfish. But if that was true . . . Samantha prayed that the rest was not. She shook her head in denial, refused to accept that she was no better.

Flames erupted from her father's eyes and then his clothing and his hair began to burn. The dead warriors had been observing carefully, weapons clutched in cold, pale hands. Now—as he began to burn—they began to close the circle they had made around Samantha and her father.

"Look what you've done," her father said, his words carried to her on the black smoke that curled up from the flames that consumed him for a second time.

The warriors attacked, intent upon killing her and destroying this abomination she had created. Engulfed in flames, his flesh running like candle wax, charring to black again, Carl Finnin shot an elbow into the face of the warrior closest to him and tore the axe from his hand. He swung the blade around and lodged it in the bloodless throat of the revenant that came at Samantha from behind. The swiftness of his motions painted the night with the flames that danced upon his resurrected form. Carl brought the axe down with both hands toward the dead thing that had held his daughter moments before. The axe split the helmet between its horns and cleaved the warrior's skull in two.

His skin split and blackened and curled up at the torn edges like tree bark in the fire. A scream of anguish tore up from inside him, but this was not the dead voice she had heard before; this was the voice of her father, the laughter of those

161

rare and precious moments they had shared, and it cried out in despair. His eyes burst and fire licked up from the gaping holes.

Cloaked in all-consuming flame, a walking funeral pyre, Carl reached out and grabbed Samantha. Where he touched her, she burned. Her clothes were set on fire and she felt her arms burning as he lifted her off her feet. Samantha screamed for him to stop, to please stop, not to kill her, though the words were lost in the roar of fire. She let loose howls of sorrow and blazing agony. As he spun her above him, Samantha caught glimpses of the warriors attacking. A sword slashed across his back, but her father only stumbled slightly and kept on. A huge, ghastly revenant threw his axe. There was a wet thunk as it slammed into her father's back and stuck there.

Fire roared up along his arms and her hair caught. Flames raced across her sweatshirt and then Samantha was burning . . . burning all over. *On fire,* she thought. *I'm on fire.*

She would join her father.

The burning man staggered two more steps and then he hurled her with unnatural strength. As she fell, rolling over in the air, Samantha saw the warriors fall upon her father, driving him down beneath their blades, fire spreading from him to engulf his attackers as well.

Samantha caught a glimpse of the moon. It was red and orange and she thought it might be on fire.

Then she struck the ocean and plunged beneath the waves. She choked on salt water and felt it burn where the fire had singed her scalp and chest and the places where her father had grabbed onto her. Her mind seemed frozen, conscious thought retreating like an animal to some shadowed corner inside her mind. But instinct took hold and Samantha pawed at the water, struggled to the surface, spat and choked and would have thrown up if there had been anything left in her convulsing stomach.

Her feet touched the ocean bottom. She stood and found that the waves barely reached her shoulders.

The tide was going out.

On the shore were scattered the burning remains of the things born of the pyre, brought forth upon the altar within that stone circle. But Samantha hardly saw them for at the rocky ledge where the waves struck the shore three translucent figures loomed, their forms rippling in the breeze like the surface of the sea itself, black hair blowing across their faces, obscuring their features. Where their crimson robes revealed flesh, their skin gleamed a pale, bluish white.

The three women turned their hands upward and deep red flames rose from their palms. They moved delicately, as though they might spill the fire into the sea, and they walked out over the waves, their steps easily a foot above the surface of the ocean.

Samantha began to swim. She was at the back of the island and so she struck out at an angle she thought was parallel with the beach, though she could not see it.

The women did not follow. They paused above the waves perhaps twenty feet from the rocky shore of the island and from there they simply watched her go. But they radiated an unmistakable sense of menace, a threat. Once before she and her friends and their little game of pretend death had drawn the attention of something here, disturbed a force that was better left to a dark slumber. Now she had roused that ancient power again, and this time she had desecrated it with her need. Her selfish need.

The tide tugged at her beneath the surf, but the waves pushed her forward. Soon enough Samantha could no longer see the fire on the other side of the island or the spectral women.

The water was over her head. Her body was scarred with burns and gashes and her bones ached with an utter exhaustion unlike anything she had ever felt before. Her clothes were heavy with water and dragged her down, threatened to pull her under the gentle waves. Several times she paused and stared at the blank, dark faces of the cottages on the distant beach and nearly surrendered to the weight of her clothes and her conscience, but still Samantha kept on.

Look what you've done. You've grown up just like me.

The words echoed through her mind, branded there, perhaps the only thing keeping her from slipping into unconsciousness and drifting out to sea. There was a truth in them that horrified her. Hollow and numb as she felt, a sharp certainty cut through her grief then. It was true that she had let what her father had been shape her, both his love and his distance, his moments of affection and his years of disregard. She had been the clay and his negligence the wheel, fired on a kiln of passing years. Samantha had never been so cold; it felt like she was dead inside. But it also felt as though something new had been sculpted now, not in the kiln but the pyre.

What shape it took, that was up to her.

In the end it was not so very long before her feet touched the bottom again. With the ebb and flow of the tide she made her way at last to the shore and collapsed, the waves washing

164

around her. As the tide went out, it swept her thoughts away with it, leaving Samantha unconscious on the beach, dawn not far off.

The ocean had delivered her to the sand and receded, leaving her to continue on her own, wherever her path might take her.

JONAH AROSE

by Tom Piccirilli

For Dick Laymon

1

The flood was upon us, and I wanted to go with it.

I watched the Works for three days of freezing Manhattan rain, lingering inside a storm that wouldn't die down. Arching rivers flowed in the streets and draped off the vaulted roofs, splashing, white-capped in the vicious wind. Whenever I looked at my soaked, prune-ish fingers I thought of the pickled punks floating in their yellow liquids, tiny fetal hands clasped in prayer.

Fishboy Lenny was having a hell of a time in the roiling gutter, bobbing and swimming in torrents of rainwater. Corpses of bloated rats rolled by, sweeping down toward the docks. Addicts and the homeless shivered themselves to pieces, beg-

167

ging pocket change from stonewall citizens and wet, heartless hookers. The downpour didn't stop the whores. If anything, it drove them out into the saturated night. They paraded through the subways and pushed across the avenue, all tits and rabbit fur and shining red umbrellas. They slogged up to taxis at traffic lights, crawled into the backs of vans, and hung at the entrance of the Works hoping to entice the curious passers-by.

Starving dogs tore each other apart in the alleys, just another fragment of the drenched tableau. Blood ran but washed away immediately, leaving no impression of life or death behind. It was nothing new. Jolly Nell couldn't take the street noise and started singing the poisoned violets scene *Poveri Fiori* from Act IV of *Adriana Lecouvreur*. I'd never realized before that she could really belt out the high notes when she put everything into it.

Male prostitutes in baseball caps or cowboy hats leaned back against the bricks, posing beneath lamplights, thumbs hooked in their jeans as the slow-moving traffic eased by like oil. Christ, they'd all watched too many movies but none of the right ones. Frizzy heads bobbed in the laps of anemic businessmen, and the world kept kicking.

I could feel the energy gathering around us, swirling, black and degenerate. The stink of displacement, of aberration, became stronger as I kept watch. I knew it was going to be bad. Any sharp noise drew my attention in the constant patter, gurgle and spray of rain.

Juba unfolded himself from where he knelt, unwinding those unholy limbs further and further until they looked as if they would never stop. Even on his knees he's taller than most men, and when he stands he towers above all normality. Anybody looking out a second-story window would be almost eye-level with him. He wavered in the air, each elongated bone and tendon showing through the thin tissue of his nutmeg flesh. His oblong head appeared poorly crafted, lopsided to the left where his shoulder was hunched. He was a tad over eight feet tall, but Nell could easily pick him up and carry him across the midway, even tossing him in the air and juggling him a bit. It had once been part of the act and drew delighted yowls from the children.

He was also an anatomical wonder. When Juba sucked in his stomach you could see his backbone thrusting through. For a quarter you could touch it. Ladies would squeal and make disgusted faces, and dream about what this freak would be like in bed, with everything so long.

His heart was perfectly defined, and you could watch the muscle beating. I'd witnessed the pounding of his anger, remorse and desire. He remained a soft-spoken godly man, but I still didn't know which god.

"Is something going to happen?" Juba asked. Even his voice was thin, a sparse whisper.

"Yes," I said. "You feel it too?"

"I can tell by your face."

"Oh."

"And I know you're never mistaken about things like this."

"We all have our talents."

Jolly Nell, forever the enthusiastic optimist, said, "Perhaps nothing bad will come, this one time."

How I loved her for that. For her willingness to offer me a chance to be wrong about the arrival of misery.

But I wasn't, and Nell understood that. She'd always been the caregiver, the brace over which the rest of us could sag or slump. Her mother had sold her to McKenna's Carnival when she was seven years old and already topping one-sixty. Falling into her arms was like being embraced by all your loves and fears at once, the power in them something natural, intense and dominant. She snapped two of my ribs in a rough clench a while back, but I needed that hug worse than anything else at the time, even while the shards of bone ground together into my lungs. I spit blood for days.

Now, at five-one, she broke seven hundred pounds easy, but never seemed to have trouble with her ankles or shins or lower back the way some of the other Jollies had. Nell moved with the consistency and gravity of the setting moon. She affected us like a tidal force.

My fingers began to tremble and the burning in my guts grew worse. It happened like this, from time to time, when the hammer was about to drop. My breath came in bites and my eyes flitted wildly, scanning the cars racing by in the seeping darkness, headlights smeared upon the slick blackness.

Nell hugged me, but my ribs hadn't completely healed yet and I grunted in pain, quivering at her touch. She said, "None of this is your fault. It's all right. It's going to be fine."

Hertzburg let out a belly full of ferocious laughter. It went on longer than it should have, there in the storm. Thunder snarled above. Finally he noted Nell's expression and stopped. "I'm sorry, but your idealism during our current circumstances astounds me at this point."

"It shouldn't," she told him.

"No, I suppose not. Some of us can clear away death as easily as finishing off a roasted pig."

"Oh, well, isn't that cute?"

"For others it gets tangled in our curls."

Jolly Nell planted herself, fists on her colossal hips. "Face up to it, you're enjoying yourself. You're having a terrific time."

"Do we have any choice?"

"That's enough," I said.

"Of course it is. Let's hold our vigil and observe further."

Hertzburg didn't brush his soaked hair out of his eyes. It hung dripping across his nose and cheeks, in the corners of his mouth, down those powerful arms and between his thick fingers. Though billed as the Wild Man, he'd never been good at appearing feral. He had too much pride for that. McKenna used to go nuts when Hertzburg wore his reading glasses in the sideshow, playing chess against himself, discussing Nietzsche with the rubes, reciting Baudelaire and Goethe. Anything to break character. Even with his large muscles corded and covered in fuzz, wearing a Tarzan outfit with big leopard spots on it, he was the definition of poise.

Stoned teens in the audience would sometimes try to test him in an effort to impress their pimply girlfriends, swinging bicycle chains or tossing lit matchbooks. Their ugly, harassing chortling would float through camp and the rest of us would know what was coming. Hertzburg never lost his composure. Not when he'd grabbed the rube kids by their throats, not when they were trying to knife him, and not even while the cops shackled him and the parents shrieked. He videotaped his performances so he could later prove he always acted in self-defense.

The street lights seemed to dim for an instant, showing the contours of shadows in the sheets of rain. It appeared almost like fire falling upon us. I doubled over and went to my knees.

Hertzburg said, "Guess this is it."

A Jeep Cherokee with bad brake lining tried to run the red, way too late. The engine roared as the gears slipped. Everybody on the street stopped what they were doing in order to watch. A yellow cab pulled out and cut it off, sending the Jeep into a wicked skid, snaking and spinning now. Nell covered her eyes but Juba leaned forward off the curb as if he might pluck out the driver with one hand.

Brake lights cast a sanguine hue against the rain. The Jeep straightened an instant before it smashed into a teenage crack-head, tires screeching and sputtering in the puddles. The girl had on a yellow slicker and it made her a good target. She'd just taken down an entire bachelor party in the back of a limo and still had the loose cash in her hand. The Jeep veered and swerved again as she rolled up the grille, bounced off the hood into the windshield, and flipped over the top.

Her arms went out wide as if trying to go with it and fly for a little while. She appeared to have caught an air draft and the edges of her slicker flapped. Her hair dipped and flung aloft. The whole scene had a brutal sense of ballet to it.

Her body bowed hideously, staying up there for a time as if grooving to '70s tunes—"Dream Weaver," maybe "Thunder Island" or "Crocodile Rock," and then she came crashing down on the curb. Bills fluttered past, crisp twenties. It looked like she'd made an even hundred for the whole party. The back of her skull parted easily, flopping open on the cement. Fishboy Lenny swam up the gutter and peered closely at her, making his noises of distress and want. "Fweep, mweee, fwsshh."

Without so much as a crack in the windshield, the Jeep gunned it and kept going straight through the next intersection.

The three guys in the limo popped out of the moon roof and glanced down at the dead whore, grinning with slick teeth. They'd put it to her, giving her a last lay to take to hell. They should've just strangled her with their Italian ties. Their high-pitched dingo laughter sounded deranged but genuine as they pulled away. They were in a mood now and would probably smack around some deaf-mutes on the way home just to keep the high going.

Blurs of black motion began to swarm up and down the avenue. The street folk were on the girl then, nabbing her shoes and money and vials of crack. They danced after the cash, pirouetting in the wind, skipping past parked cars. Nobody wanted the slicker but they hauled her corpse backward right out of her stained white thong. Fishboy Lenny watched it all with his usual wide-eyed innocence, twin nostril slashes on his noseless face quivering as he mewled.

Jolly Nell asked, "Shouldn't we help?"

Juba the living skeleton said, "We can do nothing, Nell, she's already dead. Look—"

"They're taking her . . ."

"It's to be expected."

"My God, and her . . ."

"They live off carrion. It's their way."

"Don't watch," I said from the shadows, watching.

Fishboy Lenny swam from drain pipe to drain pipe as the sewers whirled and burped, his small flippers already spattered with red. I'd worked alongside him for several years and still didn't know a thing about his past, or even if he had one. He was found treading water in the tank of the high dive act one morning and immediately became part of McKenna's Carnival.

On occasion he would mimic words well enough to sound as if he was actually speaking, but they were only strung-together, incoherent sentences. It made you wonder what went on behind those wide eyes, and just what that mind might reveal.

The rumors about the Works had made it from New York down to the southern carny circuit. They were as different and preposterous as the gaffs and ballyhoo on any midway.

Like you used to have to screw on camera to get inside, or cut open your wrist and bleed in front of your children, or quote passages in Greek from the Book of Revelation. It sounded stupid enough to be true and had all probably happened at one point or another. There was an air of East Village artistry about it, a performance piece set in motion that hadn't met up with enough resistance to slow it down yet. I wondered about that. It had the worked up promotion of an Andy Warhol–type Factory alliance, where the artisans and contrivers gathered to film themselves shitting and sleeping and then presented it as art to anybody senseless enough to fall for it. Word was now that if you went inside looking for a leather-deather 'trix to whip the hide off your ass, you could find her easy enough. She'd be courteous and sweet and spit in your face only when you asked her to, and the salted ends of her cat-o'-nine-tails would help to heal the welts up quickly. You wanted some home-stomped wine or Cuban cigars, a bestiality porno or a discussion group on nineteenth-century literature, or if you needed some guy to show you how to break your own thumbs to get out of high-tinsel steel cuffs, then you could just waltz right in, pick what you required, and then backtrack out again.

But if you went with the intention of finding anything more, maybe looking for poetry to be carved into your heart, the agony of legend or a slap-down with God, seeking redemption or erasure of a dead past, then you joined something more looming and immense along the way. Until you carelessly grew into reckless myth and couldn't make it in the regular world anymore.

A writer named Paynes knew how to work the gaff and he'd hit it big with his first couple of books—bestseller lists, movie deals, television, all the rest of it. He was out of his head, that much was obvious, but his timing had been perfect. They needed somebody to stir the pot again. Paynes bought out nearly the entire city block, four or five warehouses at least, even the rubble of empty lots where the bag ladies and the zealots and the mainliners crawled among dog shit. He'd spent time in the nuthatch and had brought the asylum sensibility back home with him. From what I'd heard, the space inside had now been split into a hundred separate areas, maybe more, including private suites, museums and exhibit halls.

There were even a couple of stages where circus acts trained, the high- and low-wire routines, dancing French poodle performances, live theater where they played out scenes from Odets and Orton. TV and film sets where they shot children's morning programs with lots of dinosaur costumes and moon-eyed puppets, and pornos with hermaphrodites as ugly as three-toed tree sloths clambering on top of double amputee toothless dwarves. It had its own irony, satire and breathless plausibility. Madhouse. Anything was possible, which I supposed was the whole point.

I watched the place engulf a Fedex carrier and two Chinese delivery kids in the course of a weekend. Anyone with a crazy burning hurt who went inside the Works never came out again.

No one except my father, Nicodemus, and he only in a dream. *Come find me, son, in the blackest heart of Babylon.*

I figured this was the right place. They said Paynes had gone so far inside that he couldn't be found again. They said a bloody messiah stalked the halls, and that the devil chose his playmates carefully here. It was about time.

The Works drew in the tormented and the lost and the defeated, and even a Southern tent revival minister in a frock coat could find a home for his insanity in this dwelling. Maybe there was room for me too, but I doubted it.

Hertzburg whispered, "They got her."

"What?"

"Somebody carried off the dead whore. Look up the block, you can watch her slicker swaying in the dark. He's got her over his shoulder."

"That gruesome bastard—"

"He's having trouble handling her weight." Hertzburg took a few steps forward until he was out on the avenue, and he finally cleared the hair from his eyes so he could see it happening. "He's holding the top of her skull in place with one hand and dragging her away."

Juba scowled in that direction. "It's to be expected."

"Stop saying that, Juba," I told him. "Who the hell expects a murdered prostitute to be stripped clean on the street and her body stolen by some maniac?"

"We do," he said, and I bit my tongue until the coppery taste flooded down my throat because he was right.

I could see why my father had chosen the Works, and why the Works had chosen him. There was a thriving audience here

that desired to be entertained. They wanted miracle and astonishment and resurrection. They wanted to fuck all the blistering
hate out of their miserable bones and so did my old man. He
could set up a soapbox in any corner and scream into their
faces and slop up their sticky spirits. He must be having the
time of his life.

Nicodemus was in there somewhere, and he had my son
Jonah with him.

Police prowled the area constantly but never at the right
times. They hit the cherry lights and blared the siren for two
seconds at a clip, barely making a ripple in the sex action.
Nobody really noticed and the rats continued floating by. The
cops scooted out of there without ever stepping from the car,
amazed to have escaped once more. News crews from the major
networks came by twice but didn't exit their vans. They shot
the doorway and would use it later as file footage. Frail and
frightened husbands hunched under their steering wheels. They
all knew this was a borderland to stay clear from, but their
peculiarities kept them coming back. I had no doubt that they'd
all eventually be swallowed by the Works.

"Are we ever going in?" Hertzburg asked.

"Yes," I said.

"And you're certain Nicodemus is inside?"

"Can't you smell him?"

"I smell piety. But that could be you."

"It's all of us."

Juba grunted. He tilted that oversized head and said, "What
do they do with their hurt?"

"What the hell kind of question is that?"

"A simple one. I haven't seen the doors open to let a single person out, not even to bring someone to the hospital or dispose of a body. For that matter, what of their children?"

"They can't be breeding in there," Hertzburg said.

"You sound so certain."

"Newborn life can't survive in that kind of atmosphere."

"No?" I asked.

"Absolutely not." He said it with a flat dullness, arms crossed over the Tarzan outfit, trying to hold himself in tight. "That ambiance is for dispossession. Ruin and havoc, not for nurturing."

It was the only time I'd ever heard him sound so completely inane and foolish. He talked out of shock, or maybe dread, which surprised me considering all he had seen. Jolly Nell giggled, a warm and small sound like a young thin girl would make. It almost brought a smile to my face as she threw her hands up, tired of us. "If a baby can be born to a carnival, it can blossom here as well. That's the nature of this place, I think. It's only another sideshow."

"Maybe you're right, Nell," I said. "It might explain why Nicodemus brought Jonah here." I gritted my teeth until the hinges of my jaw hurt. Blood called to blood, and the hammer of faith would have to fall one more time before we were through. "Let's see what this grift is all about. I'm going to find my son and then we're getting out of here."

"None of us will ever leave," Juba said from far above. "Are you fully prepared for that?"

He started into the street, followed closely by the others. Fishboy Lenny splashed after them, waving his tiny flippers at me. Juba's legs were so long that he made it across the avenue in three strides. The moon rushed into the rain and poured silver down onto him.

I tried to figure out why nobody was paying attention to any of them. Usually the whores loved freaks and made a big sloppy scene. They smoothed Hertzburg's hair, twining it between their fingers, playing with his spots.

Then I remembered.

He'd been murdered. He was dead.

They were all dead, and I was consumed by ghosts.

2

I had once been the greatest child preacher in all the South. People had come from as far as Waycross, Tipton, Nashville, Greensboro, Deep River and Gainesville to listen to me wail about heavenly fire and the downfalls of sin. The blaring prayers and saving of souls had come naturally to me. Some of us are born to judgment. I learned remorse early, but not atonement.

With a ministry that brought them bustling in across the floorboards of all-night gospel sings and tent revivals, I found I had a voice given to me by God. I never called myself a healer, nor did my father, but that didn't stop the cripples from taking pain-wracked steps across the stage. They hurled their hickory canes and sprang from their wheelchairs and flung their hearing aids into the eleventh row. I gave the imploring, inspiring sermons needed to snap bones back into place and fling cancer into remission. It was easy when backed by thousands of the devoted, everybody speaking in tongues, music swelling, arms lifted to paradise. The brain can do amazing things, even in the dying and the maimed.

There is no mystery to Christ under the Big Top. You had plenty of proof whenever you wanted it. You needed only to watch the brain-damaged come and go without undergoing any change. See the blessed who aren't susceptible to the power of placebo. Their parents hoped for the miracle of the ordinary and urged them forward toward me and my microphone. The retarded limped, as they always did, and hobbled beneath the lights and weight of my dedication, grinning before the shrieking audiences, and then hobbled off again.

My father's hands were full of cash. He accepted personal checks and money orders, and he set up a system so he could take credit card donations. He liked gaudy jewelry and wore large but flawed diamond rings that flashed the sun back into the eyes of my parishioners.

When he had both Jesus and money he didn't need the bottle anymore. Nicodemus owned forty different silk suits and enjoyed driving through the poor sections of various towns throughout the panhandle of Florida, leaving stacks of crisp dollar bills in mailboxes and stuck inside broken screen doors. He prayed with the Baptists, cleaned house with the Methodists, and baked bread in silence at a nearby monastery. He rode on donkeys and went fishing with the governor. He danced with the snake handlers yet never got close enough to the fangs.

But a child gets tired of what he's urged to do, even if he's started out in faith and love. A love for the Word, and an incinerating love for his own father. Eventually adolescence finds us all, and it drives most of us crazy in the wonderful way it's supposed to.

For others it's the inferno. I lost my golden voice when I discovered the moist tenderness of Becky May Horner and the raw rush of whiskey. I gave up God in the middle of a blow job.

I suspect it happens like that more often than anyone wants to tell you. The hidden mysteries of the tongue matter more than all the parables and allegory of the Bible. In that moment, you realize a girl with large pink nipples and a tall glass of 80-proof scotch can carry your further much faster than any arch-angel's wings.

Becky May Horner had some God-given talent of her own, for sure. She had a way of making you hold off until streaks of light crept up from the center of your brain and lit your vision with unnamable colors. She liked to make a man cry for release, and Christ, how I wept and begged, signing over bank accounts. I sometimes wondered that if my first sexual encounter had been with someone less experienced I might not have fallen from heaven's grace to an altogether different kind.

The loss of my virginity drove Nicodemus berserk. He knew it wouldn't be only my downfall but his as well. He prayed with me long into the heated nights while the willows draped full of misgivings and the cypress led toward Becky May's hovel. She and her mama were packing up their washboards, tubs and ladder-back chairs with money enough for greater glory. He went through receipts and bank books and stormed around the house. I'd given her more than I'd thought, and there were many other town girls as well. Some I recalled, some I had only brief images of after a couple of pints of Wild Turkey.

Once it started to go bad, he helped to ruin the rest. It was in our genetic make-up, this predilection toward self-destruction. He hung in while he could, but Nicodemus had always been at least half-crazy. It didn't take very long. A few months and we were pretty much finished, scraping bottom and whoring together, passing the bottle back and forth.

That was enough to drive me from my father's house, after the liquor turned us inside out and, smirking, he tried to kill me with a frying pan.

3

I found it easy going from one sideshow to another. At sixteen, no longer recognizable as the flaxen-haired, sweet-faced ivory boy preacher, I went to work in my first carnival. With my manner I made a perfect talker, calling in the marks to witness delights and grotesqueries never seen before. They put me on a little platform and let me run the patter. So long as I had a few shots of whiskey, I didn't mind all those flaming eyes turned on me from inside the faceless mob.

I was the Talker, who hauled them in. Rubes called us "barkers," but you could never get anybody to lay down money if you only barked in their faces. You talked, and the better you could gauge a person's appetite—what he might be after inside the carny—then the finer you could judge which attraction he'd be drawn to, and send him on his way.

It's why I was also a mentalist, a tarot and palm reader, a madball seer. I'd been raised surrounded by people in pain searching for a way to set down their burdens. I dressed the part in robes and a turban and looked into the crystal ball for effect, but all I really needed was to catch a glimpse of their anguish to know what to say in order to hustle them into the tents. I could sense the big troubles left behind, and those that were still coming.

And all the while I was growing more insane.

I found myself dissipating as I walked through the rain. I hadn't had a drink in three years but now I felt the way I used to after about half a bottle of 151 Rum, when my head was just starting to ease aside from the rest of my body. It still happened like that from time to time even without the booze.

The Fedex guy who'd been swallowed by the Works stood just inside the doorway, staring forlornly at the rest of the world beyond the entrance. He might've been crying or it might have only been mist on his face, I couldn't be certain. He was still holding his package, whatever it was.

As I stepped past he whispered, "Don't come in. This is hell. I'm way deep down inside of hell."

"Man," I told him, "this isn't even close, believe me."

"Then, you understand?"

"Oh yeah."

"But I—"

"It's an old story. Really."

"The agony, it's . . . it's . . . my spirit's—"

He didn't have the words. It always terrified me that one day I'd lose the Talk and forget the words and be exactly like him, waving my hands about my face and stuttering in my grief.

"Get used to it," I said.

183

"My spirit's in pieces!" he whined. "Listen—listen, you said you understood, but I think you made a mistake. I . . . I . . . listen—"

Suddenly the rage rose in me and I grabbed him by the neck. He made a soft *gkk* sound and started to go a nice shade of purple while I tightened my grip. He never let go of the package, though.

"Has your own father ever tried to cave in your skull with an iron skillet? You ever have your kid stolen from you? Has God ever reached down into your throat and yanked out your voice with a blazing fist?"

I eased up and he sputtered, gasping. "I—n-n-no, hey, I've just got to tell you this, you don't—"

"Give it a rest."

"You don't *grasp* what it's like, no matter what you think. You don't have any idea."

His eyes were heavy with all his commonplace secrets and I considered his sorrow. I could read his woe as clearly as if it had been swabbed across his forehead with Day-glo paint. There wasn't much, really, when you got down to it. "Go back home to your lackluster job and indifferent cunt of a wife and your three sneering children. They all want you dead."

"I know," he sobbed.

I dragged him to the door and booted his ass back out in the rain. He screamed as if I'd tossed him into an electric fence and I wondered if the shock of freedom would stop his heart. I turned and moved through the Works, gliding, wishing myself a little further gone with each step.

"How old am I?" I asked.

"You're no longer a child," Juba said as if I were a child.

184

"You're twenty-five years old. Your hair is already going gray. You've squinted too hard for too long and have deeply set wrinkles around your eyes."

I hadn't looked in a mirror for months. "Yes."

"Regret is an incomparable motivation."

"You ain't kidding, Bubba."

"You're at the end of your life."

"Am I? Finally?"

Juba nodded his oblong head and it wagged wildly in all the wrong directions. "Yes, but you've more to do."

"Okay."

"There is much to atone for, and you mustn't fail at this hour. We won't allow that."

"You wouldn't, would you?"

"No."

"Thank Christ."

"Leave him alone, Juba," Jolly Nell said. "He's here. We're all here to get it done. Let's go."

I kept wandering.

Sex, humanity and delusion clambered side by side with the painfreaks and broken-hearted inside the Works. This was a school, a museum, a storehouse, a rent-controlled apartment building where nobody ever managed to leave. Oils and dyes spattered the floor, walls draped with speckled blood. Piles of clay and ash sat like ancient cairns and altars.

There were dozens of separate areas, all under the same big top. Private quarters, showrooms, lecture halls, and sound rooms where musicians played harpsichords and bashed gongs. Pages of poetry lay strewn in the corridors, air currents causing a drift and tide, sweeping opera scores and pornographic cartoon faxes along. There was a time when I really could've gotten into this.

Scattered in the darkened halls and corners people were arguing, napping, drawing charcoal sketches, reading Plath and Thoreau and Lovecraft, getting high colonic cleansings, piercings, dialysis, and scratching each others' eyes out. It took a while to take it all in. There was a parlor where they received slowly spun glyph tattoos in nasty places, 3-D body art where the plastic jutted out of their flesh. I dug some of it. Whispers of adoration, vengeance and admonition floated by—death threats, suicide notes, French horns blaring out of tune, and a chorus of soft sobbing that made the pulse in my throat tick harder.

I was again struck by how this type of artistic coalition hadn't been seen since Warhol's Factory, and the Works reeked of the same posturing. They were all here in their numbers, waiting for something huge to happen. I recognized them as I did any mob. A fusion of the restless and unfulfilled, the unfortunate travelers and prying voyeurs, geniuses with and without talent, and the remarkably well-off and the utterly damned. I kept waiting for somebody to go by in a platinum blond wig. Jolly Nell was right, it was just another sideshow.

"Nice digs," Hertzburg said, enjoying the action, his hair on end. He eyed the many ladies, and perhaps they eyed him as well. People laughed and pointed, maybe at me. His leopard-spotted getup wasn't out of place, and he kept hitting poses, showing off his muscles. "I'm not sure if this is the blackest heart of Babylon, but it's probably close enough."

"I thought it might be too tame for you," I said.

He sniffed the air. "They've been killing each other in here for years and stacking the bodies like cordwood."

"No different than anywhere."

"For you it's going to be."

"We'll see."

"You're never going to get out."

"Fuck that talk," I said. "Find Jonah."

The denizens paraded by, drinking coffee, discussing the Messenean War and Scooby Doo. How the Spartans marched over the Taygetus Mountains and annexed all the territory of their neighbor, Messenia. How Casey Kasem, the unheralded champion of Seventies Saturday morning cartoons, brought a hipster persona to groovy mod rocker Norville "Shaggy" Rogers. The Messenians revolted in 640 B.C. Initial childhood fantasies revolved around Daphne or Fred or both. Velma Binkley, the perfect foil. Almost defeated, controlling the territory of a subject population that outnumbered their population ten to one, it was only a matter of time before the conquerors themselves were overrun. Shaggy and Scooby were a fine pairing in a parody featuring contests to solve mysteries at various abandoned amusement parks with the aid of Batman and Robin, Laurel and Hardy. Downfall due to a culturally stagnant, sterile oligarchy. Downfall due to the interjection of Scrappy Doo.

Some were shirtless, others bare-bottomed, carting books off to Sophomore Lit, hand-correcting papers. They played with knives and carried cereal bowls, and they hummed to John Lennon and recited the poetry of Sappho. Maybe it actually was just like anywhere else, only compacted for efficiency. Hertzburg sneezed and his eyes watered. He smelled death all over the place now.

I could tell who the doomed were. Who was meant to be here and who had strayed in and accidentally been caught in the vortex. Hertzburg enjoyed the sights and kept turning, turning, his arms outstretched and bulging muscles rising higher, ready to launch into the maelstrom. Jolly Nell looked a little scared, but she was still grinning. Juba, expressionless as usual, slid among the throng as men walked between his alpine legs.

Most of the rooms appeared to be holding classes. Small gatherings of twenty or thirty people, in folding chairs taking notes. Discussions ranged from Jane Austen novels to quantum mechanics to the correct way for a matador to sever a bull's spinal column.

Everyone enticed and taken in from the outside, together but doing their own thing, divided yet uniform in their division. I waited to hear some laughter and I kept right on waiting. People were everywhere, moving in their secured orbits, thrumming with constant activity and maneuvering.

I looked down and watched Fishboy Lenny's back flippers flapping wildly as he squirmed through the halls and circled back to us. His flopping, tiny body heaved against my ankle and he stared up at me, making quiet but gruesome sounds from deep in his bulbous abdominal cavity. "Mwaop, mwaopp, ffftteeee, mwwoop, ffftteeee." The inchoate, extraneous gashes of gills opened and closed, sucking air with a coarse popping noise.

Nell cooed, too hefty to bend and reach for him. She said, "There, shhhh, Lenny, it's all right, calm down."

Fishboy Lenny went into a caricature of speech, sputtering through the minuscule abscess of a mouth. "Mwaopp, ffftteeee."

"It's going to be fine. We'll be on our way soon. And then we'll go back to the carnival."

"Mwoop."

"Go play. It's wonderful that you want to make friends."

"Mwoop."

Nicodemus was waiting somewhere close by, with his frying pan and worn verses. He'd have a Bible in the pocket of his frock coat, well-read but misremembered. Onion-skin pages would crinkle from his fetid breath. He was the only person I ever knew who actually underlined passages and check-marked chapters. You could go through and see which stories appealed to him the most.

Genesis 4:2–8 had been entirely underlined. Cain offers the fruit of the ground to God while Abel sacrifices the firstborn of his flocks. *Lamentations 2:20* had a couple of check marks and a large flamboyant asterisk. Wherein one of the prophets dares to say to God, "Shall the women eat their fruit and children of a span long?" Nicodemus had been thinking of sacrificing his kid long before we ever got around to it.

2 Chronicles 36:15–17 was highlighted with a yellow marker. After God's prophets are mocked, the Almighty sends an army to Jerusalem to destroy the city "and had no compassion upon young man or maiden, old man, or him that stooped for age: he gave them all into his hand." *Psalms 144:1* had a check mark slashed so deeply into the paper it cut though fifteen pages. God is praised for being the one that teaches hands how to conduct war and fingers how to fight and shed blood.

My father had a real thing about hands.

I started walking faster, slipping between couples, skimming past a troupe of jugglers who tossed sharpened objects along with eggs and a bowling ball on fire. I knew how to work through a crowd. Nobody touched me.

A few rooms had drapes or beads hanging in the doorways, but almost none of them had any doors. I found one that did and turned the knob: it was a rest home, with about forty eighty-year-olds sucking their gums and shivering in wheelchairs. The smell of shit and gruel grew more distinct and I went into a coughing fit.

Shifting forces clashed, and the noise of the midway bloomed.

Just like in the carny there was a sense of history and foundation, but also the possibility of tear-down. As if it could all be folded up and carried off in a couple of hours, everything gone tomorrow. It felt as if time were running out, but I didn't see how. Even if Nicodemus could leave whenever he wanted, he wouldn't until I found him. He wasn't hiding any longer, if he'd ever been. Maybe he stood just inside the next shadow, holding his skillet.

4

We were throwbacks, my father most of all. You couldn't find a real freak show in the United States anymore, not even in the South where life still hasn't been as homogenized as the rest of the country. Now the only freaks you were likely to come across were the sadomasochists bent on changing themselves into something different. They dreamed of becoming lizards, birds, or fiends that were *other*. It might not be any better, but at least it would be startling and distinct. That counted.

Their shows were inhabited by the tattooed, the pierced, the perforated, and the glorified geeks. The kids who got off on hanging bricks off their pricks, the blockheads who ate glass and nails because their uncles fondled them at six. Self-recreation. The bearded women who took hormones because they wanted the muscle mass, the shriveled tits and that look of terror in the eyes of the audience. It wasn't fouled genetics. It was simply a way to embrace the monstrosity under your skin and still get out alive.

Timeless and resilient, yet comprised of cracked cement and chipped paint, the Works lived with a slow and steady throb. Decades of Manhattan echoes passed through and kept going. Dust rose and dissipated and resettled, all part of the same current. It was relentless yet full of mourning, I thought. The blood of the city dried here, and continued to congeal.

"The Metropolitan Museum of Art spans centuries, millennia," Jolly Nell said. It sort of surprised me that she knew a word like "millennia," though it really shouldn't have. "And this place is even larger."

"It's devoted to more gods," Juba said. "Different, warring."

Nell frowned and waved him off. "I don't know about that, but you can feel them taking the years off, adding them on, in every order here. You need to step back to see the entire picture."

"How far?" I asked.

"Too far. That's why it doesn't work."

"Perhaps you need only to step in," Juba said.

"It's still too far," she said. "They're not getting anywhere. It collapses in on itself and crumbles away."

"Hm."

"I was wrong, this isn't the real sideshow yet. I don't think you'll be able to find your father here."

"Yes, I will," I said. "Juba, what's the view like from up there?"

"Sickening."

Hertzburg let out a small laugh, the kind he made when somebody in the audience tried to rush him. "I find it stimulating."

And it was, in a fashion, like the midway at noon in the heart of a jasmine summer. The power came through, it bled into the air. You didn't have to partake of it or act on it or find pleasure here—you only had to be enfolded. Whether a willing participant, a victim or only open to suggestion.

The placebo effect was already working. The crippled could wander through the Works. Pain could be suppressed, even feasted upon, for a time. Then, the collapse. I looked into faces and wondered what would happen when all their agony came crashing back in. Would it only make them love and need this place more?

Hertzburg was already in the zone, letting it get good to him, feeding off that static charge. The hair on his shoulders stood on end, veins dark and bulging along his thick forearms.

Some kids were strumming eukeleles, gagging on "By the Light of the Silvery Moon." I could imagine Hertzburg going over and grabbing the boys by their throats, holding them out at arm's length so they couldn't touch the floor even on tip-toe. Faces going red, then purple, then black as their swollen tongues unfurled. And the wild man almost gleeful through it all, but also a bit puzzled, trying to study the situation but being too near to see the whole thing. Bringing the dead eyes closer so he could inspect them for something new or forgotten.

"This is just a front, we're only touching on the surface," Jolly Nell told us. She said it as someone who knew a great deal about surfaces. No one ever looked beyond the obesity, seeing all that corpulent flesh and being completely mesmerized by it. The only questions she ever got from the audience were *how* could she let her self get that way, *why* didn't she lose the pounds, and didn't she *fear* heart disease and stroke? Even though she received at least three or four marriage proposals a month, no one ever asked her about anything except what they saw on that soft fat surface.

Juba, taking strides that carried him over three people at a time, wriggled his fingers as if trying to part the air. "I agree, this is the bally. The sideshow is always much deeper within the carny."

"Of course," Hertzburg said. The edges of his beard seemed to be alive with sparks, and you could smell the searing ozone in the air. "But the draw is already tugging us onward."

"You can fight it," Nell told me.

"You think so?" I asked.

"Yes."

"Eh, why bother?"

My father's fragile beliefs couldn't survive intact here. The nudity and drugs and stupidity of youth itself would have scraped against Nicodemus's tender underside and made him want to break his teeth. He'd be ravaging his Bible with red pens and dog-earing the pages about eating your kids.

He couldn't exist without a place of safety, and that meant either the bottle or Jesus.

I stopped in front of a young couple, my age or so, when I am this age. Early twenties but already tired of what it was all about. They sat at the base of a small cardboard set that looked like a little girl's tea room or playhouse, but there weren't any children around. The windows had been drawn on with colored magic markers and could be opened by tugging on a piece of string.

She had plastic flowers in her hair and was coaching him on how to play Stanley in *Streetcar* without sounding so much like Brando. It wasn't going to help and she knew it. The guy wore a tight T-shirt and tried to seem sensitive without pouting, but his bottom lip hung down too far and he kind of sucked on his teeth the way Brando used to. Way too much of the American icon there to ever do it any differently. No one could play *Rebel* without doing Dean, either.

The girl kept trying to get him to forget the movie, and the more she pushed him, the more he started doing Colonel Kurtz in *Apocalypse Now*. I could picture him getting to the "Stella!" part and screaming "The horror! The horror!" instead. I sort of wanted to see that.

They both appeared to be on the gaunt side, faces thin and sallow. He hadn't shaved for a couple of weeks, but his whispy mustache still didn't reach the peach fuzz on his chin. She had warm but uncompromising eyes, and she was at least six months pregnant.

I couldn't figure out a way to frame my question without sounding stupid, so I just let it out. "Is there a church here?"

"What?" Brando asked.

"I asked if there was a church here."

His lip hung lower. "Did I hear that right?"

"I suspect you did. Is there a spot to pray? A chapel?"

"It's all holy ground, man."

That was the kind of dull answer I expected, but I really couldn't blame the guy. "How about a bar?"

"Liquor is everywhere, just look. Reach out. Ask somebody. They'll share with you."

"That wasn't what I asked."

"Well, shit."

Fishboy Lenny smiled as much as he could without lips and scuttled forward on his belly, waving happily to the girl, who sat there nodding.

It would take me weeks to search every area and space inside the Works. I wanted to sleep. I wasn't tired after three days in the rain, but I needed to pick up Nicodemus's trail in the dream.

"Where's the doniker?" I asked.

"The what?"

"A restroom. The toilet."

"What the fuck language are you speaking?"

He didn't have a clue. He looked constipated and unaware of his condition. One of these days his intestines would completely seize up and he'd keel over from a massive stroke.

Sacrifice was an inherent part of becoming something larger, and he might just go the entire distance without ever taking a crap. I could feel the same kind of counterfeit energy in this place as in any bally. The excitement was here but none of the gamble, none of the fun. The tents would always be packed. They wanted love and remembrance, shock, communion. They asked me to glance into their palms in order to get God and their own nettling consciences off their backs. I did what I could. They wanted the freak show.

The pregnant girl, though, kept appraising. I didn't like the way she stared at me. There was a sharpness there, a bit of derision, I thought, though not quite enough to piss me off. But for some reason it did. She cocked her head and peered over my shoulder as if glimpsing the rest of my life layered up behind me. It brought some color into her face and made her even prettier.

Brando reached into the cardboard playhouse and started tangling with something. He drew out a snake. "Meet Lester."

"Is it hot?" I asked.

"What?"

"Is it poisonous?"

"Damn, mister, you got a fucked-up word for everything, I bet. Nah, Lester isn't poisonous."

"Too bad."

"What do you mean by that?"

"I used to wrangle them. There's more gamble to it if they're hot."

"Still hurts like a son of a bitch if he gets a piece of you."

I was suddenly very sick of the guy's voice and wanted her to talk instead, but she wouldn't. I grabbed Lester and brought him up to my face. I'd learned a lot about handling animals, especially reptiles, even before I started eating them.

Lester was easy. After a few moments of zoning the snake, I could get him to copy my motions. He'd tilt his chin when I did, flick his tongue out at mine. Recoil and jut forward following the actions of my head. It was a trick, like everything else, but a fairly good one.

"That's wild," Brando said, defunct, almost dead.

"Yeah."

"He's even blinking when you do."

196

"That's part of the show."

"Can you teach me?"

"It would take too long."

That didn't flatten him. Brando started blinking in time with the snake, in time with me. "What else can you do with Lester?"

"Nothing you'd want to see."

"I want to see everything, man."

He was right, they always wanted to see it all.

I could've bitten Lester's head off and spit it into his lap. I had been a geek for a few years when the whiskey had worn me into a madness much different from my father's. I sweated mash liquor. I smeared myself with my own shit and vomit and shoved empty beer cans up my ass. I'd chewed the heads off chickens, mice and pit vipers and puked them into the crowd.

They loved it.

So did I.

And that's how Megan had found me.

5

I'd been dragged through the slough of cabbage palms and palmettos, where the gators clambered across the mangroves. The carnival had set up outside the broad channels of a swamp and I lived in a cage of gnarled roots sucking the spleens out of frogs. They poled their skiffs from miles around to come watch.

Whatever hit the dirt became a part of me. They thought I was too weak to wrestle the bull gators, but there were plenty of tricks. They expected me to die a hundred times over and I wouldn't go. The toads they tossed me were hot. The mushrooms deadly. The murderous stews should've put me down but didn't. And they loved me and hated me for it. The screams and cheers, the disgusted looks. Cats' entrails and children's beaming smiles. We learned a lot from one another, about how far we were all willing to go.

And in the middle of the madness, at its worst and at its best, somehow the madness ended.

Megan wiped the venom and feathers out of my mouth and held my shoulders down to the mattress while she slowly fed me soup and watered-down scotch. She knew better than to try to get me to go cold turkey. I was so far into the bottle that my heart would've stopped without it. Which might have been a good thing considering the situation.

The dreams had always been bad, but they grew worse while I dried out. The D.T.'s didn't get me shrieking or tearing at my own eyes, though. I'd eaten bugs and rats for years, what did I care if they crawled over me in my delusions?

Instead I was drawn into conversations with the prophets and lepers, kneeling at stone altars beneath a desert sun, carrying children sucking on honey-coated locusts. I decapitated the priests of Baal, climbed mountains of fire. Where was the New Testament? Where had they hidden my forgiveness? Archangel Michael aimed his fiery sword at my heart and plucked it out with one twitch of his wrist.

I was the seer, and I talked endlessly while Megan pressed icy towels to my forehead.

Two weeks passed before the hallucinations and delirium eased enough for me to realize I was no longer rolling in the mud and sawdust, covered in my own puke and blood, having pocket change heaved at me. She'd either bought or stolen me from the carny, I never found out which.

I could only see in shadow at first as she leaned over my chest, a raven figure in an even darker world.

Her silhouette moved like fluid, back-lit by silver. Occasionally I'd hear the rustle of cloth and chiming of metal. A spoon would ease between my lips as shades and dimension slowly filled my mind again.

She had caramel-colored freckles spattered across her nose and cheeks, and a smile that put me at rest like nothing ever had before it. I'd been burning my entire life—first with heavenly fire and then with lust, and finally with whiskey and poison.

But right then, in that first minute as I laid my eyes on her, she cooled my thrashing spirit, and she did it without so much as a word.

She wore a silk kimono showing off every curve, and I saw the firm muscles of her arms and neck as she dipped the spoon again and again, feeding me. I ate more slowly, watching the shape of her lips. She was a beautiful stranger.

I scanned the room. There was a black and white television with rabbit ears in the corner, some Mexican game show flashing silently screaming faces, no sound knob. Dirty venetian blinds were half drawn. I saw a stream of dying orange light. Her cooch costume was thrown over the back of a busted rattan chair, all sequins and chainlets and white plumes. We were in a flea-trap motel and I had bed sores.

She noticed that my eyes had focused on her. "You look awake. Can you see straight yet?"

"Yes." My vocal cords felt like they'd been scoured down

to threads and knotted together. I hadn't spoken a word in over a year, and my voice sounded so much like my father's that it made me look around for him.

"Good. You're strong."

Nobody had ever said that to me before. I didn't know how she could even think it, having cleaned the snake piss off my neck. "No, I'm not."

"We'll see. Now that you're over the worst of it you'll be on your feet again soon."

I thought I recognized her from the cooch dance, but I couldn't be sure of much anymore. Had she been in the audience watching me geek all the animals? Or had I sneaked under the hoof tent and seen her and the other girls teasing the marks? I hadn't had a lick of pride in years, but I suddenly felt a tinge of embarrassment. It was an odd sensation.

"You're with the carny?" I asked.

"Not anymore," she said. "Not that one. They tore down and left town seven or eight days ago."

"I'm sorry," I told her, and I was. "You must know the route. You can still catch up."

"Hell no. It was the worst one I'd ever worked. I got hired on outside of Edmond six weeks ago and hated every minute of it in that show. Dyson ought to be arrested, the way he runs it."

"Dyson?"

"The owner."

He must've taken me on, but I couldn't remember. Her accent had a nice flair. It was Southern but without any drawl. East Texas, I guessed, somewhere out in the flats and deep scrub. I kept staring at her lips, and she didn't seem to mind. "Why'd you help me?"

"You needed it."

"I'm nothing to you. I'm—"

That smile again, comforting and cooling as she pressed a damp rag to my throat once more. "I know who you are," she said. "You healed me once."

6

I felt something touch my ankle and thought it was Fishboy Lenny, but when I looked down I saw that Lester had followed after me and was now winding his way around my leg.

The girl walked alongside us. She was smiling in a self-satisfied way, as if she'd just found a new partner she could help through a Tennessee Williams play. I had caught her attention and felt uncomfortable with the fact. Her pregnancy reminded me that I was really only here to get back Jonah.

"You've got the serpent wrapped up tight," she said.

It might've been a vague reference to Satan, but that sort of crap didn't do much for me. "Not exactly. More like he's got me wrapped."

"He likes you."

"Most snakes do for some reason."

"What are you looking for here?"

"My kid."

She moved easily, even though her belly was already protruding quite far. I had the urge to press my palm there, or my cheek, and rest for a while. Despite those shrewd eyes there was a trace of naiveté to her. Or perhaps that was only my penchant for seeing innocence where it didn't exist.

"You're here to find your own kid?"

"Yeah."

"That's a new one. Usually they drive up outside and dump them off without hardly even slowing down."

There was also something about her that touched me in all the wrong places. "Listen—"

"What?"

"No offense, really. But leave me alone."

"Nobody wants to be alone."

"Terrific. Then how about if you just get the hell out of my way."

She ignored that and glided beside me, the hem of her dress drifting against her knees as she unwound Lester from my leg and lifted him into her arms and held him like a baby. I didn't think anything in the world could ever unsettle me anymore, but I was starting to get that feeling.

"You carry a lot of guilt," she said.

"Doesn't everybody?"

"No. I don't."

"You sure of that?" I asked.

"Some of us set down our burdens."

"Some of you are assholes."

She let loose with a delicate giggle that floated around for a minute like cotton candy on the wind. "Isn't everybody?"

"Just about."

She quit talking for a while but kept up with my quick pace. I couldn't shake her. I wanted to run and didn't know why.

Maybe it had something to do with her belly. I kept flashing on Megan, pregnant and cheerful, scribbling names on a piece of paper and asking me which ones I liked. One column for boys, the other for girls, and me pushing for the sonogram.

I wondered if Brando was still going through the motions, maybe trying a little of *On the Waterfront* or *The Wild One* by now. Tennessee Williams must've been spitting up bottle caps in his grave.

"You're from down south," she said. "Whereabouts?"

"All of it."

"Yeah, that makes sense. You've hardly any accent. And you've got a New Yorker attitude."

"Anybody who's dealt with a lot of people does."

"Maybe that's true."

"I think it is."

She kept on smiling and Lester glared in my direction, flicking his tongue at me. That titter slipped out of her unconsciously, like a nervous tic. It was getting under my skin for no reason at all. She really did remind me too much of Megan when Megan carried Jonah, so lovely in the pale morning light. They both had that same kind of childlike candor.

"I'm Lala," she said.

"Your parents named you Lala?"

"I named myself that."

"Oh."

"I should be in charge of my own identity, don't you think?"

"Sure."

"You can, you know," she told me. "It'll be fine. Go ahead."

"I can what?"

"Touch me."

It stopped me for a second. It wasn't a sexual come-on, just a friendly gesture. She'd sensed my urgency to hold that life close and she'd made the sympathetic offer. I didn't realize my needs were so transparent. My geek self was bleeding through, out of control and wailing in the dirty straw.

I gently laid the back of my hand against her belly and felt the pulsing of her warm womb.

My ancestry called to me in my veins. It's happened before. Nature expects value from us. I closed my eyes and was fine for a moment, standing there smirking and floating away, and then it got to be too much. A surge of memories brought up all my love and bile in one swift surge. I yanked my hand away as if scalded, but it was already too late and always had been. A moan began to rise in my chest and I choked it back down. The girl wore Megan's smile.

I was nothing but memories now, stuffed with them, fueled by them. Lala's eyes flitted, that serene gaze wafting across me, here and there. Her clothes smelled of hash and ten dollar cigars, but whether she'd been smoking or it was simply this place, I didn't know. Lester looked a little high.

"You haven't come here to find out anything about life," Lala said, "so it must be about death."

I let that one go by. "Do you know where Paynes is?"

"Paynes? Jesus, is that what you're here for?" Again her grin angled up, the fanciful glint shining in her eyes. "I should've guessed. No wonder you carry a lot of guilt, if that's who you're after."

"Where is he?"

"Nobody knows that."

"I bet my father does," I said. I hadn't meant to speak it aloud. I was slipping more and more.

"Why?"

"I've got an instinct for these things. Paynes might have seen him."

"Your father? You're after your father? Why?"

"Because the old man stole my son from me and I want him back."

"Why?"

"You're a pretty annoying cooch," I told her.

"Whatever that means. I like the sound of your voice. There's power there. You take charge."

"It's a gift."

"Is it?"

I thought about that. We could go around in circles for days. No wonder I didn't like her much. "Probably not."

Lester seemed to have a lot on his mind. He wavered as he slid into Lala's arms, rising and flowing, quietly hissing. Perhaps he'd heard about me gnawing off the heads of his cousins for a pint of gin. A thing like that got around. Lala kissed him between the eyes, nodded at me as if she'd be back shortly, and turned away. I blinked and she was gone.

Fishboy Lenny waved a flipper after her. Or maybe he just wanted to say good-bye to Lester.

Jolly Nell said, "A sweet girl. Don't get this one killed."

I wandered on.

7

Nicodemus stood tall. Barely topping 5'9 in his boots, he still carried with him an imposing will. Raw-boned and wiry with especially large hands hanging off his thin wrists. One arm was always slightly akimbo, as if he were about to elbow somebody in the ribs. He spoke hard words, inflexible and severe, yet his voice was always calm, almost mild, even when damning some poor bastard on the spot.

He took to the bottle early and only gave it up whenever he found Jesus. When he lost Jesus he'd find the bottle again, and that's the way it went on for most of his life. He knew himself but never truly understood what he wanted, and his expectations were convoluted at best.

He'd drifted across Oklahoma and Texas working on oil well crews and laying pipe for the drilling rigs, preaching to the other vagrants and runaway kids that rambled into camp. He used a trenching shovel to hurl a Rotary-rig operator off a derrick during a drunken brawl and just kept on kicking it down to Mexico until he faded into the jungles. He hooked up with a missionary in South America for a time and took a couple of poisoned blow darts in the back. Two small but thick puckered scars rose from just over his kidneys, close enough together to have been serpent fangs. Sometimes the symbol matters a lot more than the message.

He never said how he and my mother had met. For a while I assumed she was a river-bottom whore who'd begun to tire of the business. It was common in those parts. But eventually

I found a few black-and-white photos he'd cached away. There were looping ball-point scribbles on the back, and though I tried for years to decipher the words, I never did.

The photographs showed a young woman with a heart-shaped face framed by a toss of brown curls. She wore a some-what sad smile and in every picture she was looking down or away. Fingers splayed as if warding off the camera. She had petite porcelain white hands.

I took her, whoever she was, to be my mother. I needed her that much, and I thought those hands would have appealed to Nicodemus enough for him to marry her.

My mother died giving birth to me, in the center of the storm, at the bottom of a drainage ditch. Nicodemus had quit on Jesus by then, come back to the States, and started working as a fry cook at a truck stop where the lot lizard whores took home at least half his pay. He got along well with the truckers. They engaged each other in their tales of adventure and hard-ship traveling across the country, the women they laid, the jails they'd done time in. For the most part I could picture him as an agreeable and jocular man, though by the time I could talk he was neither.

Oddly enough, for someone who spent eighteen hours a day out of the house, he was home for her when she went into labor. My mother already had a small valise packed. She'd fed the cats and used a neighbor's phone to call ahead to the hos-pital. She'd blown out the candles and sat waiting on the couch while he buckled his pants on. Nicodemus had been ignoring the bills over the last few months and yet she'd never argued with him over any of it. Had she lacked the nerve? Had he beaten her into meek compliance? I didn't believe so. I'd thought about it for a long time. She must've known that the only way to handle my father was to leave him be—whether he was boozing or on the ground bleeding.

He'd been drunk for three days and driving her to the hospital in his pickup truck when they hit a muddy curve too fast, flipped on Highway 17 and went over a twenty-five-foot embankment. My father passed in and out of consciousness for the next several hours, driven by her screams, he said, while angels called to him and the tips of their gleaming strange wings brushed against his lips.

He said.

Nicodemus had been spattered and blinded by motor oil, transmission fluid and streaming water. The rain poured in through the smashed windshield and put out the flames creeping near the ruptured gas tank. When he came to again he realized they were upside down, my mother trapped in her seat belt, her twisted legs hanging wide open toward his face. I was already squirming from her shattered pelvis as her heart continued to feed the muscles that shoved me forward into the world.

With his left arm broken and pinned beneath the wreckage he reached over with his free hand and caught me as I slithered from her womb, already falling.

He managed to undo her bloody blouse and pressed me to my mother's dying breast, where I fed until long after her milk and body had turned cold. I'd been nursed by a corpse.

It was the truth, but the story had plenty of tragedy, tear-jerking melodrama, miracle and morbidity in it, which worked wonders on the stage.

How they came in droves to see the child preacher who'd

been born in the midst of lightning, with a torrent of rain washing across his dead mother, while his father slowly began to drown and held the babe up above the raging waters of that black ditch. And everybody especially liked the gleaming wings of angels bit.

It was my father's first gesture toward becoming myth, and that was all he really needed. By the time a passing trucker hauling cabbage stopped to help, and the rescue crews arrived, Nicodemus was back on the trail to God and so hopped up on Jesus that his broken arm didn't even bother him.

Neither did the death of my mother.

He had a son.

8

I walked around the Works for a day and a half. I sat in on a few classes. One instructed you on how to prepare cheese blintzes in blackberry sauce. Always put the "seam-side" of the crepes down on the wax paper, cooking the blackberries in a sauce pan over low heat until bubbling, then pulping them with a potato masher. Jolly Nell couldn't sit beside me because there was only one free seat, so she found a place in the back where she could take up three chairs.

She made such sounds of delight at each step of the preparation that the chef eventually focused all his attention on her, whether he saw her or not, and held up the plates to show off the ingredients before and after adding them together. Depending on the blackberries and your preferences, you might want to strain out the seeds using a sieve. Add sugar, mix water and cornstarch in a small cup and pour into the sauce. Serve on the side or put a dollop on each blintz.

Another lecture was for a martial arts–street fighting class that taught forty ways to kill a man with your bare hands. I walked in during the middle of it and watched two guys hold back their fervor while speaking clearly and with authority, dropping one another to a cement floor without any mats. I borrowed a pencil and some paper from the guy next to me and jotted a few helpful notes.

Striking the nasion, which is the summit of the nose, with sufficient force may result in death. Attacking the philtrum, the area between the upper lip and the bottom of the nose, may also cause mortal damage. I liked that term "mortal damage" and underlined it several times. I resisted the urge to add an asterisk. A sharp blow to the Adam's apple can cause a man to asphyxiate. A blow to the base of the cerebellum, at the nape of the neck, can bring about death.

Catch someone in a full nelson and bend his neck forward until it breaks or the supply of spinal fluid is cut off to the brain. The Russian Omelet had you cross an enemy's legs and fold him by pinning his shoulders to the ground, upside down and sitting on his legs until the base of his spine cracked. The Brain Buster placed a man in a headlock as you quickly grabbed his belt and yanked him into the air until he was vertical and upside down. Then you dropped him on his head, which absorbed your combined weight. Most effective on concrete or gravel.

I really wanted a crepe now, but by the time I got back to the first room the class had become a performance art piece. I might've been seeing things but it appeared that the walls had been let out a few extra feet. I couldn't figure out how it was done. Six ballerinas carried television sets with live video feed and mimed making love to the various faces that sprang across the screens. I kind of enjoyed watching the show, but I was still hungry for a blintz.

The size of the spaces in the Works was deceiving, the way they could run into one another, alternating, traveling, trans-forming. Construction went on overhead, workers doing some brick work. Bulky guys in hard hats moved machinery and scaffolding. Murals and posters were being put up and taken down with great frequency. Even advertisements, local sales. Who the hell cared about discounts to Six Flags Great Adventure? Who could ever get out of here and play on the rides?

Like graffiti, the process was ongoing and profitless. If one leg on the vast amount of scaffolding buckled the whole setup would drop and take out two hundred people. Kids composed haiku and smoked grass under it, elderly couples strolling along with their canes and kerchiefs.

Nell said, "I smell bacon."

My stomach trembled.

"Me too," I told her, but I knew it wasn't bacon. So did she. I tried slipping by her but she grabbed my shoulder with one of her massive hands, held me up and carried me along. It had weight and solidity. Juba's shadow fell across my face and I was suddenly cool and in darkness. At times they appeared to interact with the world and be seen by others. People bounced off Jolly Nell or gazed upon the entirety of Juba, and women flirted with Hertzburg and all his hair.

I said, "I can't remember if you're alive or dead."

Hertzburg frowned and shrugged as we passed by a barber shop. "You've said that about yourself as well."

"I know it."

"Does it really matter to you that much?"

"Sometimes."

He smelled of burned—"Maybe you'll figure it out."

"I get the feeling I won't."

"Who gives a shit at this point? So long as you finish what's been started. Don't put such a high premium on truth."

"Me?"

A new warren of paths and alleys opened. Scattered in the corridors of the Works people slept, sketched, sat reading Harlan Ellison's *Deathbird Stories*, Jim Thompson's *The Killer Inside Me*, newspapers and menus. Playing the clarinet, dropping acid and chalking pentagrams on the floor. They recited puerile passages from Crowley and LaVey. I used to do the same thing.

I expected to see religious fanatics, a few Jesus freaks going off the deeper end, but there weren't any. That surprised me. The hordes of rats hung back in the converted meat lockers knocking off the weak, and the Goth-gurrls and leather-deathers wearing their scars and vampire paleness giggled like virgins and scampered around the show rooms painting themselves with latex.

Juba said, "He won't come to you now, you know, in your vague and ugly dreams."

"Oh yes, he will."

"No, Nicodemus could reach you across all your nightmares while you were on the outside—"

"So?"

"—but now even your vengeance belongs to the Works."

212

I couldn't help it. I burst out laughing.

Not that cool clear kind of chuckling but the real rot-gut that brings up acid from the back end of your life. It kept coming and coming while I gasped and wheezed, my heart starting to hurt and my muscles locked out of place. I glanced at the enormity surrounding me, understanding that it was nowhere near large enough to contain all my hate.

Finally I settled back and wiped the tears off my chin.

Fishboy Lenny said, "Mwoop fwsshh mwaop mwaop," and I totally agreed with him, whatever it meant.

"Yeah, buddy."

"Mwoop."

I went to find a place to drop off, in order to hear the harsh and bitter words of my father.

9

Megan believed in redemption and revelation, down where it mattered. She blamed me for that. I had healed her once, she said, at twelve. Troubles in her stomach, brought on by a beating from her older brother after he'd kneed her out in the woodshed, prying her legs apart.

She'd had ulcers throughout her childhood, with her grandfather offering rags dipped in sterno to kill the pain. Hemorrhaging for months and dealing with the bruises and cramps. The constant nausea of hopelessness and loss terrified her less than something unknown. She was changing.

The discomfort and swelling in her belly grew worse each day until her parents finally dead-bolted her in her bedroom, away from the truancy officers and sheriff's deputies. Its sole window faced the woodshed, where her brother wept and howled and threw his shoulder against the chained door. He had changed too.

Her grandfather, spitting blood, sneaked her out of the house, still gulping sterno and letting her suck a soaked shred of cloth. He carried her most of the six miles to the tent revival all-night sing, where I laid my hands upon her.

The next morning she blessed my name because the pain was gone. God had become second string. A lifetime of prayers had been answered at last and heaven had nothing to do with it.

She whispered my praises as her mama bundled up the bedsheets and set fire to them in the yard.

Her brother had broken his neck hurling himself against the woodshed wall, sometime before sunrise. Her parents didn't cry. They didn't bother to bury him. They tossed his corpse onto the fire and then collected the bones and ashes and threw them into the scrub.

Megan believed I had cleansed her, and now she returned the favor.

I had taken the hideous baby out of her body, she thought, and she loved me for it.

10

Circling, I hunted for a way to get to the regions inside the Works that I hadn't been to yet. I seemed to be traveling in a well-defined rut, unable to slip out of the channel, going around and around. Construction continued in the buildings, hammering taking the top of my skull off and electric drills whining constantly. Maybe if I planted myself in this spot the rest of the Works would eventually come to me.

Brando was hitting his post-*Superman* stride, all the downhill stuff. *A Dry White Season*, *Don Juan DeMarco*, and oh my Christ *The Island of Dr. Moreau*. It almost hypnotized me, the way he brought it all into *Streetcar*. He still wore the dirty T-shirt and he looked even more constipated.

"Where's Lala?" I asked.

"Who?"

"That girl who was coaching you a couple days ago."

"Oh her. I never seen her before or since. Stupid chick didn't have any idea what it means to be an actor. Kept telling me to play it real. If I wanted to be real, then what the shit would I be an actor for?"

"Good point."

"Worse," he said, "I think she stole my snake."

"Too bad, man."

"Yeah."

Brando went back to doing his thing, now up to the Blanche Dubois rape scene. I watched for another minute or two and then backed away to the cardboard playhouse. I climbed inside and yanked the string and closed the paper window. It was dark but comfortable.

Outside, Juba leaned down to the window and hissed against it. "If you go to sleep you may never awaken again. We didn't."

"Ya pays yer money and ya takes yer chances," I said.

"You've just crawled into your own grave."

I was getting a little tired of his constant nettling. I might've felt guilty, but not enough for me to keep putting up with it. "Have you found Jonah yet?"

"No."

"Then stop pestering me and go look."

I heard the cartilage in his knees, elbows and spine crackling as he stood and stood and kept on standing up to his full height before finally moving off.

Nell talked through the ceiling and said, "Pleasant dreams."

I could still smell bacon frying, and the stink of my father's breath.

I slept.

11

Come find me, Nicodemus asked, and there was a hint of fear in his voice. *God's got us all out on the rock, he does. It started with me but I guess it's gotta end with you, that's the way of things. Sometimes our sacrifices are spurned. By God or by our kin. Just go on and ask Cain hisself. He was damned, but he was the chosen one. Just like you.*

My father liked to play to my vanity even though I wasn't vain. It was part of his myth in the making. *Jonah hasn't got any more need of you now, and for that alone you ought to get on your knees and be thankful. A child can be a disagreeable thing. It grows heavy. There's a need to drop our sacks by the roadside.* As if I could do that, as if I would ever do that.

He must've had the bottle again, something to give him a

backbone. When he said my son's name it clutched in his throat and came out like a jagged piece of terror. *You're flesh of my flesh. What's yours is mine. We's still family, despite everything. The blood in your veins runs only because I willed it to be done. But the suffering, that there is your debt to be paid, and so's mine. You owe that much.* Talk about a Christ complex, give it a rest.

Funny how he never mentioned murder. His lips pulled off his dry teeth and settled into a grim smile. I knew I was going to kill him and wondered if Jonah would eventually feel the need to do the same to me. That would be all right. *We're laid out on the rock. It's where we all wind up 'neath the eye 'a God.* I took it as metaphor. Maybe it was true.

Sometimes the old man was inside my head, and sometimes it was just the hurricane.

12

After I'd quit my ministry at fourteen, I watched my father losing his messiah inch by inch and day by day, just as I was. We drank together and got into bar brawls three or four nights a week, and as the money ran out we formed a sort of peace with our ruin. Or so I thought until the day he tried to murder me.

Nicodemus had never been any good with the cash when it was rolling in. Even when he was loaded he played the horses and gave most of it away in bizarre fits of charity. He did some hard-line preaching of his own for a while as I sat in the back pew watching, pondering what the true intent was behind his words. He chose obscure passages from the Bible and made haphazard leaps in logic trying to understand the ways of God. It got them tittering in their seats now and then. He carried his conflicts right into the pulpit, the same way I'd done.

Often when he raged about sin and trespasses he broke down into sobs or wracking laughter. If he could get away with it, he pretended to fall into a spell of tongues, but usually they caught him faking it and left him there. We shared a pint down at the river once, just before he was about to do a group baptism, and the sun and the lilacs helped us to get a good high going. He wound up holding some chunky teenager beneath the water too long and nearly drowned the kid in the muddy bottoms. Nicodemus left his congregation long before they left him.

He had plenty of guns but chose to do me in with a frying pan.

He stalked outside my bedroom one morning when I was hungover and sleeping with Miss Chastity Flo, the only town whore who still had most of her teeth. She had a way about her that kept a wounded man oozing but alive. She'd bruised a couple of my vertebrae, broken the headboard, and swallowed my last half pint of whiskey. I was down to cooking sherry. It'd been a rough night.

The agony had already started in my sleep and I awoke with my stomach twisted with the approach of evil. I fell out of bed and went to my knees, gasping and grinding my back teeth together. Miss Chastity Flo opened her eyes, yawned and started to laugh. She thought it was kind of funny and sexy, what I was doing down there, and she leaned back on the bed and spread her legs farther apart.

I was drunk and groggy and the swirling black energy of

wrongness skewered through my chest. I twitched and gouged the dirty floor with my fingernails until they cracked.

Nicodemus stepped in, wearing his frock coat and hat, ready to give his last sermon, holding his frying pan. When she spotted him she said, "Is he gonna cook us breakfast in bed?"

"Get out, go on!" I yelled.

"But I'm sort of hungry. I could use some scrambled eggs and sausage. You worked me up an appetite, son. Ain't ya at least gonna feed me after all I done for you last night?"

"Go," I moaned. "The hammer's about to fall."

"Are you two kiddin' me? You got any more scotch in the house? This sherry ain't worth shit."

Nicodemus started his swing, but he couldn't raise the heavy iron skillet high enough with his bad arm to fully connect with the back of my head. He caught me with only a glancing blow and proceeded to hunt me around the house, shrieking verse from the Old Testament and generally getting his quotes wrong. Miss Chastity Flo thought it was all very mystical, mysterious and entertaining—me scrambling with my naked white ass hanging out, the old man screaming with his pan—until he stopped in his tracks, wheeled and went after her.

I could barely see with the blood in my eyes. His first swing caught her in the mouth and there went her teeth. I was wrong, some of them were fake. I saw a partial bridge go flying. The searing in my guts grew much worse. Miss Chastity Flo tried to talk with her crushed lips, to beg or argue with Nicodemus about the evils of murder, but she didn't have much time as he brought the skillet down twice more on the sweet spot of her skull.

The pan rang out with two nice notes, one low and one

high, like a choir getting in tune. Miss Chastity Flo's ears spurted red and her eyes rolled up.

Nicodemus, whom I'd seen in all his many states of being, fooled me this time with his insanity. It was both familiar and yet altogether new. And like the skillet, he was now filled with a unique and absurd purpose. I leaned against the far wall and sat heavily as my father approached.

His face glowed with unshakable resolution. I cocked my head at him and my blood sluiced across my brow. I think I was smiling. I'd been waiting for this for a long time, in one manner or another. I wanted to die, or so I'd thought. This was an opportunity not to be missed. I couldn't do it by myself, and I'd been waiting for the finality of his fist to strike. I wondered if he would tell me that God had set him upon this righteous path or if he'd bear up beneath his own feelings. He'd always hated me. Right from the first second when I'd lunged from my dying mother's womb and fallen into his mighty hand.

On the stage, I'd offered possible redemption to those who asked and those who didn't. But as a drunkard and a failure, I mirrored only his own guilt and doom. I wore his face.

As he came closer, his fury so evident and well lit, I did something I'd never done before.

I preached at him. I hurled hellfire.

He screamed as if I'd tossed embers into his eyes and he ran screeching out of the house and down the dirt road. I called the sheriff's office but was so sick on sherry that by the time they got there I wasn't making much sense. They soon grew disgusted and worked me over some. It was understandable. Half the folks in the county were related to Miss Chastity Flo by stock or marriage, and I was at least partly responsible for her death.

But justice for whores is short in coming, and after a few days they let me go. I went home and looked at my father's footprints in the dust.

Nicodemus hadn't returned to the shack and never would. I set it on fire and watched it blaze down to ashes while my guts crawled with a hint of depravity to come. The flames would follow.

13

When I stirred again I felt clear and capable. I'd broken onto a new track and could get someplace now. The playhouse was stale and rank with my own breath, and when I pulled the string to open the cardboard window it was like letting in a new morning.

I climbed out and Fishboy Lenny happily waved to me and said, "Mwoop, ftssshawww."

"Hey, buddy."

"Mwaoop."

I could feel the awful tension building inside me again, black and seeping, but I didn't resist, I tried to ride the crest. Engulfed from the inside out, I shuddered so violently I nearly bit through my tongue. The sweat did a slow skid down my neck. Whatever was about to hit this time would lead me to my vengeance or death or salvation. I didn't much care which it would be so long as it was soon.

Lala spun past and she wasn't pregnant anymore.

"Jesus holy Christ," I whispered.

She saw me and kept walking, shambling in an odd fashion. She no longer moved quickly and easily though the obstacles of the Works. Obviously she was in some pain and a nasty hitch wrecked her careful stride.

The hem of her dress was dappled with crimson and still wet and dripping. Lester slid around in her grasp and gazed backward over her shoulder, as if he had a score to settle with someone they'd just left behind.

I got up close and Lala stopped, frowning. She didn't meet my eyes. Lester did, his head moving in a jerky way, back and forth. I realized he was imitating my own gestures, and that I was quivering badly.

Her lips were white and going blue. A crease between her eyes had deepened to where it appeared as if she'd been slashed by a razor. I shouldn't have been so blatant about it, but I couldn't help myself. I stared and inspected her, thinking it was some kind of a trick yet unable to figure out how it was done. She'd been crying and salt streaks dusted her hair.

I could see it happening—lying back in the stirrups, weeping quietly, the tears trailing through her curls toward her ears. Maybe it was for the best, but who the hell knew. Her eyes were pink and puffy and some of the naiveté had been kicked to death there. I still didn't completely believe it and pressed my palm to her trim belly. I wanted confirmation. We all did.

"Don't touch me," she said.

"What?"

"I don't want you to touch me anymore. I know I said you could before but not now, all right?"

"Okay."

"Just keep your hands off me, got it?"

"Sure."

It wasn't a gaff. She'd had an abortion somewhere inside the Works. It had never shocked or surprised me before, but now it struck an aching chord because I was searching for my own son. She was just a kid locked inside a shadow existence of eclipse and ephemera.

Symbols matter more than all your taxes. Signs and portents can carry you further than your sterno-gulping grandfather. I dropped my eyes and couldn't think of anything to say or do, so I turned aside.

Lester made a pretty good leap for a snake of his size. He coiled and snapped up through the air. I caught him in one hand and let him swing around my wrist. It was a sight that would've played out well in the carny. The audience would've given a nice round of applause even if I didn't bite his head off. I wasn't sure whether I should stop and hand him back to Lala or just keep on going. I hesitated for an instant and then walked along.

She followed me again, and when she began crying I held her while Lester twined around us both. Megan's presence became very strong, and I could feel her in my arms for an instant, her cooling touch easing my seething mind. Lala sagged a bit. The blood on her dress smeared against my knees. The pungent odor brought death back into my watering mouth.

I used my thumbs to brush away her tears. Lala whispered something I didn't catch. "What's that?"

"She wanted out."

A freeze started low in my bowels and continued growing until I couldn't feel my fingertips anymore. We were out of the rut all right, and on our way. "What do you mean?"

"The baby. I wanted to get rid of her, but I couldn't stop her either. I had to let her out."

"You did?"

"Yes. It's what I needed to do, but more than that. It's what this whole place here . . . everything, all of it around us, what it wanted her to do."

"I'm missing something, Lala—"

"You see, it should've been my choice, and that was stolen from me."

"Listen, I don't think I—"

"That's why . . . that's the reason, see? If it was her decision, that would be fine, but I don't think it was. And *he kept her.*"

"Who?"

"The man in the Clinic. The doctor, or whoever. He took her and put her in a jar."

"Oh fuck."

"He never even asked me anything, to take a last look, he just carried her away." Lala trembled and turned an awful shade of green as her legs gave out. I held her while she vomited twice, and though I tried to get her to lay down she wouldn't give in. She was still spotting a little. "He had no right to do that, the rotten bastard! It's unfinished now. I have to go back."

"I'll go with you."

She lifted her chin. "You will?"

"Sure," I told her.

But my smile must've been something heinous to see. She drew away. So did Lester.

Now I knew where to find Nicodemus and Jonah.

14

And I had been resurrected and lifted from my tomb.

Megan healed me. She hauled me away from the geek life and gave me back my Talk. She took God out of my divine voice and discovered enough of the man left to put back into it. I learned to say what I'd always wanted to say. I no longer acted simply as a vessel for some louder, larger Word. She taught me to whisper in the cold night, and to whimper as well.

She danced the cooch dances across stained motel carpets and asked for criticism that might inspire her to do better. It was actually an art form for her; that's what made it so exquisite and heartbreaking.

But I could only stare and grin like an idiot, or sometimes fall apart in the twirling light of her passion. Her small hands rubbed the dead past out of my back. Her lips entranced me when she sang along to Top 40 hits that would've made even a geek gag. I followed her mouth the way the snakes had followed mine, tilting my head toward the jut of her tongue. She returned my chatter and how she loved to gossip. We never shut up for weeks on end.

When we hooked up with McKenna's Carnival, I had the gift once more. I could size up a person's pain and haul them inside with a nod, a few carefully placed words or a glance into the madball.

Megan looked so beautiful while pregnant that McKenna didn't want to take her out of the dance tent even after she started putting on weight. He still billed her as the star. Megan would smile at me from across the midway and my enigmatic act would be shot to hell. I'd be in the middle of a darkly cryptic reading, turning the tarot and gazing into the crystal ball, peering beyond the veil with the rubes on the edges of their seats, and suddenly the giddiness of our love would tickle me under the heart and I'd boil over into laughter. I'd lay on the bed holding her belly close and dream of children in the moonlight.

It was a good life until Nicodemus found me and burned it all down.

I had the sense that I was losing years and losing ground. "How old am I?" I whispered.

"How should I know?" Lala said.

"You're still a child," Jolly Nell told me. "The congregation loves you. There's still time to revel in your sanctity."

"Yes."

"You haven't even lifted a girl's skirt yet. You're thirteen . . . no, twelve . . . and haven't found the bottle yet. They bring you their devotion. You soothe the soul with your shrieking fits. Your father is behind you, on the stage, proud and stately and satisfied."

"That's right."

"Are you doing okay?" Lala asked. "You look sort of out of it. You're scaring Lester."

"Sorry."

An August evening, cool with a storm on the horizon, the wind rising slightly and the crowds pouring in. The cotton candy machines hummed without rest. I put in a few extra hours reading futures and gaping into the madball. Megan had finally started to show too much for the dance numbers and I didn't want her exerting herself anyway. She helped out under

226

the food top and worked some of the concession stands when the crowds got thick.

But that night she was in our trailer on the far side of the lot, thinking up names for the kid. I suppose all new parents fall into the pursuit of that, but with Megan it wasn't just a pastime. She took it extremely seriously, just like the dancing. She hadn't wanted to know the sex of our child but I did and she put up with the ultrasound for my benefit. We were going to have a boy.

She had a lot of Irish in her and she kept coming up with all this Celtic: Colin, Eoghain, Dylan, Cormac, O'Connell. She stayed away from biblical names, and that was fine with me.

I'd just turned over the Ten of Swords and the Hanging Man when the agony speared me through the kidneys. I grunted and chewed my tongue. The mark was an elderly lady around seventy years old, and when my face blanched she figured I saw her death in the deck.

"Oh lordy, lordy!" she shouted. "It's my colon, ain't it? I knew that damn doctor done give me somethin' awful bad with his probin' black fingers! I got cancer of the colon!"

"Lady—help, go get somebody—"

"We needs help for my colon!" she squawked, running in circles in front of the tent. "The magic man says so!"

I smelled bacon.

No one knew where the fire had started, but the center sideshow tents went up immediately, followed by the bally platforms and canvas partitions of the milk bottle and ball game and squirt gun concessions. The roustabouts labored in a frenzy to save what they could.

I worked the hose and bucket lines, but it was already way

too late. Most of the freaks were dead from the flames or smoke inhalation. The pickled punks had boiled in their jars.

The arsonist had spread gallons of gasoline and alcohol around, possibly for hours, and no one had noticed a thing. Hertzburg had tried to save two women from his audience, but by the time he made it out of the inferno and onto the midway he was a blazing pyre holding two molten corpses. He lived for almost six hours, longer than any man should have been able to. He'd been using vegetable oil in his hair to give it a shine, and when he went up he ignited as if he'd been dipped in phosphorus.

Finally he gave up the fight. Perhaps the ghosts of Juba and Nell had talked him into slipping free from his immolated shell. Even then, it would've taken some convincing.

When I got back to our trailer I found Megan on the bed.

She had a couple of Irish legend high fantasy novels out, as well as the Big Book of Baby Names. They'd been tossed onto the floor and stepped on.

Nicodemus hadn't used a skillet. Instead, he took his time with a busted whiskey bottle. I'd kicked it aside as I entered.

A Bible had been left open on her dead breast.

With her blood he'd circled the name Jonah, and the child was gone.

15

The flood was upon us, and I wanted to go with it. I followed Lala to the Clinic where the walls and the floors and the ceilings demanded offerings. Stone and dust also needed life and lineage. We went deeper and deeper into the entrails of the Works, passing others who swept by like wraiths.

Beads draped in doorways fluttered in the heated draft. Poetry drifted around our feet, pages turning, unmerciful stanzas beckoning. A furnace roared nearby. I knew the sound of fire. Newly made pottery sat out in the halls, glazed and smoking, sacred vessels used to hold cannabis or recently removed organs. Freshly finished paintings remained tacky to the touch.

A geek could go places where almost no other man could. The serpent inside his stomach, his head inside the serpent. I was off on a tangent and yet this was somehow also coming full circle. The two ends of my life were meeting in the middle. It wouldn't take long now. The currents swirled to take on new shapes. Hollow-eyed women walked past, speckling the floor with trails of red.

Others stepped by all the more stronger for it, shaking their heads, annoyed perhaps, or strident. They'd done what needed to be done and there were other things to do now. We stood in the atmosphere of the pulpit, where belief and lunacy meshed with mash liquor and fable. It was necessity. Lala led me on. Wooden statues of Irish folk heroes appeared from out of mounds of sawdust. Faces formed of terra cotta and porcelain stared at us as we walked past. My father had found a home here—where religion and injury and flesh fused into something both living and dead.

Juba said, "Stop. Don't go any farther."

"Why?"

He didn't answer. His eyes were full of worry as he wet his lips. Juba hesitated in the air, and I could see each beat of his heart through that nutmeg skin. He grew upset, his blood coursing and his heart pounding heavily in his tissue-thin chest. His oblong head tipped one way and then the other.

I grinned at him. "Because you can't go beyond this point?"

"There are limits."

"Sure. Don't worry. I'll get it done without you."

"I know that. I've always known that."

Lala watched without knowing what she was witnessing. She said, "There are shadows. There are bones in the walls."

Nell spread her arms and I dropped inside them, holding on tight enough to break any other woman's back. But she only squeezed harder, engulfing me in the warm welcome of her soft flesh. I fell and kept falling into that feathery bed of her body, until the tears came and I could almost believe she was my mother hugging me with all the lost love I'd never known.

"Take care of yourself," she said.

"I will."

Hertzburg shook my hand and I could feel the naked power within him, the wildness, wherever he was. "You shouldn't have to be alone. I'll make the effort if you want me to."

"No need for that. You've got other things to do now. Go on."

"You're certain?" he asked.

"It'll be all right. Trust me."

He nodded and stroked his great beard, inspecting me, unable to decide whether I was strong enough or not. "Do what has to be done."

"Sure."

Lester flicked his tongue into my ear and Lala leaned against me for support. Her discomfort had grown more intense, but she didn't want to stop. She stared at the passing women with their flattened bellies and said, "All of them wanted out before their right time. A few weeks, a few months."

"Maybe it's not as bad as that."

"Is he keeping every one of them?"

"Let's go find out."

We were almost there. I caught a whiff of the old man now, his fear and pride and arrogance. The raw religion that never did enough to salve his ego. He wanted an angelic tongue but couldn't afford the price. We took another corner and walked down a poorly lit hallway.

The women congregated around us, waiting to enter, heading out. Some seemed relieved, others had a desperate savagery about them. Hands plucked at my sleeves, fingernails tearing against my neck. Hard-lined jaws went by, soft chins, frightened eyes, courage in motion. They wanted something, we all wanted something. I muttered every verse about vengeance that I knew, and though they sounded hollow and hypocritical they still got my wheels turning.

I entered the Clinic and there he was.

Nicodemus.

My father.

The preacher, the drunk, the killer of my lady.

The man who had incinerated the carny and almost everybody in it, who had murdered my love Megan and stolen my son because he hated the abnormal and the blessed, especially me, and who was now forming his own little freak show.

Even here, with his hands up inside a woman's womb, he wore his frock coat and hat. As he moved I heard two or three flasks knocking together in his pockets, but I didn't smell any whiskey.

Nicodemus had been extremely busy. He'd picked up a few new skills since I'd seen him last.

I watched him take the fetus, doing the bidding of the Works.

The kid wanted out, I could see that. Nine months was too long a stretch in a woman's body, inside this place. The children were more now, different, changed—the umbilical reached into the void and fed them sustenance from the other side of Pandemonium.

I knew more about abortionists than I really wanted to. Pregnant freaks were always having miscarriages, premature births and terminations because of what they called a "catastrophic fetal anomaly." Genetic disorders abounded. I wasn't only a Talker, but a listener as well. Maybe I'd sat in on a class somewhere between the blintzes and the how-to-kill-with-your-bare-hands lecture.

First he injected medication directly into the fetus to stop the fetal heart instantly. He'd already placed the first laminaria in, probably the day before. It was a seaweed about the size of a match stick that absorbs moisture from the body and slowly becomes larger. It helps to prevent infection. After it's been placed in, the laminaria expands overnight and dilates the cervix in a manner that reduces pain and the risk of perforation. He'd probably already changed them twice. Then the amniotic membrane was ruptured and drained. Contraction of the uterus reduced blood loss. Release of the fluid enhanced movement of the fetus and placenta into the cervix. Nicodemus performed a modified D & C using forceps to remove the fetus intact.

Then he took down a jar filled with yellow fluid and pickled the punk.

I understood why he was doing it. He too was assaulted by memories, full to bursting with them, buoyed and invigorated by them. He relived the day of my birth in that deadly storm, when my dying mother's legs hung wide open toward his face and he caught me with one hand. As I slithered into the world, already falling faster than the devil plunging into the pit.

The angles and planes of his face had pretty much dropped in on themselves. I saw only weakness there in the vapid wrinkles and sagging skin. I'd thought I would kill my father the first minute I laid eyes on him, but I found myself suddenly wanting to talk. The woman who'd just had the abortion kept silent, glancing around, unsure of what had brought her here. Maybe she was in shock, or showing deference to the mammoth history around her. She began to mewl. She looked very much like the photos I'd seen of my mother.

Symbols are all that count when you finally realize how little a mark you've made despite all your frantic thrashing. The wind blows it away. Perhaps Nicodemus had just been trying to kill me the entire time, in his mind and soul, and through the death of his son, the death of himself.

He made no acknowledgment of me but held up the punk and said, "They can't do no sinnin' now." He stared at the little hands and tapped the glass until the fingers wobbled and waved to him.

"But you can," I said. "Where's your skillet?"

"Don't need it no more."

"You might want to reconsider that."

"Naw." He let out a wracked sigh, shrugging his shoulders and stretching. I could tell he'd been at it night and day since

233

he arrived. "And we fight all the rest of our days lookin' for atonement."

"You pathetic bastard."

He pursed his lips, thinking about it some. "Yup."

The myth that he had once become seemed ten thousand years already gone. He had shrunken and withered. He was nothing more than sand and cinder that kept creeping across the face of the earth.

"None of this was necessary."

"All of it was or it wouldn't have been done," he told me. "Ain't you learned that yet?"

"You should've just let it go."

He perked up and seemed genuinely curious at that. "Let go'a what? The money? The ministry? You talkin' about them trifles? None'a that was ever mine anyways. I never held any of it so how's I to let it go?"

"Me then."

"Oh, you. Well, yup. I shoulda done that, but a father makes sacrifices. The Almighty demands that of us, I already done told you. Ole Abraham laid his boy out on the rock. He did it for love, and I done the same. And I saved you from having to make that horrible act of burnt offerings and penance. I done it for love, and that there's the truth."

"You might have yourself convinced of that but just look down. Your hands are covered in blood." And they were. I knew in my heart of hearts that he hadn't washed them since he'd butchered my lady.

Nicodemus was trying to reach back out for his own legend, and the idea of dried blood flecking off his fingers would be one he couldn't defy. Juba's death, and Nell's and Hertzburg's also clung to him along with the scorched ghosts of dozens of others.

He was the one who spoke like someone haunted, not me. "My hands, my soul, they been cleansed in blood. It's the road out of perdition. That's forever been the way of it, since the flood."

Lala could barely bring herself to raise her voice above a whisper. "I don't care about any of that. I want to see her again, one last time. You had no right to do what you did."

"Mebbe not," my father said, "but we all gotta do what's given us to do. That's the only duty we got."

"Where's Jonah?" I asked.

"Safe."

"Terrific. Where?"

"Never mind that. You can't have him. He don't want you no more. None'a them want any of youse no more."

I looked Nicodemus over and wasn't sure what there was about him that I'd feared for so long. Or what it was that I had once loved in him so much. I thought about striking the nasion with enough force to cause death. I wanted to attack his philtrum and induce mortal damage or give a sharp enough blow to his Adam's apple to make him asphyxiate.

I could imagine my father as a Russian Omelet, folded and pinned upside down while I sat on his legs until his spine broke. Forcing him into the Brain Buster might be a hell of a lot of fun, and I started to laugh just thinking about it. If I really wanted to torture him I could've given him some of that old-time brimstone preaching. I could still do it if I wanted.

Lala stood nibbling her tongue, her fists tight at her sides. The mewling woman held her arms out for the punk and Nicodemus just patted her leg and said, "There, sweet thing, there, it's all done now. You gonna go on your way without any such burden as this to hold you down to the rock." He kept drumming on her thigh, leaving crimson stripes against the pale flesh.

I thought of how he had stared between my mother's broken legs on the night I was born, watching me leave paradise and enter this ugly world inch by inch, minute after minute while the rains pounded over his battered face and nearly sucked him under. How he must've chortled in that smashed truck, gathering his wrath to hurl back into the face of God.

"What do you see inside there, Nicodemus?" I asked.

"I ain't tellin' you."

"Are the angels calling to you again? Are the tips of their gleaming strange wings brushing against your face?"

"Shut yer dirty mouth."

I wanted it to be over. "Is that redemption?"

"About as close as it gets most'a the time."

"Yup," I said. "Here, let me help you toward heaven."

"I been waitin'."

"I know you have."

I took the punk from him and gave it back to the woman. She sighed and started talking at the jar, brushing her cheek against it. Maybe it was hers, maybe it belonged to the Works, but for the moment she had something to coddle.

I wrapped my arms around my father and it was like hugging Nell before he fried her to death. I grabbed him by the throat and hauled him down to the girl's pussy and pressed his face into her.

Nicodemus let loose with a ferocious yelp and I held him

236

there, his nose and mouth deep inside where he could get even closer to his savior. He struggled and moaned but he was sporting an erection, and I figured this would be the best way all around. The woman enjoyed it too, I thought, and let out tiny growls of delight and disdain. I shoved him farther down into that mysterious place we were all trying to get back to until, at last, he went slack, stopped breathing and went on home.

16

Christ, I needed a drink.

Lala freed the woman from the stirrups and watched her nuzzle the floating fetus, droning lullabies, making promises. In an adjoining room we found the others. I looked at the rows of jars, hundreds of them all carefully sealed and stacked. The punks and their pale, indistinct bodies. Some had been gaffed with tails or sewn together with kittens and fish and squirrel guts.

Of course some were natural freaks. About what you might expect would be born into this environment, by these people in this place, with the city's weight of profane ages bearing down. The drugs had done a lot of damage to their parents' heredity, along with the lack of sunlight and the chemicals in the film and ink, all the poisons. The malignancy and mischief moving in and swirling about through the crowds. These were the children of the Works.

Fishboy Lenny peered into the containers, pressing his scaly forehead close to those unformed faces so much like his own. I remembered now. He hadn't been in the fire. He'd been swimming in the dive tank safe beneath the water. Now Fishboy Lenny tapped on the glasses with his flipper and the fetuses bobbed, turning slightly to stare at him. He gaped and started talking excitedly to them, as if he'd finally be understood by someone.

Lala inspected each face in every jar. It took hours until she found the one she was looking for. Some of the other women had begun milling about and gathering around by then. Lala and I spent the day handing out the punks to the mothers who had offered their sacrifices, willingly or not.

Some had made their choice on their own. Others had been influenced by the will of the Works. I couldn't tell which was which, and held the jars up and waited for the women to either walk by or take back what had been left. We returned dozens and still the stock of fetuses rose around us.

Lala lifted her little girl up to the light, with the viscous amber liquid eddying, and she stared upon what she'd given birth to. After a few minutes she put the jar down on the floor and walked away without a word.

The need for liquor grew overwhelming. The punks had been pickled in grain alcohol. I'd gotten drunk on it before. I searched around and found a punk that was almost a complete gaff, mostly plastic doll parts and some rubber cement. I shook so badly by then that I had to hold the jar in both hands, gripping it to my chest until I steadied enough to screw off the lid. After a few swigs I felt much better and more in control.

I was afraid to find Jonah. I could feel him staring at me from one of the rows and I wondered if Nicodemus had been right.

After a few more gulps I supposed it didn't matter. We are

driven by a human need, even us freaks. I got up and started searching and when I uncovered my son his eyes were wide and glaring.

I opened the lid of the jar. Somebody had gaffed a pair of plastic devil's horns to his head. I sat and waited.

A man came wandering in. He couldn't have been thirty yet, but his hair was entirely white. His eyes were separate abysses, something like my father's had been. He stared at me with the gaze of a sane man caught up in a madness that he never wanted, but who'd learned to feed on it until he could live on nothing else. He was in a place much worse than hell. He was stuck down in purgatory, and he'd made it himself. I knew it was Paynes.

"You look like you might make it out again," he said.

"I'm not so sure I want to."

An unpleasant sound escaped him. Maybe it was laugher. "Not many of us do."

"I suppose I know why."

He nodded. If his own fate didn't matter to him, then mine certainly wouldn't. "Hope you make the right decision."

"Guess we'll know in a little while."

"Good luck."

"Yeah, you too."

About a half hour later Lester slithered in and slowly curled himself up in my lap. I patted his head and a small patch of scales scraped off and his dark eyes brimmed. Fishboy Lenny was still going on, paddling around the room.

The Fedex guy walked by and looked just as miserable as he had before, but at least he was comfortable in this brand of misery. His kids could never knife him in the kidneys now and

239

his wife would never get his hefty insurance policy. After a minute he strayed off and headed even deeper inside what he took to be damnation, and he was happy with that.

The lights dimmed and came up again, and in the following silence, with the dead out of my head, I could hear the rain still coming down.

Jonah arose.

My son drew himself from the liquid and tore the fake horns from his head.

Dripping, he sat before me and hissed, then whispered, and finally preached in a golden voice given to him by a furious yet all-forgiving God.

THE WORDS

by Douglas Clegg

For Bentley

"What he touched was, according to his account, a mouth, with teeth, and with hair about it, and, he declares, not the mouth of a human being . . ."

— *M. R. James, from "Casting the Runes"*

PART ONE: THE NIGHT AND BEFORE

The end is like this:

After the last match goes out, he mouths the words to the Our Father, but it brings him no comfort. He remembers The Veil. He remembers the way things moved, and how the sky looked under its influence. He doubts now that a prayer could be answered. He doubts everything he has come to believe about the world.

The echo of the last scream. He can hear it, even though the room is silent. It seems to be in his head now: the final cry.

Hope it's final.

The scream is too seductive, he knows. He understands what's out there. It's attracted to noise because it doesn't see with its eyes anymore. It sees by smell and sound and vibration. He has begun to think of it by its new name, only he doesn't want to ever say that name out loud. Again.

Your flesh won't forget.

Prickly feeling creeps along the backs of his hands, along his calves. In his mind, he goes through the alphabet, trying to latch on to something he can work around. Something that will give him a jump into remembering the words.

He presses himself against the wall as if it will hide him. Rough stone. *No light. Need light. Damn.* He thinks he must be delirious because the goofiest things go through his mind: Michelle's phrase, *Unfrigginlikely, Spaceman Mark. Those aren't the words. Spaceman Mark. Hey, Space! What planet you on today? Planet Dark, that's what I'm on. Planet Midnight.*

And out of matches.

The wind dies momentarily beyond the cracked window.

The damn ticking of the watch. Someone's heartbeat. The sensation of freezing and burning alternately—a fever. The sticky feeling under his armpits. The rough feeling of his tongue against the roof of his mouth. The interminable waiting. Seconds that become hours in his mind. In those seconds, he is running through sounds in his head—*the words? What are they? Laiya-oauwraii . . . no. That's the beginning of the name. Don't*

*say it again. It might call it right to you. You might make it stronger.
For all you know. What the hell are the words?*

He clutches the carved bone in his left hand. It's smooth
in his fist, like ivory, a tusk from some fallen beast. Slight ridges
where the words are carved. Like trying to read braille, only he's
never studied. *If only I could read them. Need to get light. Some
light.*

Distracted by the smell.

That would be the first one it got.

Over in the corner, something moves. A darkness against
darkness.

Someone he can't see in the dark is over there.

Eyesight is failure, Dash once told him. *Perception is failure.
All that there is, all that there ever will be, cannot be perceived in
the light of day. At night, the only perceptions turn inward.*

The words? he thinks. *The words. Maybe if you remember them,
you can stop it. Maybe it reverses. Or maybe if you just say them . . .*

Moves his lips, trying to form vowel sounds.

The dry taste. Humid and weather-scorned all around.

In his throat, a desert.

Every word he has ever heard in his life seems to spin
through his mind. But not the words he needs. Not the ones
he wants to remember tonight.

A beautiful night. Dark. No light whatsoever but for the
ambient light of the world itself. Summer. Humid. Post-storm.
One of those rich storms that sweeps the sky with crackling
blue and white lightning, and the roars of lions. But the storm
has passed—and that curious wet silence remains. Taste of
brine in the air from the water, a few miles away.

He remembers summer storms like this—their majesty as they wash the June sky clean, bringing a gloom on their caped shoulders, but leaving behind not a trace of it. The smell of oak and beech and cedar and salt and the murky stink of the ponds and bogs. Their years together, all in those smells. All in the dark.

The night, summer, perhaps just a few hours before the sun might rise.

Might.

He wonders if he'll ever see another storm. Another summer.

Another dawn.

Those damn words.

Your flesh will remember the name even if your mind forgets, Dash had told him, and he had still thought it was a game when Dash had said it. *The name gets in your bones and in your heart. Just by hearing it once. But the words are harder to remember. They don't want you to know the words because it binds them. So, listen very carefully. Listen. Each time I say them, repeat them exactly back to me.*

He's shivering. Sweating. Nausea and dizziness both within him, the pit of his stomach. Something's scratchy around his balls—feels like a mosquito buzzing all along the inside of his legs. Twitching in his fingers. Tensing his entire body. Afraid to take another breath.

A conversation replays in his head:

"It's not that hard. Watch."

"I can't. I just . . ."

"All you do is take the thing and bring it down like this. Think of it as a game."

"I can't do it."

"Don't think of it like that. Pretend it's a game. It doesn't mean what it looks like. You've been trained to think this is bad by church and school and your parents. And the world outside. But it's not real. It is just a game, only none of the rest of them know this. They're stupid. Nobody's going to get hurt. Least of all one of us. Least of all you or me. I would never let it happen. You're like my brother."

"I know. But I can't."

"All right. I'll do it. I'll just do it. Just remember what you're supposed to do. As soon as it happens. As soon as my eyes close. Promise? Okay?"

"Okay, okay."

"And the words. After. If it's too much. You know what to say. You remember?"

"Yes."

"You know how to pronounce them? You have to know. If this gets out of hand, you can stop it. The name for me, and the words to stop it. If it's too awful."

"I know, I know."

" 'Cause it might get too awful. I don't know."

"Sure. Of course. I remember how to say them."

"And the name?"

He has no problem remembering the name. He'd like to blot it out of his mind. The name is on the tip of his tongue, and he can't seem to forget how to say it, how to pronounce it perfectly. The words have somehow vanished from his mind.

He tries to remember the words now. How they sound. The language was foreign, but he couldn't read them off the bone. Especially with no light. But even if he had some light, he knew the letters looked like scribbles and symbols. They didn't look like sounds. All he can remember is the name, and he doesn't want to remember that.

A name like that shouldn't be said in a church.

A New England church. *Saint Something. Old Something Church.* Older than old, perhaps. Nearly a crypt. Made of slate and stone. Puritanical and lovely and a bit like a prison now. Church of punishment. Rocky churchyard behind it. He remembers the graves with the mud and the high grasses and the smell of wild onion and lavender like it was years ago, rather than the past hour. Smell of summer, wet grass, and that fertile, splendid odor of new leaves, new blossoms.

The smell of life.

He is inside the church. In a room. The altar is at the opposite end.

Danny had the lighter, he thinks. *If I get it, maybe I can at least save her.*

He wasn't sure if the shape in the doorway was Danny, or the thing that he didn't even want to name. *Not Dash. Not anyone he had ever met or known. An "It." A Thing. A Creature. Something without a Name.*

But it has a name. He knows the name, but he does not intend to ever say it again. He knows the name all too well, but it's the words he keeps trying to remember. The ones that are on the bone. The words that might stop it from continuing.

He tries to lick his lips, but it's no use. His mouth is dry.

Dry from too much screaming.

Nearby, there's a very slight noise. A sliver of a noise. He is sensitive to sound.

In the Nowhere.

Someone might've just died outside. He doesn't know for sure. Who? He just heard the last of someone's life in a slight moaning sound. The open window. No breeze. Just that sound. A soft but unpleasant *ohhhhhh*.

The puppy is whimpering. Somewhere nearby.

Other sounds, barely audible, seem huge.

Branches against the rooftop. Scraping lightly.

His heartbeat. A rapping hammer.

In the dark, the ticking of his watch is too loud. He slowly draws it from his wrist. Carefully, he presses it down into the left pocket of his jeans. The watch clinks slightly against his keys. He holds his breath.

Needs to cough.

Fight it. Fight it. Swallow the cough. Don't let it out

Closes his eyes, against the darkness. Closes his eyes to block it out. To make it go away.

Holds his breath for another count. The cough is gone.

Brief sound.

Someone's breathing. Over there. Across the room. Small room. More than closet, less than room.

Her? Thank god. Thank, god. He licks his lips. Mouth dry.

After a few minutes, he can just make out her shape.

He's staring at her, and she's staring at him, but they can't really see each other. Just forms in the dark. *Michelle?* Ambient light from beneath cracks in the walls creates a barely visible aura around her as he stares.

Dead of night. Dread of night.

The dread comes after the knowledge. He remembers the line from the book. That awful book that he thought was fiction.

But the words do not come to him. The sounds of them, just beyond his memory.

Breathing hard, but as quietly as he can.

Smells his own breath. The stink of his underarms. Glaze of sweat covering his body. Shirt plastered to him. Hair wet and greasy against his scalp.

The chill that hasn't left him, not since he came up out of the earth. Burning chill.

She's going to do it.

Or I am.

One of them is going to scream again. He knows it. He wasn't even sure if he had stopped screaming a half hour before.

Problem is, when the screaming starts, it happens.

And neither of them wants it to happen.

But the puppy is okay.

It doesn't want the puppy.

That's what someone said before. How many minutes ago? Did he say it? Had he said it and just not remembered it? *"It doesn't want the puppy."*

She whispers something. Or else he imagines she whispers.

Or it's the sound of the leaves on the trees, brushing the rooftop.

If it's her, it's wrong for her to whisper. Neither of them knows what decibel level it needs to find them, but she whispers anyway, "Please say it's a game. Please, god, say it's a game."

He's not close enough, but he wants to hold her. Hold her tight. Rewind the night back to day, back a year or more, so he can undo it all. He wants everything to turn out okay, but he knows it won't.

Most of all, he wants her to shut up. He wants to hold her and press his lips or his hand against her mouth and keep in whatever she's trying to let out.

Silence. Come on, silence. Don't . . .

Even her whisper is too loud.

And it hears her.

And it wants to make her scream.

If she screams, it's all over.

Not just the game. The game will never be over.

If we can just hold out 'til daylight, he thinks.

But the noise begins. From her throat. He wants to shut her up, but he can't. He can't. She's over there in the dark, and he's on the other side of the room from her.

The scream is coming up from her lungs in a staccato gurgle. A hiccuping gurgle.

She can't hold it in.

That's when he hears the sound.

Not her scream.

Dear sweet Jesus, do not let that noise out of your mouth. Do not scream. It is inside here. With us.

He hears the sound it makes as it moves. Wet, popping sounds, like bones springing free of joints, and then that stink of overripeness. Rotten. Steaming. Then that awful thumping begins again.

And the steady hissing, as if dozens of snakes trail behind it.

He leans back against the wall, wanting to press himself into the wood as far as he can go. Wanting his molecules to change and move through the wood so he can just escape. He's praying so hard he feels like his skull is going to crack open, only the prayers are all messed up, and he's sure they don't work if you get them wrong. *Dear God, Dear Jesus, please help this poor sinner, Hail Mary, full of grace, Hail Mary, full of grace and the fruit of thy womb, Jesus, Our Father who art in heaven, hallowed be thy name.*

Then it whispers something in the darkness.

He begins shivering when he hears the words.

The girl in the corner finally begins to scream as if she already knows the game is up.

It sweeps toward her. *Sweeps.*

He can't stop it. He's too scared. He's so scared he's afraid he's going to pee his pants and start giggling because something inside his head is going a little haywire.

And then he feels the wet fingers—he hopes they're fingers—along his ankles.

He tries to remain perfectly still.

Perfectly still.

Like a statue.

Like I'm not alive.

Like I'm not even here.

Remember. Come on. Remember. Remember.

Damn it, the words.

1. Before the Night

1

All that screaming and darkness happened one night when they were eighteen, but the truth was, it started long before, at least for Mark.

The longest day of the year; the shortest night of the year. But they didn't take off for the party until the dark had fallen. No one in his right mind went to a party early.

But that was the end of it.

The beginning was a game. A game within a game.

The game was about darkness.

2

There was a history of minor corruption between Mark and Dash that began when they were thirteen. Dash was named, he told Mark early in their friendship, for Dashiell Hammett, a writer. Dash refused to read anything Hammett had written. Mark was called the Spaceman because, he assumed, he must've seemed spacy at times. He didn't do any illegal drugs, but other kids were sure he did. Dash only called Mark "Marco."

"Names have power," he told him. "Only I can call you Marco."

Back when they were a bit younger, Mark was completely unnoticeable. He had few friends and tended to mumble in school. Like the other students at the Gardner School, he had been pulled from public school for one mysterious reason or another. He had arrived, newly thirteen, at the Gardner School in Manosset Sound, at a spur in the Massachusetts coastline. It was nearly a forty-minute drive from his home, which was in an outer suburb of Boston. Some nights, he slept over at the boarding department, but most, he went home. Sometimes his mother or father drove him to school; sometimes he carpooled with another older student who had a car. The Gardner School was the only school that would take him after the little incident with the knife.

"I found it out on the blacktop," he'd told the guidance counselor at his previous school. "I did not bring it to school. I didn't threaten to kill anyone. And I didn't stab him. I held it up and I wanted him to get away from me. He was a bully. He tried to push me. He got cut because he pushed me on the blacktop and then he was about to hit me and I put the knife up between us."

Dash told Mark that he was at the Gardner School for something fucked up, too. "I have an IQ of one eighty, so I'm apparently really smart, only I'm bored with school already. Why don't they get better teachers here? It costs a fortune to go here. You'd think they could hire a better group."

They'd bonded immediately. They both turned up in French class, sitting next to each other in eighth grade. Then they found themselves with lockers side by side. Mark was an altar boy at St. Peter's, and as he got his robe on one Sunday, there was Dash, inside one of the confessionals, his head craning out from behind the narrow doorway.

"Wanna smoke?"

"How'd you get out here?" Mark asked. Dash lived closer to school than to Mark's neighborhood.

"Bus."

"I didn't know you were Catholic."

"I'm not," Dash said. "I don't believe in that stuff. I was just waiting for you to get off-duty. And have a smoke. I saw you smoke in the stalls at school. I like to hang out in grave-yards, and there's a nice one behind this god place. I was having a smoke, and I saw you troop in with all the other god people." Dash had a funny rhythm to his speaking voice, even then. As if he were preparing lectures, an old professor in the body of an adolescent.

"We're too young to smoke," Mark said. "And it's bad for you."

"Like I said, I saw you smoke at school. Or at least, I thought it was you. Do you have vices? Self-destructive ones?"

Mark only hesitated a moment. He had never smoked a cigarette before in his life. "They might catch us in there."

"Nope. Confessional's all empty. Come on," Dash said. He held up a pack of Marlboros. "This is the slowest way of killing yourself. One cigarette at a time, but if you start young enough, it'll help."

"Not everyone dies from that," Mark said.

"Everyone dies from something. That's the problem of life. You're just going to die," Dash said. "Me, I'll get hooked on any number of things if I can. It's always good to improve the odds if you want to succeed."

"That's like suicide. That's a sin."

"For you. You're Catholic. You have that whole resurrection

of the body thing and the life everlasting, choirboy," Dash said. "Not that I don't find that appealing. I'd love to die and then come back. Conquering death should be the alternate goal if dying is the common one. I'd love to be a messiah. It would suit me. Now, come on, let's have a smoke."

3

In school, they went into the janitor's closet—a deep broom closet that had stacks of *Playboys* beneath a pile of cleaning supplies. The closet stank of Comet and bleach and oil.

"Just shut off the lights."

"Why?"

"Just shut 'em off."

"Okay."

Off went the lights.

"Listen," Dash said.

"To what?"

"Just listen. Hear my breathing? Now?"

Mark mumbled something about bad breath.

"See? This is the Nowhere," Dash said.

"This definitely is nowhere."

"*The* Nowhere. It's a different place than when the lights are on," Dash said. "Different rules apply. Hell, there are no rules. With the light on, it's all rules and regulations and laws and order. But with the dark, it's a different world. When you're dead, you're in the dark."

"When I'm dead, I'll be somewhere else."

"You think so?" Dash asked. "Now here's the thing. I know these people who believe they talk to the dead."

"Psychics?" Mark said.

"No, none of that crap. I mean people who actually believe they talk to the dead. Who call them up from corpses. They believe it. I don't know if I believe it yet."

"Are they in school?"

"Don't be ridiculous. I met them in a graveyard. Manosset has more than just the rocky beach. There's the Old Church. They were there. Doing a ceremony. They were sacrificing a turtle."

"Gross."

"It wasn't as gross as you'd think," Dash said. "They told me all about the Nowhere. How it changes the world. Darkness. Night. Absence of light. And in the dark, they think they talk to the dead. They have an old religion. Older than, well, yours. One of them told me that people still practice it, only no one ever talks about it. Bands of believers, basically. It's not so different from yours. Only, they believe in a messiah of darkness. A savior who comes by night."

"You making this up?"

"I wish I were. I don't really believe it. But they do. I find it a very attractive kind of belief system. It's this interesting idea. And you know how I like interesting ideas. And you've got this absolute connection between death and life. Bringing back the dead." Dash said this last part in full old, professor mode. Then he asked, "Do you believe in God?"

"Of course."

"Well, then you might as well believe in the Nowhere. I mean, virgins and miracles and rising from the dead. It's not so far from what they believe."

"You mean your made-up people who sacrifice turtles?"

255

"Not just turtles," Dash said. "Other stuff, too. Goats sometimes. Chickens. I'll introduce you to them one night. Did you know that a man named Crossing actually wrote several stories about their group? More than a hundred years ago. He was one of them. People thought he was writing fiction, but apparently, none of it was made up. I'll loan you one of his books sometime. He said that the darkness has a reality to it that lets illogic through. Isn't that a cool way of saying it? The darkness lets illogic through. He called it The Veil." He paused, smoking. "It's not so different from anything else. It's *almost* logical. There aren't any virgins in it. But there are some miracles. Take the streets, lights on. It's normal. Boring. At night? Lights out. No light. No moonlight even, it's a place where you make up the rules. You define the space. You create what's there and what's not," Dash said, his breath all warm. "You create what's there. And maybe it creates what's there."

"It?"

"The Nowhere. There's something out there. In the dark. And if you're in it long enough, it comes out. That's why they had to do the sacrifices. They told me it stops worse things from happening. You know about Eastern philosophy?"

Mark did not.

"Some of it is about how it's all an illusion. Everything we think we see. It's not what's really there. And if that's true, maybe what's really there is something else. Only we don't see it because we're too busy perceiving the crap we expect to see. We're taught from an early age to see things a certain way, and we name things so that they stay that way. But the darkness is fluid. It defies perception. You know how your eyeball works?

How everything you see, you're really seeing upside down, only your eye somehow adjusts it back again?"

Mark had never heard of this before. Sometimes, Dash's ideas went right over his head; or else they hit him square in the head and gave him massive headaches.

"Or a rose. They're not really red. How it's the absense of some pigment and how all the other colors are there, and it somehow makes it red? But if you turn off the light, is the rose still red? Or is it no color? Is it even a rose? Does it become something else in the dark? And do you become something else in the dark?"

"Cool," Mark said. "But, I mean, I'm . . . me. I'm me even now. Even in the dark."

"Are you? Are you sure?"

Mark laughed a little.

"I'm not joking. Are you the same you in the dark as you were when the light was on?" Dash asked. "Would you do the same things in the light of day that you'd do if no one could see you? Do you ever wonder why people have sex in the dark?"

Mark didn't answer.

"Maybe it's 'cause they can be something different in the dark. Or maybe they really are something different in the dark," Dash said. "Maybe right now, you're not even Mark. Maybe you're something else. Do you believe in life after death?"

"Well." Mark fumbled with his thoughts. "I'm sort of Catholic."

"Sorta?"

Mark shrugged. "I believe some things and not others."

"The only thing I believe about Christianity is the resurrection of the body. I mean, I think dead bodies still have some-body in them. Maybe we do them a disservice by burying them."

"What, you mean if you didn't bury a body it would just be fine?"

"Not saying that," Dash said. "If you can't think deeper than that, Marco, I don't know about you. I just don't know. I mean, what are those caskets for? They're like little traps. What if we could all roll the stones away from our tombs after we die. Maybe there'd be more messiahs around. Who knows? Let me give you a rundown on deity. First, God's name is not God. Second, in the Old Testament, they called him Yahweh or Je-hovah. In Greek, Deus. The Greek name for the top dog god was Zeus. Pretty close to Deus, don't you think? And Jehovah is pretty close to the Roman god, Jove, alias Jupiter. I won't even go into what I learned about the goddess Ishtar and her relationship to your Queen of Heaven. You don't want to know what the word Easter comes from, trust me. It would blow you out of that little churchworld you're in. God, Yahweh, what have you. And none of these are the names of God, and even with God, there are other gods. That's why you have this com-mandment, 'Thou Shalt Have No Other Gods Before Me.' It's because there are other ones. And people can't say their names because no one really knows how to say the names. They used to. That's what priests in ancient times used to do. That was their power. They knew the real names of the gods. And naming them means bringing them. Invoking them. And that's what these people in the Nowhere have. For centuries, they've kept alive the name of a particular god. Maybe it's 'the' God. I don't know. But the name of the god is the power. And the god of the Nowhere is all about death and resurrection and darkness."

Dash had been reading a lot. He claimed to have read the Bible three times 'til he knew it backward and forward, and a book called the *Aegyptian Book of Darkness*. He spoke of Kierkegaard and Kant and Buddha and Hesse and Yeats and Eliot and someone named Robert Graves and someone named Colin Wilson and about quantum something, and about transformations and chiaroscuro and shadows. He loaned books to Mark, and asked him questions about what was in them.

Mark found it irresistible, although he thought the books tough going. Only the short stories by Wacey Crossing seemed to be any fun. In them, Crossing wrote about ancient practices that called up creatures of beauty and malevolence. He even mentioned Manosset Sound by name, as if these practices happened there in the 1800s. T. S. Eliot and Robert Graves were a little more difficult, although Mark loved a book called *Demien* by Herman Hesse.

Dash told Mark that, in the dark, everywhere was Nowhere. And it was better to be in the Nowhere than in the Somewhere. Particularly if you were like one of them. A bit outcast. A bit funky. A bit eccentric. A bit different.

"Nowhere guys," Dash said. Their favorite song became *Nowhere Man*. They loved to say to their parents, when asked, "Where are you going?"

"Nowhere. Honest. Just Nowhere."

And the Nowhere was always dark, and always somewhere else.

4

But Mark didn't ever get to meet these "people of the No-where," as he began to think of them. Dash mentioned them now and again; he acted as if he was getting close to them in some way that wasn't expressed. He became secretive about some of the goings-on when Mark wasn't with him. "There's a ceremony they have, called the Tempting. Each of them cuts his left arm open and spills the blood over a newly dug grave. They say some ancient words and begin chanting something I still can't make out. They have these stones and they put the words on them, and dip them in this syrupy mixture, and then put the stones under their tongues, and the words are always inside them after that. Their bodies memorize them or some-thing. They don't even use their minds. It's weird. And then one of them becomes possessed by the dead person."

Mark assumed it was made up, stolen from Wacey Crossing's stories, and as a year or so passed, he grew to ap-preciate Dash's offbeat and dark sense of humor.

Once, together again in some dark place, hanging out, Dash asked, "Do you love me?"

"Excuse you?"

"I don't mean that," Dash said. "I mean, do you love me? Like a brother. Like we have a bond?"

Mark thought a minute, feeling uncomfortable with the question. "Sure. Like a brother."

"We've got to have that bond to make any of it worthwhile. I mean, we'll get married to some babes someday and do all kinds of stuff, but if we love each other like that—like brothers—then we can move mountains."

"Sure," Mark said, but decided to turn on the light on the back porch at his parents' house.

He was surprised by what he saw.

Dash sat next to him, but he had a hypodermic needle in his arm, just withdrawing it.

"What the hell is that?"

Dash held the needle up. "It's not for you. Don't worry."

"You a junkie? Dash? What the hell is that?"

"It's not heroin. Jesus, it's The Veil," but Dash would not explain further. He took the the needle, covered it, and pressed it into a plastic case that looked more suitable for a toothbrush. "See? I'm not tripping out or anything. Don't freak."

Dash reached up to shut the light off. Dark again. Mark sat there in the dark wondering if he shouldn't end the friendship or talk to someone at school about what seemed to be Dash's latest self-destructive habit.

5

But he didn't. He did what others probably did when their best friends were on drugs—he somehow just put it out of his mind because Dash never seemed high or wired. And Mark didn't see much evidence of the hypodermic needle again. Nor did he look for it. After a few months or so, Mark had blocked that moment from his mind. Everything seemed normal, in its own messed up way.

Dash was his only real friend at school, anyway.

6

On a night-smitten country road, Dash would flick the head-lights off.

Suddenly, it was as if the world had disappeared. They were in a car with the world gone around it. With just a sense of "road." A sense of "nowhere."

Dash started doing the headlight trick before he even had his license. This was back when he had managed to steal his brother's Mercury Cougar and sneak out in the night. He'd pick Mark up down the hill from where he lived. Always after midnight.

Mark would be out there waiting for him, waiting for the adventure. "I waited here forever," he'd say.

"Forever must last about fifteen minutes," Dash would respond, giving him a gentle punch to the shoulder.

They'd go to parties, or sneak off and grab a burger, or find out where some of the other guys were hanging out, smoking, drinking, making out with a girl or just watching others make out.

Neither of them did much wild stuff. Not real wild stuff. Mark even wrote down what he called the Nowhere Manifesto, but he tore it up one afternoon, worried that his mother might find it. At the end of most evenings, they just called it a night and Dash dropped Mark off at his house.

But, on some nights, Dash took Mark to the graveyard behind the old church. Mark never saw him draw the needle out again, but he knew that when Dash asked him to wait in the car a second, that he might be going into the darkness to shoot up with whatever he used. *The Veil.*

262

But Mark could ignore it. It didn't matter. They were friends.

Mark got out of the car, and Dash, up near the church, whistled to him to come on up the path to the graves.

7

It was not Mark's church, nor was it Dash's. It was older and more of a historic landmark than a functioning church. It was made of stone. All Mark knew about it was that the founding fathers of the area had built it, or built the original building, which no longer existed. The graves behind it had those names like Goody Something and Sir Walter John Something, but most of the gravestones were rubbed smooth and coated with a slimy ooze of moss and yellow-green muck. A bog, just the other side of a thin line of trees, had flooded the area recently, so they walked in mud and damp weeds.

"This is where I saw them," Dash said. "This is where they spoke to me. They showed me The Veil for the first time. Here."

Mark glanced around, but they were alone together.

"They asked me to tell them my heart's desire," Dash said. He went over and sat on a long flat stone. He patted the area beside him. Mark went over and joined him. "They told me that the Nowhere needed guys like me. Maybe like you, too."

"Are they some kind of witch cult?" Mark asked, his chin in his hand. He stared across the expanse of field and wood beyond the old church. "Do they worship Satan?"

Dash grinned. "No. Not witches. Not Satan. That's all fairly new stuff. This is older than that. Long before. They're wise people, though. They know things. They believe that they talk to the dead. They believe the dead tell them things. They know the name of twelve different gods. The real names. The names of power. I don't know how they do. They knew things about me that even my mother wouldn't know. Even you wouldn't know."

"Like what?"

"You don't want to know," Dash said. "There are some things I wouldn't want people to know. But they knew."

"Is it about why you had to leave the other school?"

"Want to know something funny?"

Mark shrugged.

"They told me about you. This was before we met. They told me about that thing you did."

"What thing?"

"You know," Dash said. "With the knife. Don't worry. It's kind of cool."

Dash put his hand on Mark's shoulder. Felt Mark's breath against his ear. "I did something terrible when I was twelve," Dash whispered. "Something you can't ever tell anyone else in the whole world, or I will hunt you down and kill you and tear out your heart and cut the eyes out of your face. Understood? We're fifteen, but when you're a kid, I mean a kid-kid, you do things without really knowing why. You're changing. Everything is changing. You have these impulses. You do things because something inside you tells you to do them. I once saw the most beautiful dead woman in the world, lying on the ground. She had killed herself, but it left no marks on her because she took pills. She was naked. I was caught doing something to her. But it wasn't what you think. Nothing perverted. She was so beautiful I didn't want to hurt her, even when she was dead and beyond hurting. And they knew about what I did. They had spoken to her. The Nowhere people. After she died. They had gone to where she was buried, and they'd dug her up from the grave, and she told them about me, about what I did, and they think I'm some kind of messiah because of it, like it was a sign that I was the golden child or something."

8

On the phone, the next afternoon, a Saturday. "I made it all up. None of it's true," Dash said to Mark, and then hung up.

9

Mark didn't see Dash for a while, but eventually he saw Dash's car idling on the street beneath his bedroom window. Mark was furious with his father for taking away his stereo because of a drop in grades, and he snuck out the back of the house and got in the Cougar and told Dash, "It's about time you showed your sorry face."

10

Once, they narrowly missed being hit by a car that was following the Mercury Cougar too closely. They then followed the car for miles just to annoy the driver. They planned raids on some of the guys' houses, too. When a family was out of town, Mark and Dash would go out in the dark, late as they could stand and still feel awake. They'd break in, out in some suburban enclave. They wouldn't take anything from the home. They'd just get in through some window—it was easy to jimmy one open—and just see what the house was like on the inside. They wouldn't disturb anything. They just kept the lights out and wandered the house. Dash said he wanted to see how the people in suburbia lived, what they owned, what they had. Mark once said it seemed psycho to do it, but Dash reassured him that they weren't doing any harm.

Sitting there, on someone else's sofa, Dash would sometimes say some words that weren't English, and they weren't any kind of language that Mark had ever heard. He would say a few words, and if Mark asked about them, Dash would say that he hadn't said anything at all.

Sometimes, they'd move a book around on a bookshelf. Or they'd pull a CD out of its case and put it on a windowsill. Just enough that it might seem curious to the family, returning from a weekend away.

But this was the worst of what they did together, and it really wasn't much. Some of the other guys at school regularly shoplifted. Others were smoking marijuana half the school day. Others were doing much worse. Mark reassured himself that what he and Dash did was fairly innocent. It really hurt no one. He tried not to think about that needle that Dash had. He didn't really see it, although sometimes he noticed the plastic toothbrush carrier inside Dash's green army jacket.

Mark and Dash loved girls and talked about them as much as any other guy in school, but they really adored each other. They could've been brothers. Before they'd met—at thirteen— nobody would've thought they resembled each other. But by fifteen, they could've been twins.

Dash made Mark promise to be his Best Man at his wedding, whenever it happened; Mark asked Dash to be the godfather of his first kid, whenever it came into the world.

In the Nowhere, sometimes, Mark would say things to Dash that he never told anyone else. When Mark got dumped by Emmie, he told Dash first.

When Dash decided he was going to kill himself rather than grow up, he only told Mark. "That's right," Dash said. "Why turn into some corporate robot and end up like our dads? I'd do it with a knife. I'll become one with the Nowhere. You?"

"Hanging. The front staircase."

"Do it at my folks' place. In the foyer. From the chandelier," Dash said. "In the dark."

They had a good laugh about it, and then shared a cigarette.

"What about those people?"

"What people?"

"The ones," Mark said, grabbing the cigarette from Dash's mouth, "that were in the graveyard. The ones you told me about."

Dash flicked on the light. He regarded Mark with a nearly mistrustful look. His eyes were bloodshot. "Listen, they're dangerous sometimes. They showed me some things that were kind of nasty."

"Like what?"

Dash shivered slightly, but Mark couldn't tell if he was just joking or not. "Just some really bad shit," he said. "They have these ceremonies that you have to study. I've been studying them for a long time now, and I still don't completely understand them."

"Why haven't I met them?"

"They decide who meets them and who doesn't," Dash said.

"I thought you made them up." Mark laughed again, puffing on the cigarette. "Back in eighth grade. To scare me. You told me you made it all up."

"No," Dash said. "I made up the other thing. The priests of the Nowhere are real. They're practically holy. They're really good people, but they do some nasty shit. I'm sort of into what they do."

"Sort of philosophically," Mark added.

"Maybe," Dash said. "Give me that cig back, or go buy a new pack."

11

Dash would end the night out in the middle of some godforsaken nowhere, spinning the car in the mud, or glide down an icy patch of road, the back end of the car fishtailing. All around them, the dark, like they were driving inside their own minds, and the world existed around them only for them.

The connection between them came with it. They could talk about their deepest thoughts, argue philosophy, their sense of the meaning of life and if there was one at all. They determined that there was no meaning to life, but to truly enjoy life, they each must act as if there were a meaning to it. Their understanding of girls became legendary, as they discussed sexual availability versus the sacred virgin as it applied to the girls they knew; misunderstanding of other boys in school, which manifested in an open contempt for jocks and their football parties;

they shared their love for Herman Hesse's novels and Joan Armatrading albums and this writer with the unusual name of Wacey Crossing, who wrote *When Nowhere Comes*, and other books in the 1800s, which Dash swore were true. He had three Wacey Crossing books, all short stories, and their bindings were leathery and cracked like old Bibles, and inside, people had written messy illegible notes all in the margins and drawn what looked like dirty pictures of naked women with huge breasts in the front and back of the books. The Crossing stories were about a mysterious cult that had survived centuries of persecution, misshapen creatures that lived beneath graves, and ancient ones that prowled the darkness. Mark borrowed each of them, and read them thoroughly, enjoying the terribleness of the punishments meted out to those who treated the Nowhere people badly. There were seven primary deities in the Crossing stories, all with nicknames: The Devourer, She Who Befouls The Night, Hallingorianang-the-Eater-of-Souls, Oliara-the-Sword-of-Fire, The Swarmgod of the Thousand Stings, The Pope of Pestilence, and Julaiiar the Conqueror. Mark began calling Dash the Devourer, and he in turn might call Mark Swarmgod. It definitely sealed their fates within weirdohood, and Mark was perfectly happy with that. They dreamed together, aloud, of what they'd do if they had the powers of Julaiiar the Conqueror, who came in Shadow and cut the heads off friend and foe; or if She Who Befouls The Night decided to make it with Oliara-the-Sword-of-Fire, what kind of kid they'd produce.

It all happened when the lights went out.

Heading down some lonesome road, the headlights off, they'd light their cigarettes, and the world would change from its unsubtle self to some kind of dark wonderland.

269

Even though Mark might be in the backseat with Emmie, making out and doing everything two teens can do with each other while still keeping most of their clothes on, it was Dash who made him feel as if it were just their world: in the car, on a dark road, with nothing but the unexpected wonders of night around.

And one night, Rachel Cowan had a big party out at the country place her folks had, a few weeks after graduation, and everybody they knew was going. Michelle and Danny needed a lift, and even though Dash and Rachel used to date and now didn't get along very well, Mark convinced him to go. "This is a perfect night for this," Dash said.

"Yeah?" Mark asked, grabbing a cooler of beer. He checked his watch: *10:15.* "I figured the party'll be hoppin' by eleven."

"It's a sacred night to the Nowhere. It's a night they call Lifting The Veil."

"Oh," Mark said, used to Dash's tales of the Nowhere and its priests.

Dash whispered to him, as Mark slid into the front seat next to him, "Let's have some fun with them. Okay?"

Mark couldn't reply because Danny had already opened the back door, and Michelle rapped at Mark's window for him to unlock her door. In her arms, a plastic and wire cage. She had brought a stupid puppy from her sister's kennels as a surprise birthday gift for Rachel, who had just turned nineteen, and whose dog had recently passed away.

"Just a little fun," Dash said. "For a sacred night."

Then he reached around to unlock the door for Michelle.

2. The Night Begins

1

Dash flicked the headlights off. The night came up like veils of shadow against shadow—purple darkness, black darkness, and the curious ambient light of the earth itself—particles of illumination from unknown sources. Reflections of slivered moonlight off distant ponds. It was beautiful, Mark thought. The narrow, winding road was ripe with potholes and wounds, and the June-fat trees hung low over it—it was a beautiful world as far as Mark was concerned, and he felt comfortable there with Dash in the front seat, their world, their Nowhere surrounding them.

Mark glanced over at Dash beside him. Dash in his green army jacket, with holes throughout it. Beneath, he wore a black T-shirt. Even in the summer he wore the jacket, his emblem of weirdohood, of not abandoning his outcast nature. Smoke from his mouth. The red glow of the cigarette lit Dash's features. His hair had gone from brown to dark blue with fiery tinges where it flopped around his eyes. His eyes seemed to have a light of their own. He smiled, showing all his teeth.

It was not pitch black quite yet, for the moon half-lit the world. Its light, diffuse behind scalloped clouds, hinted at the outline of a dilapidated farmhouse with its property cut in a ragged square from the encroaching forest, and a balding fringe of dead trees at the edge of the road before the property. A single light was on in the house, and it somehow made Mark think about loneliness, despite being there with his friends. He wondered what he would do—now that college loomed, and he and Dash would probably grow out of their friendship, as all friends seemed to after high school. He didn't want it to happen, but there was an inevitability to it—they would move on and stay friends but lose that closeness, that brotherhood they felt. The farmhouse became a blur as Dash recklessly swung the steering wheel to negotiate a curve in the road.

Then the woods appeared again, thick and dark, and another turn, another break in the woods cut by a stream and ditch to the left. They passed what seemed at first an empty, desolate field, and there came the moon across it, a white sickle of moon. The field was not empty, but some kind of cemetery—Mark didn't recognize it at first, but then knew he had been there before—*of course*, he thought, *it was here, the Old Church is here. Saint Something.*

They had been mostly silent in the car—*me and Dash in front, our world, our night world.* Mark grabbed another beer from the back, and nearly stuck his hand down Michelle's shirt. Suddenly something stank like a dead animal in the car, and Mark knew it was the puppy, in his crate. It was whimpering. Michelle, after nearly slapping him, reached back and thrust a finger through the small Kari-Kennel opening and murmured, "That's okay, baby, that's okay." Then she reached up and flicked on the car's interior light. "Some light in here would be nice. What's this thing with darkness?"

"Darkness is cool," Mark said.

"Friggin' Goth," Michelle said; but Mark was not a Goth. He was just a guy who felt better in the dark. With friends. In the car. It was his comfort zone.

"Are you sure Rachel wants a new dog?" Dash asked. "She can't exactly take it to college with her."

"I already talked to her mom about it. Her mom's going to keep it while Rachel's at Smith."

"She got into Smith?" Mark asked.

"Last minute," Michelle said. "With me."

"Where are you two going?" Danny asked, fairly innocently. With the question, came the unspoken: they were a couple to some extent. Mark and Dash were paired in the minds of their classmates.

"How could you not guess?" Michelle huffed. "They've practically been talking about it since sophomore year."

"Oh, yeah," Danny said. "I thought maybe Mark might go to Georgetown."

"I didn't want to go to Georgetown," Mark said. Then he added, "Really. I didn't."

"U-Mass for us," Dash said.

Mark sniffed at the air. "Who farted?"

"That dog crapped," Dash said. "He needs to go outside. Not in the car."

Mark laughed, popped open the beer, and reached for the radio buttons. Dash rolled down a window, and the humidity poured in—a gentle steam. He switched the air-conditioning up to a higher level.

Michelle began lecturing Dash on why the puppy was in the car in the first place; how Rachel had wanted the puppy ever since her last dog was hit by a car out on the highway; and how, even though we were headed for "what no doubt is going to be some kind of brawl," the puppy would be fine, and when they got to Rachel's house, she'd let it out to do its business in the wild.

"Whoa!" Dash cried out. "That was close!" Another pair of headlights, in the opposite lane from them, fast approaching and crossing the invisible line in the road. Dash swung the car to the right a little too hard, and they all felt the car leaning into the ditch on that side.

Then, back to normal, driving in the dark.

"Do you really want to hurt me?" Mark began singing along with the radio, which he'd very wisely turned up slightly to drown out Michelle's whine. "Jesus, nothing but oldies." He punched the radio buttons, but the best he could find was heavy metal.

Briefly, he turned the sound up high; Dash reached over and switched the radio off. Then he switched it back on, and a voice came up that was nearly monotone, "And the angel carried a crown and a burning sword, and sayeth unto . . ."

"Jesus radio. I love it. Selling God on the airwaves without really knowing all about God," Dash said, switching to a soft rock station. "I like oldies better."

"Look," Danny said, rising from the back seat. "I think that's Carbo's truck over there. Hell, did Rachel even invite the dropouts?"

"That redneck," Michelle whispered, as if no one would hear her. "Carbo is such a hillbilly. I'm surprised he ever even got into Gardner." She drew the little yellow puppy from the crate into her arms. She let it lick her all over her face. Her shirt was unbuttoned, and she wore no bra. Mark could make out the roundish mounds of her breasts, glancing back at her for a second too long. He found them unappealing. They weren't as big as they looked when covered up.

2

Perhaps it was because it was Michelle, who Mark found generally unappealing.

She had a well-bred look, as if her parents had never been in love, but had known that between their checkbooks, their inheritances, and their basic health, they should mate and produce offspring with equally good checkbooks, inheritances, and health. Like some alien lifeform that must have progeny in order to conquer the earth. Michelle was the natural product of this loveless but purposeful union. He had seen her type throughout high school—she was not a prototype the way Dash was, or even Rachel, who was a true original. She was just one of the herd. Dash had a thing for her, but he said that his interest didn't go much past the flesh. "She's a copy of a copy of a copy. But with an especially nice rack," he'd said at some point.

Michelle was mass produced. She was one of many rich girls with not a lot going on other than her birth certificate and her trust fund. She had teeth—and a lot of them—and hair, and a strangely seductive little jaw of determination that waggled side to side when she was pissed off. She dressed like she was hot stuff, even in her khaki shorts, with visible panty line, and white top wrapped for maximum breastage. Mark supposed there were boys with the low expectations of a Danny, who found her completely irresistible.

But she was no Rachel.

She wasn't even an Emmie, Mark's girlfriend who had dumped him on prom night right after they'd made love on the golf course at the country club. Right after he'd lost his virginity. Just dumped him, and left him on the moist morning grass as the turgid sun rose somewhere—Mark, there, near the seventh hole, his tux jacket somewhere else in the world, cummerbund lost, shiny black shoes in a sand trap, and carnation shredded from passion. Still, he had his cufflinks and a hazy memory of his first time. Emmie had given him that, and she was more of a human being than Michelle could ever hope to be.

Unfortunately, Michelle and Emmie were best friends, so Mark knew that Michelle knew about his getting dumped in that way; she probably knew about how badly he'd fumbled with Emmie's shiny blue prom dress, how he probably was less-than-perfect at the whole sex thing, and how he may have said something stupid in the throes of coitus that really made Emmie dislike him once and for all.

3

"You know, that dog has worms," Mark said to her, in the car, still looking at the sloping mounds of her breasts through her open shirt. "And you letting him lick your face could put wet puppy spit full of miscroscopic worm larvae on your skin, and from there, they could get inside you. And when they do—"

"Only someone like you could come up with something that disgusting," Michelle said.

"I want to hear," Dash said. He drove the Cougar with one hand; he had a cigarette in the other.

276

"The puppy has roundworms, and maybe tapeworms," Mark said. "Almost all puppies have them. The puppy will get wormed soon, but right now, the poop inside that little crate probably has tiny strands of spaghetti—that wriggle."

"God!" Michelle shouted, kicking at the back of his seat. "Stop now. Just stop."

"I want to hear it," Dash said. "So what do they do?"

Mark shrugged. "Well, to dogs and cats, a lot, but worming pills will take care of it, most likely. But when they get into people, it's harder. They make little canals under the skin. They like to go for the eyes."

"You're making that up," Danny said.

"No, for some reason, the roundworms can't mature into adults in people. So the larvae just make do, and they seem to really like getting the tissue around the eyes."

"If," Michelle said, slowly but with her usually dominating force, "you. Do. Not. Shut. Up. Right. Now."

"I won't even go into the tapeworm possibility."

"Jenny Patterson had tapeworm when she was twelve," Dash said. "Remember?"

"No," Mark said. "I didn't know her back then."

"She had it, and she lost twenty pounds practically overnight. She was sick for a long time. She said it was pretty nasty."

"They grow inside you," Mark said. "They grow as long as they can. They can fill your intestines and just eat at you."

"I once saw a dead body that was opened up and it was full of worms," Dash said. "I almost took a shit when I saw them in her mouth."

"Shut up!" Michelle shouted; the puppy began whimpering;

Dash laughed and accidentally dropped his cigarette; Michelle cried out something that Mark thought was "What," and that's when they hit something in the road.

3. THE DEER

1

The car didn't just hit something in the road.

It slammed into something like a brick wall. The car made a squealing sound, and the sound of glass breaking filled Mark's ears. He felt the world spin a bit, and his head knocked back into the headrest of his seat. He was thrown against the glove compartment, to the front of the car, almost to the windshield; something flicked against his scalp; Michelle screeched, or else it was the tires screeching; Danny made a noise like he'd had the air knocked out of him. Dash whooped as if he enjoyed the ride; Mark wondered if the puppy was going to be okay.

But it was over in a second.

Mark opened his eyes and saw something dark and liquid covering the windshield.

Not the windshield.

His eyes.

He reached up. "Shit." He was bleeding. Something had cut his forehead.

Someone touched him on the scalp. "Not much, Marco." It was Dash. "Just a little blood. It just seems like a lot to you." Then, "Everybody okay back there?"

No answer.

Whatever they'd hit had darted out in front of the car from the edge of the bundle of trees at a bend in the narrow road. It was dark, but even so, Dash didn't turn the headlights back on. Perhaps they didn't even work. Mark wondered if something awful was going to happen now. If one of them was dead. Or if they'd killed an animal. Or if Dash's parents would ground him and take away all his privileges for the summer and beyond.

Mark wiped his face. It was a lot of blood for a little cut, but he felt the irregular slice at the top of his scalp, and it was, indeed, not much of a wound.

"Lots of bleeding at the scalp level," Dash said. He took a facial tissue and daubed it on Mark's forehead. "See? All better. You knocked it on the dashboard."

"I thought I was dead."

"Maybe you are," Dash said. "Maybe we all are. Maybe we're dead but doomed to stay right here in this wreck and never leave the dark road."

"Hmm," Mark said. "I think I saw that old *Twilight Zone* episode."

From the backseat, Danny gasped, "Oh my god, we hit a deer."

Michelle shouted out "Fuck!" The word seemed to stretch into an eternity of several seconds.

Outside the car, the world was dark.

For just seconds, they were all silent again. Mark closed his eyes and wished it away. When he opened them again, he was still in the car, feeling bruised, a throbbing at the front of his scalp.

A few seconds, which felt like minutes.

Complete silence.

"Is everybody okay?" Dash asked a second time, breaking the quiet. He didn't bother turning around to check. He adjusted the rearview mirror and glanced back.

"I guess I'm ok," Mark said, although the back of his neck hurt from the way he'd slammed back against the seat. His scalp stung.

"Just a little upside down back here," Danny said. "More beer, please."

"I'm fine. The puppy's fine. As if you care," Michelle said, coughing. "My arm hurts a little. And ow. My knee."

Dash began cussing up a storm. When it subsided, he looked at Mark, tapped him on the shoulder and gave a slight squeeze.

"Shit, and I forgot to pay my goddamn insurance this month. I am so screwed."

2

It wasn't a deer.

At least as far as they could tell, although Danny insisted it had antlers, and since he was the drunkest of them, he was the least believed.

3

Mark got out last, generally pissed off that they wouldn't make it to Rachel's party at all. They were somewhere between school and the Sound, and it was a section of road he couldn't quite identify. There were no lights in the distance. There was no sound of traffic on some nearby highway. Trees all around, thick with leaves; the moon existed somewhere, but not where Mark stood. It seemed darker than dark.

But Dash had a flashlight and was waving it around the front of the car.

"This car is fucked," Dash said. He spat out some more choice words, and Mark thought it was a bit like watching a three-year-old have a temper tantrum, the way Dash stomped around in a circle, muttering and shaking his head.

"It is, truly," Danny said. He hoisted a beer to his lips, and seemed to drink the entire bottle in one gulp. Then he belched.

The damage to the Cougar was extensive. The front end had completely smashed inward, practically wrapped around the engine; the front axle was bent; and Danny made a joke that it was a miracle none of them was hurt. "Even the puppy," Danny said. "Man, that was a hell of a deer."

"I didn't see a deer," Michelle said. She had put the puppy on a short leash and walked around the front of the car. "I saw some people. A few of them."

In the flashlight's beam, she looked like a doll that had been through a windstorm. Pale white, her shirt half unbuttoned, her hair a mess. For a second, Mark thought her lip was cut, but it was just an odd shadow.

"Well, they'd be lying here," Danny began, but Michelle gave him a harsh look that shut him up fast.

"I saw these people. I didn't see their faces or anything. I just saw a group of them. Maybe three. Maybe more." She had begun crying a little, only not so much that anyone could notice. When the moon came out from behind a cloud, beyond the trees, casting the slightest amount of light across the road, Mark noticed.

"Somebody hold me," she said.

Danny obliged; his arms wrapped around her. "No, babe, it was a deer. I'm sure it was."

"We killed some people," Michelle said, but even as she said those words, it didn't sound like she really believed it now, seconds after saying it. "They all had shaved heads. They might've been monks or something. I know. It sounds crazy. Maybe it wasn't people."

"We're not far from the old church," Danny said. "Maybe it was some monks."

"I didn't see any monks," Mark said.

"Monks, skinheads," Michelle said with a bit of venom in her voice. "I saw faces. And maybe one of them had antlers on." Then she laughed. "Oh, my god, it sounds ridiculous. I've had two beers exactly and I sound ridiculous." She looked at Mark and Danny. "You would've seen it if it were people, wouldn't you?"

"Antlers?" Mark grinned.

"What?" Dash let out a huge laugh, like a ballon popping.

"Okay. Something on his head."

"It was dark," Mark said.

"Maybe," Michelle began. Then she seemed to change her thought. "All right. If I had seen them, they'd still be around."

"Well." Dash clapped his hands together. "Mystery solved. You got bounced around back there. Maybe it jogged some memory or made you hallucinate."

"Well, I guess you three have talked me out of my mania," Michelle said.

"It was pretty dark, 'chelle, and it happened pretty fast,"

Dash said. He shook his head, chuckling. "Antler hats. Pretty good. Skinheads in antler hats."

Mark looked at Dash, but couldn't read anything in his face.

4

It was only later, when Dash went to take a leak with Mark, that Dash said, "It was them. The priests of the Nowhere. This is the night." They stood at the edge of a mossy embankment that encircled what looked like a bog. Thin trees all around. Mark had the uncomfortable feeling that they weren't alone. He kept looking off in the woods as if he would see Danny or Michelle standing there.

Mark toggled his zipper and let loose a stream onto some twigs.

"This is fun, no?" Dash asked. "We're going to be part of a ceremony."

"What are you talking about?" Mark zipped up.

"I guess I didn't tell you. This is Midsummer's Night. A sacred night. Remember in the Wacey Crossing story?"

Mark did. There was a Wacey Crossing story about Midsummer's Night, and how it was the weakest point of darkness in the world, so the Nowhere gods had their moment to come into the world of Man. It was a bit of a shivery tale, and Mark had a few nightmares after reading it. "It was just a story," Mark said. "You nut."

"Everything Wacey Crossing wrote was true," Dash said.

Mark nearly looked at Dash straight on, but didn't. It looked like Dash was pulling that toothbrush case-that-didn't-hold-a-toothbrush out of his inside jacket pocket.

Mark didn't want to see the needle come out.
Or see Dash use it.

5

*Excerpt from "The Night of Changing" by Wacey Crossing
from the collection* In the Grave of The Devourer & Others *published 1882, N.M. Quint & Sons Press, New York,
NY. Used here with permission.*

. . . The one called Rowen motioned to Petra, a flourish-
ing movement of hands that reminded me of fish, swimming. Petra left my side, and I was loathe to let drop
her hand, for fear, for the terror I had begun to feel in
my heart. She was my beloved, and she was too innocent for this night of madness. Her mind would become
twisted from their heathen perversions and dark callings.
I looked upon her in the shaded and sickly moonlight,
upon her luxurious dark hair, her figure so lovely and
dress of gossamer. I was afraid of what this Unholy Man
would do to her, what he might take from her, as he
had taken my peace from me.

But it was too late. She had persuaded me to bring
her, for she longed to speak again to her father. She had
begged me with tears and cries and silence, until finally,
weak man that I am, I allowed her to come with me to
this ceremony.

Gudrun took her hand, and brought her into the
sacred circle, drawing down her cloak, and painting
strange figures upon her face and neck.

I did not know what to expect, for although I had been an initiate for nearly a year, I had not borne witness to this highest of their Holy Days, the shortest night of the year at Midsummer. From my studies, I knew that this was the sacred veil that flowed the thinnest between the world of the Nowhere and the world we human beings occupied. The gods were at their most powerless to resist human intervention in their affairs. I was well aware that invocations would be made, that the Names would be said, and the seven words of power would be intoned over the exhumed grave of one of the early Masters.

The bones of the Masters had been given, reliclike, to the handful of followers left in the world—on some distant European shore, hundreds of thousands of years ago. Each bone, whether a toe-bone or knuckle or entire skull, had been held in secret, and buried with one of the followers, and the circles of belief arose around the grave that held the relic.

I had known that this particular spot of worship held a rib from an early Master. On the rib were the runes of Boediccaeringon, the last words uttered in a time of famine and torture in the west of the British Isles centuries previous. It was used, they said, to ward off the invasions of Romans and Norsemen. I had never seen this sacred rib, but now Gudrun held it.

In the darkness, I saw only its knifelike appearance, curved slightly at the end.

Then Rowen drew close to her. I saw their shadows

nearly touch, and it filled me with both jealousy and dread.

And I knew what he was about. He had lied to me about what this ceremony was—yes, there was truth to his lie. But I knew in that instant that I would forever regret bringing Petra to this bloodthirsty tribe of worshipers.

He was telling her the Names, and the Names were sacred and known only to the few.

And these were the names of the Gods, the TRUE NAMES, THE NAMES OF TERRIBLE AND SWIFT POWER, THE NAMES THAT SHOULD NEVER HAVE BEEN REVEALED TO MANKIND!

To know the secret names of the gods, to be able to say them aloud, had been brought by one who had come back from the dead thousands of years ago. The legend of the Names was that the one who brought them could not get rid of them. They were accursed to the one who knew them, for he could not resist saying them. Could not resist intoning the names of the gods, and this brought terror and panic into the world, and with it, disease and ill-begotten monstrosities. So the first Masters had found a way to put a lock upon them, so that only part of the Names could be said by one, and the Masters knew the completion of the Names— but no Master knew the entire Name to himself alone. The priests that followed the Masters shared the Names as well, and for each gathering, two priests or priestesses would know the Names, and could perform the ceremony if times were needed to invoke the Wrath of

Gods. The flesh of the one who heard the Names could not resist saying them, for the sounds went wormlike not into the brain, but into the lips and the throat, and remained there until the point of Death.

Only in the last throes of Death would they emerge.

I knew then to what end they used my beloved Petra.

God have mercy on my soul that I had ever taken the woman I loved into their corrupt circle! Petra had been living within a world of despair since her dear father had died so horribly! Had I but known the lengths she would go to in order to reach him, in order to be with him again!

She herself took the sharpened bone and thrust it into her breast, and as she died, I heard her utter some insane language, a string of vowels and consonants that made no earthly sense. She fell; the others held me back, though I fought them dearly to get to her.

Rowen crouched down, a lion over its kill, and leaned into her ear to whisper something.

I struggled free and escaped my captors. I fled deep into the bogs and woods, ran from the terror and the evil of it all. The visions of what I'd seen in the dark, of the dancing and singing of the priests and their minions, their shadows against the darker shadows of night, and within their circle, Petra, dying—and with her last breath, the demonic language!

At my apartment on Broad Street, I locked the door,

and shuttered the window from the night. I lit candle after candle and lamp after lamp, to bring the brilliance of day into the late hours.

I heard a rapping at my door at nearly three in the morning.

She had found me. She had returned to me.

How could I resist her? She was my heart. She was my soul.

For her, I snuffed the candles and turned down the lamps.

I let the Nowhere into my room. My soul.

Petra found me before the morning had come.

And she showed me the true visage of a god whose true name should have been destroyed millenia ago, in the ancient tongue of the Chaldeans and Babylonians, a savage, devouring god whose hunger for children and the innocent is never-ending. . . .

4. SHELTER

1

They found nothing in the ditch on the side of the road—neither any people nor deer dying in the woods.

"Whatever it was, it was big and strong."

"Brilliant deduction," Michelle said.

"A bear, maybe," Dash said.

"We got bears out here?" Danny asked.

Michelle flipped out her cell phone. The green light came

up, and she began punching in numbers. "You have triple A, Dash?"

"No."

"Who you callin'?" Mark asked.

Michelle turned her back to them.

Then she said, "Rachel? It's 'chelle. Listen, Dash wrecked his car out—no, we're okay. Oh my god, I know," she said, her voice dropping to a whisper as she said stuff that Mark was sure had to do with what geeks they were and how she'd been stuck riding with them because Danny was too drunk to drive. Then her voice returned to normal. "No, no idea. We're not far from some farmhouse. And a graveyard. Yep. We have a special gift for you. I'm not telling. Can you send your brother out to Route—Rachel? Rach? You're breaking up. Damn it," Michelle said, slapping her phone shut. She spun around. "You guys have a cell phone?"

"I'm technologically challenged at the moment," Dash shrugged, and went to grab a beer from the back of the car. When he got there, scrambling around the backseat, he shouted, "Jesus, Danny, did you drink two six packs?"

"I don't think so," Danny said, looking at both Michelle and Mark with the look of an innocent puppy. "Did I?"

"Found one. Wait, found three. No, five. Who wants a beer?"

"I do!" Mark shouted.

"Yeah," Danny said.

Michelle opened her cell phone again, and tried dialing. "We're in one of those dead areas."

"Dead?" Danny grinned.

"Can't get through," Michelle said, practically under her

breath. She went over and stood beside Mark, and touched him lightly on the shoulder. "I guess we can't just walk to the party? Jesus, Danny, you always have that damn cell phone."

"I have my beeper," Danny said. He reached into the pocket of his shorts and withdrew the small plastic case.

"That'll help. Yeah."

"We can find another phone," Dash said. "There's that church."

"Or the farmhouse."

"Church is closer. There's either going to be a pay phone or an office phone in there."

The sky began dripping with rain. The soft distant rumble of thunder.

"It's comin' back," Danny said. "One one-thousand, two one-thousand."

A few seconds later a flash of lightning so bright it seemed to illuminate the forest, and for a moment, Mark thought he saw some people standing there, behind some trees, just standing there.

Danny began counting again, and a louder rumble of thunder sounded.

The rain began coming down fast, and Dash called out, "Come on, this way," and Michelle put the puppy in the little carrier; Danny took it in his left hand and held her hand with his right, and they ran together. Mark jogged behind them all, down the now-slick road.

Within minutes, Dash ran to the right, up the grass-covered path that led to the Old Church. Mud sloshed all around. The rain came down in sheets, and Danny was laughing and running, and the puppy in the carrier was barking; Mark held the flashlight up so they could see their way up the path, and couldn't wait to get inside the church and be dry again.

As they got closer to it, Mark noticed that there was a flickering light from within the church.

2

"God, we should've just stayed in the car," Michelle said. She was soaked, her hair, dripping strings, her shirt pasted to her breasts. "This feels a little déjà vu in the junior high department. I can't wait to get out of this place and get to Northhampton. May this be my last rainy night in Manossett."

"Yeah," Danny said. Then he added, "God, I feel wasted."

"I'm amazed you're on your feet," Michelle said, nearly cheerfully.

"I can always go down the road to that farmhouse, too," Mark said, not breaking eye contact with Michelle.

"No need, Marco," Dash said.

They huddled inside the arched doorway of the church, Mark pressed against the thick wooden door.

"This is more of a chapel than an actual church," Dash said. "It's one of the oldest in this area."

"It's locked," Danny said.

The windows were all shuttered and locked from the inside, as well—Mark had checked when they'd first arrived.

Lightning illuminated the night again, and Mark saw the rocky graveyard lit up. Again, he thought he saw people—a group of them there—but they seemed blurred to him, and he wasn't sure if perhaps he should not drink more than a couple of beers in any one night.

"This kind of place," Dash said, "has to have a key. This isn't the kind of place people worry about getting broken into. Not way the hell out here." He felt around in the recesses of the arch as it peaked and then dipped, and cried out, "Gotcha!"

He held up a thin round key. "Ask and it shall be given to you."

"Thank god," Michelle said. "I just want to be somewhere dry."

Mark kept looking out through the heavy rain at the darkness of the graveyard. He heard the door open behind him. The puppy whimpered in its carrier, and Danny made baby noises to it as he lifted it and took it inside.

One one-thousand, two one-thousand.

The sky lit up with whiteness.

There, in the graveyard, were shadows of people.

And what looked like an open grave.

Then darkness. Rain. The grumble and crack of thunder.

3

"The world's smallest chapel," Dash said. "You probably know its history."

The chapel was one oblong room, with angles cut into it to create recesses with shrines along its gray stone walls. Mark noticed the windows first—barely slits to let in light, with stained glass in them. The shutters outside were deceptive—they were large, and had made Mark think the place had large windows as well. When he and Dash had been in the graveyard before, they'd never thought to venture in the church itself. It was a plain, nearly bare church, with flat, long benches for pews. The altar looked very much like a wide flat stone of four or five feet in length, and two feet wide.

The light they had seen from the road had been from candles—there were fat long candles in brass holders up and down the aisles.

"If the windows were shuttered, how did you see the light?" he asked Dash.

Dash grinned. Winked at him.

"Well, there's no phone here," Michelle said. "At least it's dry."

"Yeah. And it's better than being out there."

"How's the puppy?" she asked.

Danny crouched beside the carrier and looked in. "Doing fine. Chewin' on his rawhide."

"Damn," Dash said. "My ciggies are ruined." He held up his pack of Marlboros.

"I have some," Mark said. He reached into his pocket and drew out two cigarettes. "Got a lighter?"

"I do," Danny said, feeling in his pockets.

"I got matches," Dash said, withdrawing some from within his jacket. "And shockingly, they're dry. Five left." He struck one against the matchbook, and Mark passed him a cigarette. "You keep these." He passed the matches to Mark once he'd begun puffing on the cigarette. Mark thrust the matches into the back pocket of his jeans. "You got four more cigarettes and four more matches. Perfect, Marco."

"I hope Rachel appreciates the effort we go to for her birthday," Michelle said. She reached into her handbag and withdrew a comb. She ran it through her hair, her head tilting sideways. She wandered over to one of the pews near the front of the chapel. "So now what?" She patted the bench where she sat, and Danny hobbled over and sat down beside her. Soon his arm was around her waist, and she leaned against his shoulder, looking up at the candles at the altar. "This is one ugly chapel. Those puritans really—holy crap, look at that!" she pointed toward the curved wall behind the altar.

Mark immediately looked there. Behind the flickering candle, there was a painting that reminded him of something from his sophomore European History book. It was nearly medieval looking—a faded painting of what seemed to be several monks, their heads shaved in tonsure.

"Those look like the guys I saw," Michelle gasped, and then giggled. "How bizarre."

"Oh yeah, the monks we hit," Dash said, his voice brimming with contempt.

"Gives me the creeps, a little," Michelle said. "Now I *really* wish we'd stayed in the car."

"And risked getting hit from behind by another car. No thank you," Dash said. "What good would that do? Your cell phone won't work. I know this place. I'm sure there's a phone in it."

Mark said something about how seeing a painting of monks in a chapel was not the strangest thing in the world, but the whole time he felt like he was lying. He wasn't sure why, but there was something funny about the painting. He walked up the aisle to get a closer look, then stepped up the worn, uneven stone steps to the altar.

The monks had faces like softened inverted triangles and

large wise eyes. There were four of them. In one of their hands, there was what looked like a thin white flute or recorder that bore markings—*Hebrew? Latin?*—Mark had no idea. As he gazed at it in the shimmering candlelight, he thought it might be the thin tusk of some wild animal rather than a flute. The next monk held a round stone in his hand, or perhaps it was a large wafer of some kind. Again, this had strange markings upon it. The third monk held both his hands out. The artist had painted in that flat style of Norman invasion paintings—that's what it had been, the picture in his history book of William the Conqueror invading England. The third monk's hands were merely presented as having nothing in them.

But the fourth monk in the group held a small human skull.

And the skull had small bumps along its scalp—two just above the forehead. And its front row of teeth seemed unusually sharp, nearly wolflike.

"It's funny," Mark said.

Behind him, Michelle. She had gotten up and looked around the altar, too. "What?"

"I was sure I'd been in here once. A long time ago. Some time. But I guess I never have. I've been outside before. But never in here. I've never even seen anyone go in here before."

"Look at this," Michelle said. He turned, and she was reading something off the top of the altar.

He went to look. The stone tablet of altar was rough, and covered with a stubble of what might've been mold or some kind of dusty lichen. Michelle brushed some of it off. "Look at that, Mark," she said, pointing to something carved into the stone.

Mark thought the drawing was a squiggle of circles and lines intersecting—some abstract Christian imagery. He noticed that it had eyes.

"It's some kind of bird," she said.

"Or bug. Look at its wings. There are four of them," Mark said. In his mind, the words *Swarmgod of the Thousand Stings* seemed to surface. Words beneath the carved figure. "Is this Aramaic or something?"

"It's Latin," Dash said from the back of the room. "Or Greek."

"I took Latin in ninth grade," Michelle said. "It doesn't look like anything I remember."

"Then it's Greek," Dash said. "I've been in here before. I got a guided tour. This is one of the oldest churches in New England."

"How old?" Michelle asked, idly, her eyes never leaving the altar top.

"I would guess the sixteen-somethings."

"No, wait, I know what language this is. This is just French," Michelle said. "It's just carved in the stone with such a strange script, I didn't notice it. Let's see, this means, no, maybe it's not French. It's something I recognize." She leaned against the stone tablet. "Why would the pilgrims write in Greek? Or French?"

"I'm sure more than just pilgrims have been using this in the past five hundred or so years," Mark volunteered.

"That's right," Dash said.

"This is Latin, this part of it." Michelle's fingers traced the engraving. "VE. DEU. VI. Well, it's all broken up. It could mean anything. And what the hell is that? It looks like a round mouth full of sharp teeth."

"Deu is probably Deus," Mark said. The words seemed to be in his head: *The Devourer. She Who Befouls The Night. The Pope of Pestilence.*

"Maybe," Michelle nodded. "These drawings are fascinating. They almost look like caveman paintings. This word—AMOR. That's easy. Unless it's part of a longer word—too bad it got rubbed away here. I just wish I could figure out the letters in between."

"I didn't know you studied Latin," Mark said.

"Two years, but I switched to French junior year. I stopped enjoying it," Michelle said. Then she arched an eyebrow. "What, you think I'm just some dumb rich girl skating through life?"

"No, no, really, I don't," Mark said.

"Well, there's always more to people than you think. Even you and your buddy." Michelle offered a sweet smile. "I'll probably major in comparative lit at Smith, if I can take German and handle it at the same time. Someday, maybe I'll translate great works of literature. Or be a foreign correspondent."

"Or a spy," Dash said.

Mark almost wanted to tell Dash to shut up. He had his own interest in language and had been studying Spanish in school, but had wanted to learn French, too. He looked at Michelle carefully, as if seeing her for the first time. She noticed, and laughed.

"I guess it takes a car wreck and a storm for us to get along," she said, and he felt a warmth from her, just standing beside her. Connecting in some way that he never thought he could with a girl like Michelle.

"Well, obviously, there's no phone here," Dash said. "Maybe we better take a hike."

"Yeah," Mark said, feeling a bit more like a man.

"I'll be fine here. I'm going to try and decipher this stuff," Michelle said. "Danny, you want to go with them?"

Danny, the puppy in his lap, made a motion that seemed to indicate that the puppy needed him.

"Me and Mark will go to that farmhouse," Dash said. "You two stay here. What, it's maybe a mile down the road?"

Mark nodded. "Yeah."

"We can run."

"Sure," Mark said, but dreaded the rain.

"You two just continue the party here, dry off, and we'll be back," Dash said. "Feel free to chug the last beer, Danny."

4

The rain had slowed to a steady but light sprinkling. The lightning was off in a distant sky, barely lighting the path from the old church.

"Okay, now, here's what we do," Dash said.

"What's all this?" Mark said.

"Huh?"

" 'Huh?' You planned this," Mark said. "I know you did. What is all this? The church. The crash. Huh?"

"Come on, Marco, I told you, we'll have a little fun."

"It's not fun. It's the opposite of fun. Fun would be the party. Fun would be anywhere but here."

They walked out among the graves. Mark kept the flashlight on the ground to avoid any rocks and stones.

"She's a bitch, you know that? Don't let her fool you with all that Latin shit. She spent half of high school thinking that guys like you and me are less than toads, so don't suddenly get all sugary just because she shows you her rack."

"Aw crap, maybe we are less than toads sometimes, Dash. Maybe we are. Maybe all this weirdo Nowhere shit is just the kind of crap that toads do."

"Blasphemy," Dash spat, and reached over and slapped him hard on the face.

It stung. Mark reached up and touched his cheek. It was numb.

"What the hell?" Mark said.

"Tonight is the night," Dash said, and grabbed him by the elbow and pulled him close to him. The flashlight fell from Mark's hand. Dash's breath was all beer. "Look, you've known since you were thirteen that you were going to be part of this. You knew. And tonight is the night. Just like in the book. It's the Night of Lifting The Veil. It's nearly midnight. It's Midsummer's Night. The shortest night of the year. The night when the veil between our world and the world of the Nowhere is thinnest."

Mark laughed. "Come on. Come on, Dash. Come on."

He pulled away from Dash, walking ahead on a narrow, scraggly path between gravestones. "Get real."

Then Mark thought he saw something before him—some shape that was all shadow, and he saw that at the edge of the graveyard, like a gate, there were people standing there, in long coats or cloaks, he wasn't sure, but he could see them.

He heard Dash groan behind him. Sound of sudden movement. Mark was about to turn around to see what was wrong, when something hit him hard on the side of the head, and he was out.

5

Mark awoke a few seconds later, but felt dizzy. His vision blurred, but it was all shadows and scant moonlight around him. The rain kept coming down. He lay in mud.

He thought he saw others there, those people, those monks, whoever and whatever they were, and it seemed nearly natural to see them. He almost expected them. Had it all been true? Had everything Dash told him about the Nowhere—all those stories—been true?

He lay there, blinking, in the rain.

Of course, a cult could survive. There were people who practiced witchcraft who believed their religion had survived despite burnings and centuries of torture and murder. There were all kinds of cults and religions in the world—he knew that. But right here? In Manosset, near the Sound, in the twenty-first century? And could they be so backward and ig-norant as to truly believe that there were gods with such ridiculous names as She Who Befouls The Night?

But those were just nicknames. He knew that from the Wacey Crossing stories. All names for the gods were not their true names. Their true names were only known by those who held the power.

The back of his head throbbed.

He looked up into Dash's face, shadowed with night.

Were they alone? He felt alone.

"Here's the thing. You've got to listen very carefully, Marco.

Very carefully. There are words, and they're on this," Dash pressed something into Mark's hand. His fingers curled around it instinctively. "Sometimes, the god that enters gets out of hand. And has to be stopped. The words will stop the god. The words are the only thing that stops the god. Listen. Just lie there and listen or I will hit you again so hard so help me god Marco you might never wake up. Listen! This is so important," Dash said. Was he weeping? Was it rain? Mark couldn't tell. "I have to fulfill something here. It is my destiny. I am chosen for something, and tonight is the night. When this happens—and it has only happened nine times since the dawn of recorded history, Marco, nine times. I will be the tenth. I will be the tenth, and this hasn't been arrived at lightly. They are very smart people. They have waited more than a thousand years in their religion to allow this to happen again. They feel it's time. And I am the one. But you have got to remember the words when you hear them, Marco. I can only say them once. You are the only one who can stop this with the words. Only the one I . . . I—" Dash's voice broke. Then strength returned. "Only the one I have given my heart to can stop this once it starts. And the words have got to be remembered. These others," Dash nodded to darkness, although Mark saw no one, "they have had their tongues cut out lest they utter the words. The one who told me, taught me, drilled me in this, is dead. I can say the words to you, but you must remember them. And with the words, I will tell you the names of the gods. This is an enormous responsibility. The world is corrupt. The time of human life is nearly over. The gods want to return and end the stupidity of this race of men. The names of the gods . . ." He leaned into Mark's face, and pressed his mouth to Mark's ear. He began

301

whispering something that Mark tried to remember as soon as he heard it.

"There's really a Nowhere?" Mark asked, pleading in his voice.

"Oh," Dash sighed. "Marco, wait 'til you see it. I mean *really* see it. There's something you need to drink. Here, sit up."

Mark felt Dash's hand slip behind his neck, pressing near the throbbing. "It's easier to see like this."

Mark moaned a little—the pain at the back of his scalp intensified. "You hit me too hard."

"Sorry." Dash withdrew the hypodermic needle from the plastic case.

"What—what are you—what—don't," Mark whispered.

"It'll take the pain away. And you'll understand. You'll see. You will really see," Dash said, and he held Mark's arm down, tore his shirt sleeve up to his bicep. Dash squeezed his bicep, and then Mark felt the needle go in, twisting into his flesh. "This isn't junk. This is ambrosia. Believe me," Dash whispered. "You'll have a taste of the Nowhere. What it really can be like."

6

The sensation of floating, but not floating.

Hands moved in birdlike blurs before his eyes.

It was already morning. The rain had stopped. The sun was out.

But the sun was white, not a warm yellowish gold, it was white—all the light was pure white in the sky. There was no sun. Mark sat up against the gravestone. The throbbing in his head was gone. The trees were funny; the woods seemed funny. Something moved along the bark of the trees. Snakes and worms wriggled along them.

The strange thing was: some things were missing. The trees themselves didn't move in a light wind; and there was no rain, although there had been seconds before.

Dash was there, only he was Dash with a difference: he seemed better looking. Color in his face. A rosy glow. His eyes were like a little boy's—all happy and expectant. Mark's eyes went in and out of focus, and he heard a strange humming in his head. He looked at his hands, and he saw them as liquid, contained within some invisible boundary that defined "hand." When he waved his hand, some molecules of flesh dispersed— just a few and seemed to form into an insect of some type in the air—a ladybug, flying off.

"Ain't it cool?" Dash asked. "It's like the world, only different. If you stay still, you disappear. Watch." Dash closed his eyes and mouth, and clasped his hands together. Within seconds, he seemed to evaporate like steam.

Then he laughed, and suddenly was there again. "The world we're used to has to move a lot or make noise for things in The Veil to see it. It's a strange place, no?"

Dash kept laughing, but it all seemed to move slowly, and Dash reached into his own chest, and drew back his black T-shirt, tearing it, only it didn't tear like fabric. It formed droplets of black goo that absorbed against his green jacket. Dash pressed his hand against the skin of his pale, hairless chest and drew back the skin—not as if it were cut or scraped, but again, in that liquid medium, as if Dash himself were a bubble of soap, with the image of flesh and clothing poured into him—malleable and shifting, but within a boundary that kept the liquid in place.

Dash's fingers went deeper into his flesh, and drew out what appeared to be a pulsing mass of purple and poppy red. Smiling, Dash brought it closer to Mark's face. "My heart," he said. "My heart and your heart." Dash reached into Mark's chest, and it tickled. Mark laughed, and felt Dash's fingers inside his flesh, moving along the organs within his ribcage and up. A featherlike tickle of his heart. All the while, the liquid between their bodies, the floating droplets, merged and mixed, splashing together.

Dash held both hearts for Mark to see. "We're brothers," Dash said.

"The Veil," Mark murmured, feeling particularly good, as if he had never known, what it meant in life to feel good.

Dash nodded. "Yep. The Veil. From a garden that existed thousands and thousands of years ago. A garden destroyed by mankind when it learned the secret names of the gods. But the wise ones who knew its value rescued this flower and its seed. And they've planted it and cared for it in secret all these years, Marco. And it shows you the real world. The Nowhere. If I told you this was Eden itself, wouldn't you believe me? Look, we flow. Look at the sky. This is night, Marco. Not daylight. This is true night. The blackness is an illusion. See? Look—" Dash pointed to the sky. An eel or snake of some kind wriggled in the white air as if it were moving through rippling milk. "This is the realm of the gods. This is what we're blinded from. This is what the Nowhere people know. And always have. We can't be here long. We can't take The Veil too much. It's addictive, but it can be horrible as well as beautiful. Do you see now? Marco? How beautiful? Marco, I've seen magnificent cities on the surface of the sea—I've seen creatures that have only been drawn in ancient texts—sea monsters, mermaids, all here, all within The Veil. And the gods, too. They cause what happens, in our world, but we are blinded and cannot see—we see through darkness. The Nowhere is the true light."

"I feel a little sick," Mark said, reaching to his stomach. "Sick."

"It's your first time. But you'll get used to it. You'll enjoy it more. Right now, you can only tolerate a few minutes. But later you'll be able to have more of it. I'll show you amazing things, brother. Amazing. Each one more beautiful than the next," Dash said, and then he held something in the air. It looked like a white horn of some type. Writhing around it, tiny red insects, mites of some kind, thousands of them. "You'll come out of this in a minute or two, Marco. When you do, you must say the names as soon as I've said the first part. And if it gets too out of hand, you can stop it. There's always a way to stop it. Just remember the words. They're here, on this bone. The names you can't forget, even if you try. Your flesh hears them once, and your molecules take in the names of the gods and hold them. You have to say the names as soon as you see me die."

"Die?" Mark looked at him, uncomprehending. "You're going to die?"

"Not really. Not die like you think. You ready?" Dash held the bone in front of his chest.

He began saying what Marco realized were the first halves of the names of the gods of the Nowhere.

Alone, with Dash, in the rain. Out of The Veil. In the real world. The ordinary, awful world again. Mark sat up. Sky, black. The earth, sucking mud.

Taking the smooth thin bone, Dash pressed the sharpened end of it into his chest.

Mark reached for the bone, pulling it out. "No, Dash, please, no!"

As he let out a final breath, Dash whispered the beginning of the names of the gods.

When Dash's eyes were closed, Mark said the last half of the names. He didn't know how he could remember them—they were a long string of sounds and clicks and howls. They hurt his ears to say, like a strangely out of tune sound of pipes being played from his throat—or a saw twanging across the vowels of the names.

He almost wanted to say the words, as well, out of fear.

The words that could stop this.

But he hesitated.

Then Dash opened his eyes again.

They glowed like the ends of cigarettes in the dark.

5. CHURCH OF THE VEIL

1

Mark began shivering in the darkness as he watched what had been Dash rise to its feet. It no longer seemed to be Dash, not in the sense that he had felt Dash had been. It had the glowing eyes, and its teeth were sharp at the ends, small nails of teeth, and even in the moonlight, Mark could see the way spurs burst from his joints—elbows and knees—and writhing worms, long nightcrawlers moved along his fingers.

"Nowhere is here." Dash grinned, and for a second Mark thought it was a trick. The drug, perhaps, still lingering in his system. *Of course. The drug. The Veil.* The needle that had gone in his arm.

"Jesus," Dash said. "I'm hungry."

2

Dash turned, glancing toward the church. Then back to Mark. "You're not going to understand this, Mark. If you could see what I see, you would." The red eyes burned and then seemed to fade into Dash's normal eyes.

Mark heaved a sigh—it must've been the drug. It must've been. He was still hallucinating. He still felt weak and dizzy, and he had to sit down again. His head was spinning. It was the drug. That's all it was. None of it had happened.

"Look, give me a minute," Dash said. "You need to rest. You're going through a lot. Shit, *I've* been through a lot."

Mark turned and threw up onto a gravestone. He wiped his mouth; a sickly sweet taste lingered in his throat. *The Veil.*

When he turned around, Dash was gone; by the time Mark rose to his feet, he thought he saw some enormous winged bird—almost a pterodactyl, given its wingspan—landing at the door to the old church; but it was a man—no, it was Dash.

Mark walked toward the church, lurching with each step,

stopping every few feet to cough. *God, what if I die? What if that drug kills me?* He slid in the mud and had to pick himself up. His heart beat rapidly. *It was poison. I'm going to die.*

By the time he reached the door to the old church, he heard Danny's shout.

3

The candles along the altar were lit. It was warm and humid within the church, as if the summer storm had turned it into a steamroom.

"What the fuck?" Danny laughed. "Holy shit, what the hell have you been drinkin', Dashy? Or maybe it's me, maybe it's just me!" He was beer-soaked at this point; the last couple of bottles lay beside him on the stone altar. Michelle glanced up— they had been making out, which is what they seemed to do whenever they had five minutes to themselves.

"Dash, don't, just—just—get away," Mark shouted from the doorway. He stepped into the back of the church. "Just come outside!"

"Oh Danny boy, the pipes, the pipes are callin'," Dash began to sing, and practically skipped into the church. Danny had his pants off, briefs intact, button-down shirt still on with a few buttons missing; Michelle's shirt was open; she made an annoyed sound in the back of her throat.

"Sorry to interrupt, lovebirds," Dash said.

"Get the hell outta here," Danny said, but he began laughing—it must have struck him as funny to be caught nearly doing it with his girl on the altar of this rat-hole church. Michelle pushed Danny away and began closing her shirt.

"Enough," she said.

"Just a little fun," Dash said. Mark stood at the entrance to the church, watching Dash, unsure of what he was really seeing. Dash seemed to move with a grace he'd never had before, like a dancer or gymnast, and he went right up to the altar and pressed his hands down on two of the candles to snuff them out.

Only one left.

"Dash!" Mark called out. "Come on, let's go. This won't be fun."

Dash turned back to him, and in the final candle's glow, laughed a little—laughed the way he would when they'd first met, back in eighth grade, a let's-have-fun laugh, and said, "Oh, wait and see."

Then he snuffed the last candle out. The room was plunged into darkness.

"Hey, who turned off the lights?" Danny shouted. Mark saw shadows against shadows. Michelle started cussing and saying she just wanted to get the puppy and get to the party, and why didn't her cell phone work? Danny began laughing and telling her that it was going to be better in the dark, but Mark heard a strange groaning sound—perhaps a creaking of some door?

The door behind him slammed shut, as if by a great wind.

But there had been no wind.

And then the screaming began.

The time moved swiftly, for Mark's first instinct was to run away; but he moved forward in the darkness, hitting one of the long benches. He dug into his pocket for the matches, and drew them out. Only four left.

He lit one, and for a fizzing few seconds, the light lit the room—there was Michelle, screaming, and something with enormous leathery wings, and crablike appendages studding its body. It was Dash, but it was no longer Dash. It had hold of Danny by the throat and was shaking him hard, side to side.

The match went out.

Another match; he struck it, and it flared for a moment.

Michelle was halfway to him—her eyes were wide and seemed to have lost all intelligence—

A creature that seemed both insect and dragon—it was only an impression, like the flash of a dream—chewing on Danny's scalp—

Mark dropped the match and was again in complete darkness.

Gurgling sounds followed, and then the tearing sound of meat and a cracking of bones.

Michelle ran past him. He felt a revulsion toward her, as if in her sudden madness, she were no longer human.

Dash's voice from the darkness:

"Yessssss," snakelike and hollow. "Marco, the Nowhere is here, you helped bring it, it's all true," and then the sounds of a dreadful slobbering and gobbling, as of a wild dog swiftly devouring some prey.

Mark drew out a third match, and struck it in the matchbook.

Dash stood so close to him that they were practically touching.

Shocked by the closeness, Mark dropped the match, and it went out.

In that second, he had seen the white and pink worms

encircling Dash's throat and hands, growing in pulsating movements from his flesh, and soft fuzzy tendrils gently fluttering from his bare waist and ribcage.

His mouth painted a dark red.

In his arms, he cradled what was left of Danny's body. Torn and ragged and more meat than human.

"Any shape I desire," Dash said, and tossed Danny's remains to Mark when the darkness again engulfed him.

Mark felt the nausea sweep through him; he dropped the body, and turned to run, but fell to his knees instead.

"Pray to your little god," Dash said. "Pray like a good altar boy. But you're in the wrong place, Marco. This is the altar of the Nowhere. The Church of The Veil. Now, where do you think Michelle's run off to? Not outside. I made sure the door was shut tight and locked. She must be here. Hiding. Oh, yes! This makes it more of a game, doesn't it? But I can see with more than eyes now. You know that, Marco. You've been through The Veil. You know that it's a world of liquid white now."

Mark wanted to cry out or scream, but his voice had abandoned him—or else he had screamed so much in the past few moments without realizing it that he had no voice left. He felt cold and hot at the same time. *The words. Remember the words.*

You can stop him with them. They're the words of ending. The god will return to The Veil. The words.

"I can hear her breathing," Dash said. "She is gonna love what I do to her. I hope you're there to see it, Marco. I hope you'll partake."

Mark thought he heard Michelle cry out from behind him.

"Run! Get out! Michelle! Just get out!"

The sound of her sobs echoed. "It's locked!" she cried, banging on the door, "Somebody! Somebody help me! Help!"

"Michelle! Shut up! Just shut up!" Mark yells. "Stay still and shut up!"

It needs movement and noise. Maybe it will leave now that it had Danny. Dear Jesus help us. Help her.

The words. Remember them.

PART TWO: THE ENDING

1

And so, in the room in the church, it feels his ankles. He has pressed himself against the wall, halfway between scared shitless and ready to do something—anything—to keep it from going after Michelle.

Slick and sticky and wormy, it seems to lick his calves with its feelers. Michelle by the door, moaning out little noises—and the thing that Dash has become is slithering and feeling its way over to her. In Dash's mind, he must be seeing the whiteness of the darkness. He must be seeing the liquid move and slosh, and the unseen things that move in the air and along the walls. He must see Michelle, too, not as a terrified young woman of eighteen, but as some collection of molecules to be devoured, to be fed upon, to increase its happiness and its mission as it moves through the world.

The last of the tendrils that Dash-thing drags with him, slide away from Mark's foot.

Leaving him. Letting him go.

Moving toward her.

She is groaning as if she can't contain her fear.

And then she lets out a bloodcurdling scream—and another and another in quick succession.

He hears the throaty laugh. "Come on, it's only me, Mielle, come on," Dash says, and for a fleeting instant Mark thinks that it might be a game. It might just be all fake. *The drug! Yeah! It's the drug!* What he saw, the heap in the corner, wasn't Danny at all. It was some kind of illusion. Some trick of light and dark. A bad acid flashback.

This is some kind of trip. This isn't the real world.

Michelle's sobbing, with screamlets in her voice, jagged shards of sound.

Get to Danny. In his jacket. A lighter.

It's afraid of light. The Nowhere can't exist where there's any light. Any genuine light. If darkness is light to it, than surely light is its own kind of darkness.

"You always wanted me, Michelle, you always did," the thing that Dash has become says. "Rachel used to tell me how you thought I was quirky and cool, and when she did, when she whispered those things to me, it got me so revved up, baby, and I knew that someday, you and I would have this moment." As he spoke, Mark heard the whirring sound again—a soft, rapid fluttering. He'd once had a junebug fly into his ear, and it was a sound very much like that.

If I just get to Danny's jacket, Mark thinks. *The lighter.*

"Please," Michelle is whimpering. "Dash, please. Don't hurt me. Please. Oh god. Please." Her "please" becomes the sound of bleating, and in a horrible way it's funny, it sounds like a joke, but Mark knows it's not.

Why doesn't she try to run? Is it blocking her way? Mark estimates that he can get to the doorway, to where Danny's body rests. He can grab the jacket and thrust his hand into the pockets. He can get the lighter, flick it up, and scare it away.

Scare that creature away.

"Oh, Michelle, baby," it says. "I want to love you so badly. I want you to be my girl, don't you know that?"

"Please," she says such an awful tone that tears come to Mark's eyes even as he takes a step toward the opposite corner of the room.

"Take my hand, Michelle, don't be afraid," it says. "I want to love all of you in every way."

The sound changes—it feels like an alarm has gone off somewhere. A sound like hissing and spitting and the crack of a whip.

"No!" Michelle screams, "Oh my god, oh my god, god, god, god, god!" Her screams turn into giggles and jets of laughter. Mark races to Danny's body, pushing through the wetness, tearing the jacket from what remains of him, sifting quickly through the pockets until he finds something cylindrical and hard.

The lighter.

Hang on, Michelle.

The sounds are wet and bubbling. Michelle is moaning, as if she has been swiftly gagged.

Mark turns, flicking the lighter. It doesn't light.

Flick! Again no light.

Then it catches.

A small flame erupts from the lighter.

He cups it in his hand, a yellow and rosy glow around his palm.

He calls out to it, but the noise—the splattering noise and that whirring—has begun again.

Mark brings the flame up to see—

Shadows cast against the old bare wall of the room.

He sees what looks like the spread wings of a shiny beetle and long white and pink worms—or slender tentacles—moving between Dash's body, which floats barely a foot in the air— holding Michelle—caressing her—she struggles against it—the worms inside her mouth, her nose, tearing her shirt off, scraping at her skin until it is flaps hanging down—the wormy tendrils shooting and pulsing from Dash's mouth and eyes and ears— his ribcage opens like two doors creaking apart—and long feathery whips emerge and stroke her skin—Mark feels frozen in terror—the worms are wriggling, but they are from Dash's ribcage—boring out from them, and feathery, barnacle-like fans—moving swiftly, tickling her breasts and sides—and her eyes are wild and the worm-appendages of the thing reach into her ears—and they are—

Mark shouts, "I have light! You have no power in the light!" He waves the flame around, his arm outstretched, his body taut. "I'll set you on fire."

He moves over to Dash, what Dash has become, to the beetle-like wings, four of them, spread wide, with a layer of nearly transparent wings in between. Bone in one hand, lighter in the other, the flame shooting up high. He tries to read the bone, but he can't—not while Michelle is still . . .

315

But he tries—the symbols on the bone seem different from before. They seem to have smudged or moved around, and he can't quite see them for the flickering light.

With the light, he can see the markings—the sores and pustules along Dash's spine. Dash turns for a moment, his face covered with many small black eyes, and he says, his words rapid-fire and ripe with excitement, "The light has no power over me, Mark. Not once the incarnation has happened. All the world is white light. Once in the flesh, I'm indestructible. Unless you know the words. But you don't, do you? You will never know them. You will never read the bone, will you? How can you? Only the priests who have studied for decades can remember them, can speak them." And then the creature turns about to Michelle's beatific and glowing form, the blood shining along her body, and begins devouring her like a spider feeding upon a wriggly fly caught in its web. "Oh, so delicious, such a deleecious treat," Dash says, his mouth foaming with white and red. Then, his opening body, like a mouth, covers her, like a Venus flytrap, like a devourer.

Shivering, Mark moves toward him and thrusts the flame against his neck, but the worms shoot out from beneath the wings and tear the lighter from his fingers.

The creature turns—its face bubbling with sores, its eyes blinking in unison. It regards Mark with some interest.

The wings close, and it floats inches downward until it touches the floor.

Then, with the dark that encircles the small yellow flame like a cloak, it shoots tendrils around Mark's ribs. He presses against them, but he can't pull free. It lifts him up, and he feels the invasive, parasitic wormy fingers moving against the holes in his ears, pressing onto his lips, forcing them open. Lower, his navel is stretching as the worms push inward. Wave after wave of nausea hits him.

The slick, wet tendrils pry the sacred bone from his fingers. What feel like bundles of worms thrust down the back of his throat. He feels the sharp jab against his stomach—

the bone—

Going into him.

Dash's voice, nearly sweet, whispering along with the dreadful humming of the wings as they move rapidly, "I won't let you hurt for long, Marco. I want you and me to be together. We can do anything now. Anything. And we'll bring the Nowhere into daylight. We'll tear The Veil."

2

Dying? Blood is pouring from his stomach and legs.

Dash, in the dark, seeming human, seeming not to have a thousand wormy tentacle arms and barnacle feathers, lifts up Mark. Lifts him with two arms. Broken bones shift; freezing pain. No screams left in him. Mark is sure now that he screamed the whole time the creature was slaughtering Michelle.

Through the narrow hall. Smell of fresh air. Outside again. Sky is clear. Moonlight, very little, but enough.

Dash strips off Mark's shirt, and with his fingernails scratches markings on his chest and stomach. "You can be like this, too. Just like we said. We never have to be apart. We can be in the Nowhere."

"No." Mark tries to lift his head, but can't. "Please, I need help, Dash."

"The words," Dash says. "Just remember them. Your body will die soon." He lets out what can only be a sigh of contentment. "None of this has to change who we are. This is just the god thing. It's what gods have to do. Look, Mark, I know things now. I gained knowledge. Yeah, it hurts some, and part of me feels bad, but when it takes me over, man, you have got to experience this. It's like . . . like fucking life. Like there's no darkness at all. There's a whole other world you can see when you're like this. You can see things without your eyes. You have feelers. You have these parts of you that can stretch out and find things without even opening your eyes. And them? Michelle and Danny? Shit, they're in another place. Death isn't bad for them. They're the food of the gods, that's all. They're chow. Gods eat life. That's how it goes. The god of grass eats grass and the god of the flesh eats flesh. You can't have life without this. It's something we've all gotten away from, but the worshipers, the priests of the Nowhere, they've known. They've kept the ritual. They've put themselves at one with the gods to do this. We are anointed ones, we are gods in flesh. You can't be afraid. You can't look at this with the same eyes you had before, not once it's happened. It's stupid and human of you to do it. When you die, you're not going over there. You're going to come back here. Do you know what the gods are? Do you? Do you?"

A hiss that might've been contempt came from Mark's lips as he looks up at the dark figure.

"The gods are creatures, just like us, but they don't have boundaries. They reshape themselves at will. They let their hunger loose. Their lusts. Their wants. We think things happen because we do them or there are natural laws, but Marco, there aren't natural laws—the gods make things happen, they make it all go. But their names are power. I have the power. It's within me," Dash says, passion swelling in his voice. "I can be anything, Marco. Anything."

3

Mark, in the muddy grass, at the edge of the grave. He looks up at what once had been Dash.

What is still Dash.

The moonlight is soft around his face. Dash has a beautiful face. Dash has an ugly face.

Michelle. Danny. Gone. In less than an hour.

It still looks enough like Dash, with his hair, stringy from rain, matted with mud. His longish jaw and his eyes that seemed to shine even in the absence of light. Just two eyes. Two human eyes. No thousand eyes of some monster. Darkness around his lips. Blood?

"You're dying," Dash says. "Don't be afraid of it. Just say the name. Just say it, Marco."

"Mmm," Mark says. "Nuh. No."

"We never have to live anywhere but in the Nowhere again. Not ever."

"You're dead." Mark isn't sure if Dash can even hear him. Mark feels so weak, with his life draining from him.

"The name," Dash says. "Remember? You say it as you die. The first part. I say the other half of the name after you breathe your last. I know all their names now, Marco. I know each of the gods, and their wonderful hungers and the way they look—I can see them all around us. We are their children. I have them incarnate within me, too. I can be a thousand different things. I can be a hornet or dragon, Marco. I can bring up a wind or burn with fire. I can see clearly, more clearly than I could in daylight, see with more than just these useless eyes. I can smell my sight, I can feel sight. You will, too!

"We can go to Rachel's party. We don't have to miss it. We can bring her the puppy. I'm not going to hurt the puppy. It's not like that. What's inside me now, it has meaning. It doesn't want puppies and turtles and goats and chickens. It wants more than that. Everyone will be there. Everyone from our class. And we'll show them that we're not just there for their pecking order and social put-downs. We'll be there to show them the faces of the gods. We could even bring some more of them back, if we're careful with their bodies. We could make all of us live forever, if you really want. I mean, yeah, it's too late for Michelle and Danny, but I let it out too much. I hadn't learned how to pull back on the reins yet. But I think I understand now.

"And the Nowhere is with us. They think I'm a messiah. They'll know you as my lieutenant. We'll change everything. Everything in one night if we have to. We'll pull back The Veil. You and me, both. After you say the name. And then you'll be here again. We can fly now. We can swim under water for hours. We can turn to liquid or move within the bark of a tree. We can become the darkness. Or light. And it'll be you and me. Brothers. In the Nowhere. We'll be gods here, Marco. We'll do things we couldn't have imagined before. Before it was just a game. Now it's real, and we're real, and the others, the people in the world, your mother and father and mine and the teachers at the Gardner School, they're the unreal ones. We can go on to Rachel's next. Just the name. Let me whisper it to you."

Mark closes his eyes.

Soft rain falling. Just drips of it. On his face. Cooling rain.

The feeling of Dash's wet slippery hand touching Mark's face.

"The name," Dash says, as gentle as the rain. "Just say it for me. I love you so much. Just say it." Dash may have tears in his eyes, or perhaps it is the raindrops falling gently on Mark's face.

He opens his eyes. The shadow of Dash's face is all he sees. The smell of his breath—the same stink of the dead body, its flesh torn open.

Mark mutters something.

"Marco?"

Mark says it as loud as he can. It comes out a whisper. "You. Not my brother. I don't love you. I don't want to be with you after I die . . . far away from you."

All his energy in those words. He feels smug. Numb and smug. A worm of pain somewhere in his gut, but otherwise, he's ready to go. *In the arms of Death.*

Mark wants to close himself up.

To die without remembering the name.

To die without Dash's whisper against his ear.

The image of Michelle's face, covered with tears. Michelle, who was beautiful and wonderful, only Mark couldn't see it because he'd let Dash infect him all those years. Michelle, who was not stupid. Michelle, who was not trashy and snotty all at once. She was a beautiful human being, a shining human being, who had deserved more than eighteen lousy years on this earth. She had deserved a life after high school, a life after college. She might've become something magnificent if she'd had the chance.

He loves her right then. That night. That moment of dread, of fear. He knows what love is. It isn't sex and longing and a feeling. It isn't the empty thing he had thought, of wants and needs and kindness. It is deeper than anything he thought before—deeper than all the philosophies that Dash had spouted, the empty words, the babblings of Wacey Crossing, it is richer than any of that. It is the understanding that in the extreme of life, all of them are connected somehow. All of them are within the same skin. That is love. That is what love is. Not what Dash had sold him on. Not this . . . darkness . . . this death god. Danny and Michelle, swept from the earth as if they didn't matter. He had loved them, just because he had understood how he was brother to both of them. In that awful moment. He is connected to them by the invisible cord of humanity, a cord he has never felt tugging at him before, but now it is all he feels.

Dash has trampled all that with his magic and words and runes. Stupid figures scratched on bones and somewhere in his mind. Words from some best-forgotten tongue. A tongue no doubt cut out by invaders and new religions that supplanted the darker ones, the ones that burnt children alive and devoured the innocent, and no matter what Dash said about cults and religions, they were more advanced than what was worshipped in the Nowhere.

The people of the Nowhere. Insane people who believed

322

they were priests and worshipers, but they were merely spreaders of filth. They were like worms and flies themselves—traveling to shit and making a home within it. Dash had become some not-dead creature that fed on human flesh and had no conscience, followed by disgusting people within a perverse tradition, a twisting of the universal laws of brotherhood and sisterhood by which they were connected to all human beings, and by the ultimate law of life, to which every creature of flesh, every stalk of grass, was bound.

Dash had his high IQ twisted into triviality, into a monster's basic needs of hunger and domination. That was all. It wasn't God, or even god.

It was idiotic and yes, evil, Mark thinks, *Evil*, as he fights for air—a heavy weight of something upon his chest, as if stones are being piled upon him. *Evil. Nasty. Stupid. With the mind of Death, and nothing more.*

Dash is holding him now, cradling him, mouth to ear, practically kissing his ear as he begins to whisper something that Mark can't quite make out.

Dying. Please take me, God. Take me now. Break me out of life. Crush my spirit and body and slam me into another place. Or just cut off whatever it is that life is within me. Keep me from the Nowhere.

But even as he dies, Mark, without wanting to, without desiring this, parts his lips.

No! something within him fights against it. *Don't say it. Don't say the names!*

But his flesh is at war with his heart, and he realizes that Dash's remark had been true: *The flesh remembers the names.*

Mark utters the names. The unspeakable names of the gods of the Nowhere, of The Veil. Like the worst profanity coming from his tongue.

Permission to be called back.

He cannot remember the words that would stop this.

Only the names that would begin it.

His life slips away, just as if it were dropping into a pool. A rock in water, hitting the surface and slipping down into the murky depths. He's angry as he goes down to a place where the lights dim and flash and dim.

The lights are nearly out.

He can't even sense that he is breathing, or that Dash holds him now. Dash, singing some painful song in an unknown tongue as if he'd been singing it his whole life.

Mark has a sense of the others that are there—the priests and believers of the Nowhere. Standing in a circle around them both.

The part of Mark that still has a speck of thought and life feels terror and calm all at once, knowing that after he goes, that thing that Dash has become will hold him in his arms and intone the other part of the names, the response—*the litany*—until Mark's eyes, once again, open.

PART THREE: THE PARTY

1

An hour or so later, several miles away, a girl of nineteen, her arms around a boy of roughly the same age, says, "Oh my god."

The lights in the house go out suddenly.

The boy kisses her again, his breath all beer. "Rachel, you know what? I hope we spend every night together this summer. Our last summer together."

"Damn, I'm not even sure where the fuse box is," the girl says, pushing her boyfriend away.

"It's a brown-out."

"It's just a black-out."

"Lights!" someone shouts, laughing. "Somebody hit the lights!"

"What happened to the music?"

"Party must be over. Nice hint, Rachel!"

"Yeah, you want us to leave, you can just ask us."

"It must be the storm," somebody says, a drunken slur to his voice.

"Looks like somebody forgot to pay the bill."

"It must've been the storm."

"Yeah, or maybe a burglar."

"I love it in the dark. There's more to kiss."

"Perv!"

"Got a flashlight?"

"In my car. I'll get it."

"Jesus, it's nearly two. I better get home."

"We've got candles down in the basement, and some under the sink in the kitchen," Rachel says.

"Get your hands off me, Josh. And go get me some more beer."

"Somebody's knocking at the door. Somebody get it."

"No, something at the window. That a seagull? What the hell is that?"

"A bird hit the window."

"No, it's the front door."

"Come in!"

"Where are the candles?"

"The kitchen!" Rachel shouts. "Under the sink. There should be six of them."

"Here," some boy says. He flicks on a lighter. For a second, the small blue-yellow flame lights his face. The shadows of others, around him. In the mirror on the back wall the reflection of the light reveals more: the enormous living room is packed. "Everybody light your lighters."

"Don't be ridiculous. Just get some candles."

"Knock knock." A boy, a junior, from the Gardner School, reaches the front door. He draws the door inward.

A gust of steam. Humidity has risen.

Two figures in the dark, on the front porch.

"You're late," the boy says sleepily, not quite recognizing them in the dark. "Party's almost over."

For a split second, the boy who has opened the door has an instinct, but he ignores it. He thinks he should shut the door and lock it, but he doesn't know why he'd think that.

2

And then it begins.